For Whitney
fine writer & the
beginning of a great
friendship

The Long Journey

Wayne Greenhaw

8-26-2002

Montgomery

The Long Journey

a novel
by
Wayne Greenhaw

RIVER CITY PUBLISHING
Montgomery, Alabama

Designed by Lissa Monroe.
Printed in the United States.

Library of Congress Cataloging-in-Publication Data:

Greenhaw, Wayne, 1940-
The long journey : a novel / by Wayne Greenhaw.
p. cm.
ISBN 1-57966-028-2 (alk. paper)
1. World War, 1914-1918--Veterans--Fiction. 2. Teenage boys--Fiction.
3. Brothers--Fiction. I. Title.
PS3557.R3948 L66 2002
813'.54--dc21
2002001364

River City publishes fiction, nonfiction, poetry, art, and children's books by distinguished authors and artists in our region and nationwide. Visit our web site at www.rivercitypublishing.com.

Wayne Greenhaw's recent book *My Heart Is in the Earth: True Stories of Alabama and Mexico* is also available. Order via e-mail at sales@rivercitypublishing.com or phone us at 1 (877) 408-7078 toll-free or 265-6753 local.

For Sally,
Once Again,
With Love

Springtime

North Alabama

1919

BOOK ONE
A Higher Calling

<u>One</u>

The letter came on the first Friday in April.

Papa's liver-spotted hands quivered as they unfolded the paper. He read the words haltingly, although his eyes had perused the sentences over and over since he'd retrieved it from the post office early that morning.

"Your son, Bosworth Alexander Reed . . ."

His gravel-throated voice caught.

He repeated, "Bosworth Alexander Reed," saying the name with proud intonation. His bespectacled eyes glanced over the tops of the half-moon glasses toward me.

I didn't move an inch, waiting, listening.

". . . will arrive on the Thursday train from Louisville, Kentucky, arriving in Decatur, Alabama, in the second week of April," Papa read.

He looked up weary-eyed and gazed across the lantern-lit parlor at me and said, "Son, you'll have to go fetch him."

I twisted in my seat and frowned, worrying on the proposition.

I glanced toward Mama, sitting in her caneback rockingchair busying her hands with a pair of knitting needles. I knew that she too had read the letter when Papa brought it first to the privacy of their bedroom before sharing it with the rest of us. I knew they would have exchanged words about what it meant and who would be sent to retrieve him.

"You'll ride Jed and pull Jenny along behind," Papa said. He didn't ask. He didn't inquire of his children what he assumed

11

they would do without question. But the prospect of such a trip bore deeply into me. It was no easy matter.

When I didn't speak right up, Papa growled. It came from deep down in his throat, a dissatisfied sound, like a sullen, angered dog. He bared his teeth below his bushy brown mustache. I knew he was not happy with the absence of my eager response.

After supper I went to Mama, thinking she'd form a boundary between me and the old man, but she was stoic as a tree trunk. And her eyes, if possible, were even more accusing than his.

Mama was a mite of a woman, but her spidery fingers and bony arms and frail little face belied the strength of her will and her heart. She'd come from the same kind of pioneer stock as Papa, and she held her children close, fed them like a mama bird, and hesitated 'til the last moment before she pushed them from her nest. Whenever there was a hint of communication from the warfront, Mama nervously awaited word from her oldest son, whom I'd always suspected was her favorite. I'd heard Sister and the other girls say that Bosworth was "suckled at the teat until he was past four." I knew enough to know that was long past usual weaning time, but I didn't question. I figured it was something most females knew about, and the mysteries of women lay hidden in the darkness of my brain as yet unencumbered by knowledge.

After the letter-reading, after supper of leftover chicken and warmed-over beans and peas, our usual fare on a weekday night, Papa sat in his chair and unfolded the Bible in his lap. After hooking his glasses around his ears, he looked over at me and said, "Bosworth's your brother, your oldest brother, my first born." His voice shook a little as he spoke, a sound that raked against my backbone like Miss Ella Gray's chalk against the blackboard. "Looks to me like you'd take off without my having to beg. Bosworth's a fine Christian gentleman with a great future in front of him. He's smart and applies himself. He's always been a credit to his family. He was a quiet and dependable boy. Your Mama and I, we always counted on Bosworth, and he never let us down. He was on his way to becoming a successful businessman when this war came up and took him away." His voice, low and guttural now, almost broke between words. As an afterthought, he added, "I'll tell you this: Bosworth's no slacker. When his country needed him, he went. No questions asked. No lollygagging around. He just dropped everything and went, following his duty. Frivolity was never a habit with him."

Mama said nothing. Putting aside her knitting, she took needles from her hair that was silky black as a crow's breast and meticulously combed it out, down to her waist, in her nightly ritual. The hair that each morning she wrapped in a tight knot at the top of her skull shone like the coat of a new colt in the lantern light, each strand a fine thread that demanded individual care.

After I went to bed and watched ghost-like shadows climbing the wall as the moon moved across the sky, I remembered the words of the letter. I remembered Papa's nervous reading: "Your son, who has spent months recuperating at the hospital near Baltimore, will ride the train from here to Louisville with two medical officers accompanying him. He will be placed on the Louisville & Nashville and sent south to Decatur, Alabama, the debarkation point nearest your home. You will need to meet him there. Signed: Dr. Albert C. Steiner, M.D."

The words, cold and clear, sent chillbumps over my body like a December wind. To me, they were too cold and too sharp, like a well-honed straight razor cutting into a man's skin.

Thinking on the words of the message, void of adjectives that might have given us some notion about the condition of my brother's health, I cringed.

It was a long trip to Decatur. At least two days. I'd have to spend the night along the road, in some strange place, then find Bosworth at the depot, then return, having to camp once again on the road, constantly watching for highwaymen known to rob unsuspecting travelers, or renegade Indians known to wander from their settlement north along the river, or other dangers that lurked in the thick woods or in the open fields.

It wasn't the kind of trip you took without some strong thought and mighty consideration, even when the ultimate goal was of a higher calling. I'd never been away from home alone. Not overnight. Once, when I was eight—more than half my lifetime ago—I'd ridden on the wagon with Papa and Martin and Ida Mae to Decatur. At first, Papa had said it wasn't a trip for a youngster, but I begged to be included. The day before we left, I heard Mama say, "John, Harold's got his mind set on going with y'all. He loves you so. I see it in his eyes, the way he adores you. I don't think he could stand to watch you leave." I knew by the softness of his reply that Mama's persuasion was final.

To me, we left on our journey in the middle of the night. I was groggy when Papa put me on a pallet behind the seat and I slept to the Courtland Cutoff a few miles down the road east of Town Creek. When I finally awoke the first light was shining in my face. Papa's hands swept out toward the horizon. "Look out yonder, boys and girl; that's not just woods you're looking at." Ida Mae said she knew what she was seeing, and Papa, glancing toward her with a touch of disdain, said, "Maybe the school girl's getting a wee bit too big for her britches." Ida Mae did not reply.

"That out there," Papa said, pointing toward the woods between the road and Courtland, "is where the greatest general of the War Between the States fought back the Yankees in a little-known skirmish that saved north Alabama from being taken over entirely by the Union army." I listened to Pa's words with excitement building in my brain as he told about General Nathan Bedford Forrest and his band of Confederate cavalrymen saving this countryside where we now lived in peace. Of course, I recognized the name of Forrest from my studies and also from the words of Old Louisa Dot, the former slave who lived down the Bynum Road from us. It was Old Louisa Dot who talked about General Forrest like he was somebody she had had tea with. She remembered him with a quiet reverence.

We spent the first night at General Walker's plantation, Home Sweet Home, arriving after dark, and it had been nice and warm and cozy with burning wood crackling in the fireplace. The general's daughter, Miss Annie, was sweet to me and put ice and chocolate mint in my tea, a special treat. Papa and the general sat up and enjoyed a smoke and talked while Miss Annie took me up and tucked me in the down-soft bed where a few minutes later Ida Mae crawled in next to me.

After Ida Mae boarded the train heading for college in Nashville, Papa and Martin and I stayed in Decatur in the same room at a boardinghouse, where once again Papa stayed up late and talked into the night with the lady proprietor, an old acquaintance from an earlier trip when Papa was a young man. Before daybreak the next morning, we headed back west toward our home.

On the return trip, I again slept in the bed of the wagon, until an axle broke at a place called No Business Creek and Papa and Martin lifted me out and put me on the ground while they fixed it. Martin said it was called No Business Creek because once, years before, a man had found it flooded and was unable to

15

ford the deep water in his wagon. He got down, dove in, tried to swim against the current, and drowned. When told the story, a pioneer who lived nearby commented, "He ain't got no business trying to swim this creek when it's swollen with rain. It's dangerous." Ever since, Martin said, it'd been called No Business Creek.

Another time, several years ago, I'd ridden westward from Town Creek with Mama and Papa to Muscle Shoals where we crossed the Tennessee River on a ferryboat to Florence, where Mama picked out dry goods and a bolt of colorful cloth to make dresses for the girls and where Papa bought plows and other implements for the farm. Papa did his own farming at our place at the edge of Town Creek, and Papa helped out with planting, harvesting, and ginning for Mr. Melvin Saunders, who owned the gin and a huge plantation that covered much of the valley. He was by far the richest man in Lawrence County, and his daughter, Sarah Lynn, was the prettiest girl in Hazelwood High School.

The farthest I'd ever ventured out alone was down to Bynum, about six miles south, to Saturday afternoon baseball games, which I loved almost as much as barbering, and even then I was accompanied by my best friends, Raiford Bradford and Peter Morgan. After the game, traveling back on mule or horseback, we'd talk excitedly about the play: how Jason Greene had snagged a fly ball in left field, or how Billy Dee Johnson hit a home run into the pine thicket so far back that Bynum's best fielder couldn't outrun it, or how J. D. Sumner, catching for Town Creek, got his windpipe busted when one of Mike Ritchie's curve balls dropped, hit the dirt in front of home plate and bounced up, catching J. D. in the throat. For a few seconds it looked like J. D. was dead as a doornail, then his hands flew up to his throat. He sucked wind, wheezing like he had tuberculosis. He was finally declared okay, but he couldn't talk plain for nearly a month.

I didn't care much about being out in the vast cottonfields alone, especially early in the morning or after nightfall. Matter of fact, I hated it. I didn't like lonesome one bit. That's why I got a job in Mr. Carl Guyton's barber shop in downtown Town Creek when I was eleven. I talked an old Negro man, J. P. Snowhill, into teaching me the tricks of being a shoeshine jockey, and I cottoned to it fast, although I think that my choice of profession turned Papa's better judgment of me. By the time I was fourteen, I fashioned myself a two-foot-high box to stand on where I could easily reach men's heads in the tall chairs, and I soon proved I could cut hair as well as most seasoned barbers. But to Papa that wasn't proving much.

"Bosworth's a serious young man, always has been," Papa said. "Finished high school early, got a head start on others his age, went off to college, then the war came along and took him away, interrupting his life." Papa was not an educated man, but he read books and taught himself the intricacies of the English language, and knew the Bible better than most. He was quiet and steady and contemplative.

I was just the opposite. I liked to talk. When I was shining shoes or cutting hair, I'd talk up a blue streak. I was never at a loss for words, unless I was in school with my friends. And I also liked to listen. When customers who came in the shop talked, I'd turn my head ever so slightly in their direction and nod, letting them know I was hearing what they said. It didn't matter whether they were cussing President Taft or the state legislature, the unfair transportation tariffs levied on the South by Yankee politicians, or the weather, which could blow up a storm before you could turn around on your heels, I took it all in. For me, it was better than any classroom. When I saw by their expectant nature that they wanted an argument, I'd take an opposing view. But usually I'd just listen, until someone came in who obviously wanted to be entertained, then I'd start in on the topic of the day, or I'd make something up, if need be. It was all according to the person and the time. As Mr. Guyton always said: "Let the fellow who wants his hair cut determine your demeanor. It's not up to you to take on a braggart's soap box."

As long as I stayed in Town Creek and close to the barber shop, I was safe. I knew nobody in this cruel world would bother me there. It was my place. I knew my way around Town Creek and Carl Guyton's barber shop. In a few weeks I'd be seventeen. Then I'd ask Papa if it'd be all right for me to quit school and barber full-time. I knew he'd balk. But I was pretty persuasive, when I needed to be.

I lay there and thought about the journey. While the moon cast shadows through the windows, I wondered about the dangers of the road, dangers I'd heard about while shining shoes and cutting hair at Carl Guyton's barber shop. From time to time travelers came through and stopped to be refreshed on their way across the Tennessee River valley. They were given to talk about the problems of travel: horses being spooked by rattlesnakes or gusty winds, trees falling or outlaws lying in wait for innocent passersby, Indians gone mad, or gypsies with nothing to do but fleece a passerby, or mean and ornery criminals waiting for easy prey.

I'd known from the time Papa'd first read the letter that I'd go, even though I questioned it in my mind. I had never been able to say no to him. Few people ever did, with the exception of Mama. While I debated with myself in the silence of my mind, and told Lucy about my fear of talking to the animals, I knew deep down that the trip was inevitable.

And that's what I told my boss, Carl Guyton, at the barber shop on Saturday morning. Mr. Guyton said he understood perfectly well and added that it was a long twenty-eight to thirty-two miles from Town Creek to Decatur. And if I took a wrong turn somewhere along way, it would be longer.

As I was cutting the gray hair back from Caleb Andrews's ears, I thought: *Twenty-eight? Thirty-two miles? Maybe farther.* I tried to measure it out in my mind, but nothing I could fathom satisfied my trepidation. It was too much distance for my small mind to comprehend.

We were busy all day Saturday. People from all over the valley piled into Town Creek. Wagons and buggies pulled by horses and mules lined River Street. Even Mr. Melvin Saunders's Ford motor car was parked in front of the gin office. I saw Sarah Lynn sashay by in a perky yellow spring dress, her golden curls bouncing in the sunlight. I watched every step she made and eased over to the window to peek at her from behind. Mr. Guyton said, "She sure is something, ain't she, Harold?" but I slid back to my position behind the third chair and didn't comment.

Late Saturday afternoon Mr. Guyton remarked about my silence. "You've been brooding over your trip, Harold," he said. "You'll just be gone a few days."

I frowned. "Three, four days at most," I said.

"That's what your Papa says, but if Bosworth's train's late, or if something's happened to him . . ." I couldn't imagine what, but it was a heavy thought.

That night I asked Papa.

Mama looked up from her crocheting at Papa, who'd been reading the Florence newspaper.

"Didn't that last letter say he'll be arriving on Thursday morning?" he asked.

Mama lifted the envelope, pulled out the paper, read it, and nodded. "That's what it says. The second Thursday in April. The army people could be wrong, but that's what it says."

Without hesitating, Papa said, "Bosworth's always been good at his word."

I nodded.

Like a giant, Papa unfolded his long body from the chair on the far side of the fireplace. He stepped across the room and put his huge hand on my shoulder and held it there. "He'll be there, son," he said. "Sooner or later, he'll be there. If not Thursday, the next. "

I nodded. "Yes, sir," I said, and I rose and began preparing for my trip.

Just in case his time of arrival was later, I fixed my portable shoeshine box into a traveling case that would hang on Jenny's side, balanced by some clothes and food that would hang on the opposite side.

Two

Late Sunday afternoon we sat in the parlor. While Papa read the Bible and Mama pulled her chair up to the four-foot-high spinning wheel, I thought about my brother.

But it was hard to put the all details on his face. He was the oldest and the smartest and the wisest. He'd been gone almost two years. It seemed like longer, because he was off at college before the war started, coming home only at Christmastime or in the summers when he helped with farm work. He left for the army when I was fourteen. He was skinnier than me. His face showed cheekbones that looked as fine as a robin's, and his nose was narrow and long, like a hawk's. He had a wisp of light brown hair that fell in a curl onto his widow's peak.

Mama kept a photograph of Bosworth on her bedside table. When I came to her sometimes and leaned across her bed and held her small body in my arms, I'd look over to see Bosworth staring at us. She said, "I look at him every night before I fall asleep. He was such a tall, slender, handsome boy. He could shoot his rifle straight and true. But he displayed a deep sweetness, a love for his Mama, Papa, sisters, and brothers. I think he's blessed spiritually. I keep thinking Bosworth'll make a preacher. When the time's right, I keep thinking, he'll get the calling. That's probably the reason the Lord brought him through the misery and the horror of this war. It's probably the reason the Lord is sending him home to us. The Lord always has a purpose, it's His way. When I look into Bosworth's face every night, I say a little prayer for his safety, for the Lord to watch out for my boy." Her words were like tender reeds in the wind, a high-pitched whisper, hard with truth, brittle and breakable.

I could tell she missed him worse than I missed Missy, my little spotted mixed-breed dog who walked in my shadow during most of the years of my growing up, until last spring, when she got sick and crawled under the house and died. I buried her out by the barn and cried every night for a week. Finally, one night, Papa came to my bed and put his hand heavy on my shoulder. He looked down into my face and said, "Son, that's enough now. A dog's a dog. Missy was a good one. But she's gone." He patted me gently. "You're nearly grown. You don't have to weep any longer." I tried to stop, but late at night I'd awaken and think about Missy and feel her weight near my feet, but when I looked she wasn't there, and I'd cry with my face buried in the pillow so the sound wouldn't carry.

In the early mornings, when I was doing my chores, emptying the slop-jar or carrying garbage to the dump or bringing chopped wood to the kitchen to fire up the stove, I'd linger near Missy's unmarked grave and think about her kind eyes, when she used to put her head to my lower leg and look up at me, nuzzling gently. And sometimes I'd stop in the evening, when I was bringing ham from the smokehouse or corn from the crib. But I never wanted Papa to catch me. I wanted him to think I was strong enough to have forgotten about her by now.

Now and then, when I'd bring a pail of fresh milk in, either Lucy or Sister would be waiting on the back stoop, where they'd drawn water from the well, and they'd smile at me and nod. Both of them knew how I felt. Neither chided me for it.

The last remembrance I had of my oldest brother was the night before he left to enter the army and go to war. It was a hot August afternoon in 1917. He sat on the back steps, cleaning his gun. He asked me to sit next to him. "I'm gonna put this gun up high in my closet. You know where I keep it. It'll be wrapped in flannel so it'll stay oiled." I nodded. "If you want to use it, climb up there and unwrap it and take it out. It's a fine gun, got a good bead on the sight." I nodded again. "Before you put it back, be sure and oil it good and wipe it down and wrap it back in the flannel." I said I would. But I had never taken it down. I had never even thought about it until now.

PAPA SMOKED his pipe. Mama raked bolls of cotton between wire-spoked brushes, which she worked together, combing until the white bolls became thin, gauze-like wisps which she fastened onto a spool. Then she began working the cotton, pumping a pedal with her right foot, until the cotton formed threads of yarn. Her tiny fingers twisted and turned, her bony elbows fluttering through the air like a butterfly's wings, making the wheel sing, turning the cotton into yarn she would knit into socks or sweaters or mittens or bed covers.

I watched, as I usually did, fascinated by the concentrated beauty of her work. After she'd finished with a comb of cotton, she flicked back a strand of hair that had fallen onto her forehead. She glanced toward me, smiled, and said, "I guess that's enough for one evening."

After she tucked the wheel back into its place in the corner and took down her hair and brushed it out, she said, "Goodnight," touching my shoulder lightly as she passed.

Papa finished his pipe and shook it clean of ashes.

As I started to excuse myself, he said, "This is the first grown-up duty of your life, Harold."

I stared into his dark, solemn face.

"You're sixteen. Be seventeen soon. Old as I was when your mama and I got married," he said. "I was only a few days younger when I made my first trip to Decatur," he said.

"Was it a long journey for you?" I asked.

"It was a long, meaningful trip for me," he said.

I kind of shivered.

He reached into the bib pocket of his overalls and pulled out folded greenbacks, unsheathed them, and counted five ones, which he handed to me. "Be careful with every penny you spend. We know that your brother will be arriving in the next few days, but we are not sure of the exact hour of arrival. I doubt he'll have any money, although one communication stated something about 'mustering-out pay,' whatever that is."

I started to say something but held my tongue.

"You may have to stay in Decatur a day or two," Papa said. "Your money'll run out fast, if you squander it. Money usually goes faster in a city. And there'll be plenty of quick and loose people, trying to get what you've got. They work nights, thinking of ways to pilfer, especially from young innocents. Keep in mind, you're not in Town Creek no longer. You'll be in a city, where folks are not as naturally friendly and kindly as they are here."

I looked into Papa's face. He was serious as a funeral preacher.

"Always remember: the good Lord's up there looking down on you, and He's carrying your mama's sweet heart and my right fist. He can love, but He can also swing hard and deliver a mighty blow."

I nodded. I reckoned He was a mighty Lord, just like the one Preacher Sims spoke of on Sunday mornings.

Papa reached back into his overalls and extracted an old bone-handled single-blade knife I'd seen many times in my years. When Papa took to contemplating a subject on the front porch, after he'd packed and lighted his pipe, he took out the little knife with the worn handle and carved his fingernails to a fine curved edge.

He opened his palm, revealing the knife. "Take it," he said. "Every man needs a knife."

"Yes, sir," I said, and reached out tentatively. When I touched it, I half expected it to disappear, a magician's trick. But Papa was no magician and took little truck in trickery.

I handled it gently, looking at it as though it were pure gold.

"It's sharpened to a fine edge," Papa said.

I nodded. I opened it and looked at the silvery tone of the blade and nodded again. "It sure is fine," I said. "I'll bring it back in good shape."

"It's yours: now and forever."

"Yes, sir," I said. I closed the blade and palmed the handle. It felt good in my hold.

"Now," Papa said, leaning slightly toward me. "We don't know the exact condition Bosworth'll be in."

My forehead pinched.

"That little note from his physician brought a lump to your mama's throat. And it settled in me pretty hard. We didn't say anything about it, but I know one thing: when Bosworth left here near-about two years ago, he was a smart boy who could write pretty good for himself, had no need for someone else to do his writing for him. The last letter we got from him was from somewhere in France. It was sad. We could feel the loneliness in his words, but we could tell he was all right—physically."

I wasn't sure why he was telling me all this; I'd heard Mama read Bosworth's letter out loud, and I'd read it myself. I'd felt the cutting words about "laying here in this ditch with my friend's blood soaking through my trousers," and about "my heart jumping every time I hear an explosion, each one closer and closer, until you'd think it couldn't get any closer," and about "my buddy screaming out in the middle of the night, I thinking he was having a nightmare until I saw the hole in his stomach big enough to put my fist through, and then knowing that it was me who was crying, screaming inside like a frightened little boy waking from a dream, wishing you were here with me, Mama." I had lain in my bed at night, thinking about poor Bosworth over there in that foreign country, shells exploding all around him, my brave brother defending his country from some terrible German enemy. I'd known only one German: Hans Krackenbush, a traveling vender of pots and pans, who stopped by the house a half-dozen times when I was a boy to try and interest Mama in his wares. He always seemed a friendly person, although his face was hidden behind a salt-and-pepper beard, and Papa, although he wore a thick mustache above his lip for as long as I could remember, said a man who hides behind a thick beard has too many secrets to be entirely honest.

"Ask the workers at the train station about the military transportation units," Papa said. His eyes squinted as he looked straight into my eyes. "Don't be afraid to ask for help. When you're out there in a world that cares nothing about you, step up to a stranger and ask. More'n likely, folks are friendly, although there are always some shysters lurking in the dark. Folks in the city may seem cold and uncaring. But deep down inside, most of 'em are just like you. And if a man has the knowledge of something, he'll generally be glad to impart it, even if he does so pridefully. Remember that he is giving you something that he owns; his information is a part of himself, and it's of value to him. When he shares it with you, accept it humbly, and always thank him for it."

I nodded, listening carefully. I had never heard Papa say so many words at one time. Most times, he kept ideas to himself. Now and then, particularly on Sunday evenings, after a long morning of sermons, when Preacher Sims took parables from the Bible and likened them to problems in daily life, Papa would speak to us after supper while he was enjoying a pipe. But I never once thought he was speaking directly to me.

Usually Ida Mae and Martin and Lucy and Julia or some of the others were here, and Mama would be swinging easily, doing her sewing while he talked. When Ida Mae came home for Christmas, we'd all sit in the parlor with the fire, and Mama would tell about Preacher Sims's daughter Evelyn running off with the Mayfield boy to get married over in Mississippi, or about Lee Everett failing out of the University of the South at Sewanee, where he'd gone to become an Episcopal minister, or about Miss Edna Roswell, the third-grade schoolteacher having a vision of Jesus and the Virgin Mary, then crying out, speaking in an unknown tongue that no one could understand. By the time Ida Mae caught her ride back to Decatur with three friends from Sheffield in a buggy, she knew all the latest happenings of Town Creek and the surrounding communities. But now, Papa was speaking straight at me.

"There's many-a sinful place in Decatur," he said lowly. "There's places in that town where the Devil himself wouldn't go." He hesitated for a moment. "Hard liquor and gambling, harlots and hell-raising, all of it's found down by the river in what they call Moccasin Alley. And it's just like a moccasin: it'll reach out and grab you and squeeze around your throat in a death-choke grip, all the while dancing in front of your eyes like Delilah, enticing you with its strange and elusive charm."

I wondered how Papa knew all of this about Decatur. While we were there—taking Ida Mae when she first went off to school—I'd never seen anything like this Moccasin Alley he spoke about. Papa had never traveled away from us on his own, yet he had said he'd gone there once when he was just a little younger than I. *Perhaps* . . . I tucked my runaway thoughts into another pocket of my mind for later use.

"You go to Mrs. Prudence Longshore's boardinghouse. Just ask anybody where it is; they all know Mrs. Prudence, a fine widow woman who runs a fine establishment. She'll bed you and board you for fifty cents. If you have to stay for more'n five days, which I doubt, she'll let you pay later, when you return home, or after Bosworth gets there. He may have some of that mustering-out pay."

I nodded, figuring I'd find out soon enough what "mustering-out pay" was. Right now, my mind played with the idea of "sinful places" on a street called Moccasin Alley.

"Mrs. Prudence Longshore will feed you well, and she'll put you in touch with a preacher, if you're in need of spiritual guidance."

"What for?" I asked, astonished by the idea.

"Well, you never do know about a young man off on his own in a city for the first time in his life. There's many-a temptation out there, wandering around, waiting on him to stumble. Mrs. Prudence knows about such as that."

"I don't plan to stumble," I said weakly.

"You never know," Papa said.

In the privacy of my room I lay awake, thinking. I lay awake, holding the hard weight of the knife. Then I thought more, wondering about a place called Moccasin Alley.

Three

It was still dark when Mama shook me awake. I stumbled into my clothes and through the lantern-lighted house to the back stoop where Papa had already drawn a pan of water. I shivered as I splashed my face with the cold water, brushed my teeth with a sweetgum brush, and readied myself, smelling eggs and bacon frying. By the time I finished breakfast, washing it down with strong coffee, I truly did not wish to leave the warmth of the wood-stove. But Papa had the horse and mule packed and ready. I hugged Mama and felt her damp lips against my neck. At that moment I thought I'd hold the feel of her next to me for a long, long time. I shook Papa's hand and climbed aboard. "Now, remember," Papa said. "Bosworth gets to ride Jed on the return trip." I nodded and said I remembered everything he'd told me.

"Mrs. Prudence Longshore," he said, his heavy warm hand on my thigh.

I nodded and repeated the name.

I sat proudly atop Jed, my back straight, my head high, the wide brim of my hat parallel with the road, and I kicked the horse forward, holding the rope tied to Jenny's halter, to let her walk slowly behind us. I did not look back. I was a warrior riding off to war. It was like the days when I was a boy, playing Confederate soldier with my friend, Peter Morgan, when we'd be either General Forrest or Robert E. Lee or J. E. B. Stuart. We liked Forrest best, mostly because of old Louisa's personal descriptions of him, but any one of the others made for a challenging afternoon of warfare. We never thought for once that the South had lost; to us, each of its generals was the personification of chivalry, and that was all we cared about: we wanted to be heroes.

By the time Jed and Jenny and I got to the crook in the road that made the lights of home disappear behind, a great emptiness expanded in my chest. I pulled Jed to a halt and turned in the saddle and gazed back, hoping to find one last twinkle of light from the back bedroom window where Mama and Papa slept, but I couldn't find it in the darkness. I took a deep hard breath of fresh cool air that expanded my lungs to their capacity. As alone as I'd ever been in my life, thoughts of chivalry vanished. The moon shone bright as a silver dollar in the sky. My thoughts were of Mama and Papa, seeing their faces clearly in memory, still feeling Mama's lips against my neck, I told myself that I'd never forget them, no matter what happened out here in the world.

I faced the road that led away from Town Creek. I was heading into a world that I had never known. Suddenly, in my mind, things lightened. I kneed Jed and felt him step out into the world. There would be adventure ahead, like in the books Miss Margaret Anderson read to us when I was little, like travelers venturing into foreign countries, knights in the days of old, going off to fight in the Crusades, like Richard the Lionhearted. I'd always liked that idea: lionhearted; it sounded strong and righteous, noble and graceful. When Miss Anderson read about the Crusades she pronounced the words full and round, like they were being spoken with purpose.

The black world turned to shades of gray. Birds came to life in the thick blackberry bushes in the gully that ran next to the road. Sparrows and robins fluttered in trees that bordered a fence between a pasture that kept milk cows and neat, narrow rows that had been freshly plowed. A flash of gold light in the distance signaled the first sight of sunlight. Then, as fast as the snap of finger and thumb, it faded. The world fell dark again and the scuttering, rustling whistles of the birds died as quickly as they had started. I shivered and frowned, wondering.

Papa had told about the false dawn, how sometimes the sun flickered, then disappeared. It was so sudden and sullen, it made my heart flutter and my arms shiver with chillbumps. I hugged my arms against my chest. Jed snickered. Jenny answered. The animals knew. It was a strange world into which I was wandering.

I kept an even gait, a slow but steady walk, directly toward the east, following the twin paths of the hard-packed dirt road. Moments later the first true sign of the sun formed a silver sliver across the distant horizon. It too gave me a quick chill as the birds fluttered to life again. Then the light spread like molten metal in a blacksmith's shop, growing brighter and brighter, until it filled the world. Slowly, we moved directly toward it.

I'd heard men around the barber shop talk about the fickle weather here in north Alabama. I had known it all my life but never spent much time thinking about it. As quick as a twitch or the flick of a horse's tail, a northwest wind could whip up and bring high winds and rain. Especially in the spring, when a tornado could form a funnel in the middle of a wide-open field in an instant, and pick up strength enough to blow a house away just as fast. Lord only knew what it could do to a boy riding a horse and leading a mule. Dewey Free, a pool hall jockey who wandered in and out of Mr. Guyton's barber shop from time to time, talking about all the places he'd been and all the women he'd been with, told about seeing a man from Moulton walking down the road one Sunday afternoon. "Before he knew what hit him, he was covered by a jet-black tornado cloud, and when it left, traveling south, that man had been picked clean of his clothes and left just as naked as the day he was born," Dewey Free said. All the men nodded solemnly at his story.

Jed lowered his head and made a nasal sound, shaking his head. At full light, I kicked the horse to a faster walk. He could see the road easily now and shouldn't be in danger of a misstep. Jenny jogged along behind, shaking her head, making her sounds, as if trying to break the monotony of the trip.

As Saunders Castle came into sight, I wondered what Sarah Lynn Saunders was doing at this very moment. I knew with no doubt she was the prettiest girl in Hazelwood High School. A cheerleader with short page-boy-styled golden blonde hair that flipped up at the ends, she was pert with rosy cheeks and eyes as blue as a summer sky. She put on airs constantly, but I'd never call her down about it. Her voice jingled, always edging toward a giggle, which disturbed me rather than delighting me, as it did most boys. I'd have been more pleased with a quiet, mellow voice, but she'd never asked me. She hardly regarded me at all; as far as she was concerned, I didn't exist, the way I saw it. But I could hope that in the distance of time I could make myself known to her, and she'd do something besides laugh at me. Perhaps, after this journey, I could delight her with tales of a new and sophisticated world.

Now, however, I watched her from afar. When I was out on the football field blocking for Billy Ray Sims, the preacher's son who played quarterback, I watched Sarah Lynn out of the corner of my eye: how she'd twist and turn her hips beneath the full pleated gold-and-black skirt, how she filled out Billy Ray's letter sweater, how she'd jump and make the hem of her skirt fly up high enough to expose naked calves. Once, not long ago, I dreamed about her, but I never told a soul; not even Peter Morgan, who'd confessed that last fall, after the game against Moulton, he'd kissed Laura Sue Holt, holding her close and feeling the pressure of her breasts against his body. His telling me the details made me excited. Thinking back, I squirmed in the saddle.

Smoke was drifting skyward from the kitchen fire at Saunders Castle. I wondered how late it would put me if I trotted up the drive between the twin rows of cedars and begged a cup of coffee. Perhaps even a warm biscuit, a slice of ham, a patty of sausage. I'd linger there with a view of Sarah Lynn in her wide-awake morning look. I laughed aloud and kneed Jed, who threw his head up and glanced back at me with his big bulging black eyes. He knew I was thinking something I shouldn't, my imagination getting the better of me, and I laughed again.

Papa didn't like me playing football. "A waste of energy," he called it. But I carried on about how my best friends played the sport. Mama said she thought it was all right, as long as I didn't get hurt. Martin talked to Papa, telling him these were modern times, that boys needed such outlets to keep them busy. "He's busy enough with his chores and his job at the barber shop," Papa said, but reluctantly agreed to let me play, as long as I fulfilled my house duties in the mornings and worked downtown several hours on Tuesdays and Thursdays and all day most Saturdays. As for football, we didn't do much practicing and played only on Friday nights. Mr. Abernathy, the history teacher, was our part-time coach and didn't have great expectations of our team.

Jed, Jenny, and I slowed to a creep at the Courtland Cutoff. I looked down the road toward the south to see if I could see the town. The only sign was smoke drifting up into the bright sky in the distance. A trio of buzzards circled a spot a half-mile down that way, and I figured a varmint must have been killed during the night, or a dog had lost a fight with a wolf or fox.

I gazed through the gray-shadowed woods where General Forrest had fought to hold off the Union troops, and in my mind I saw the battle unfold as we clip-clopped down the road at our leisurely pace. It must have been something to see, that gallant officer with his hat sporting a feather as white as the

33

angel Gabriel's long-flowing robe. It was said that he not only looked the part, he was as courageous as he was handsome. Once, when the Union soldiers were swarming through the Confederate ranks, Forrest leaned down and snatched up a blue-coat and held him clamped to his horse's breast, using him as a human shield as he swung his polished blade through the afternoon air. In that single day of battle, legend had it, Forrest killed more Yankees than any other dozen soldiers in a half-dozen battles.

By late morning, after I'd stopped twice to water Jed and Jenny and they had settled back into a slow walk, I fell asleep twice, letting my chin fall to my chest. I snored myself awake, threw up my head, blinked my eyes, and sucked in a good swallow of fresh air. Traveling alone, I decided, was a boring ordeal. If I'd been in a buggy, I would have fallen asleep and napped without worry.

And then I came to a fork. One road veered to the right and made me wonder where it went. The other turned in a north-eastern direction. It was less traveled. If it continued in the same direction, it would eventually run into the river. But if it straightened to run straight east, it would go to Decatur and would be shorter than the road on which I now traveled.

I wondered why Papa hadn't told me about such a problem.

As I remembered it—and as Papa had described it—Decatur was on the river. Therefore, if we took the left turn, even though it was the path that fewer travelers had taken, we'd meet the river at some junction. Then, if the road ended, we could just follow the river eastward until we found Decatur.

It seemed simple enough.

And I knew it did absolutely no good whatsoever to stand here idle with an undecided mind.

I pulled Jed's reins, guiding him onto the road that ran north-east.

Within three miles, the road faded to a path next to a newly plowed field that would soon be sprouting cotton plants. Within another half-mile, the path disappeared into scraggly hardwoods dividing one cotton field from another. I knew I'd taken the wrong road.

Without further thought, I turned Jed back, retracing our steps, looking for the turnoff.

Gazing up toward the sun as we got back to the turn, I figured I'd lost several hours of daylight. It wouldn't be long before I'd start looking for a good place to spend the night on the road.

It was late afternoon before I met another traveler: a man and woman in a buckboard heading toward me.

I spotted them a mile away. I watched them coming, trying to figure out where they'd been and where they were going. By the time we met, all of us were eager for conversation. We all started at once: the woman asking where I came from, the man wanting to know where I was going, me seeking advice about a place to bed down tonight, whether there was a spring down the road a piece, and if they'd seen any other strangers on the road.

The man and I stopped.

The woman asked her questions and I answered, "It's been a long day," wiping my forehead with my kerchief that was already damp with sweat. Jed and Jenny took the opportunity to lower their heads and find a snack in a few sprigs of leafy grass.

"We come from Aiken, South Carolina, looking for some land my uncle died and left us over in Mississippi," the man under a wide-brimmed hat said. "He homesteaded it years ago."

I lifted my own hat from my head, which I wiped with the sweat-soaked kerchief that I retied around my neck.

"It's a far piece to Mississippi," I said. "I'd venture two, three days, if you keep up a good pace."

"Pontotoc," the man said.

"Four days best," I said. "A man from Pontotoc stopped in at Mr. Carl Guyton's barber shop where I work in Town Creek. Year or two back. He was a dude. Sold men's shirts made in a factory."

"Do tell," the woman said. "I make all of Hiram's shirts myself."

"Mama makes mine," I offered.

"Factory-made shirts," the man repeated.

"Wonder who buys them?" the woman said.

"He sold a few in Town Creek," I said. "There's a gambling man everybody calls 'Simple' Simon who bought several."

"Probably don't have a family," the man said.

"Not that I know of," I said.

"I hope there's not a world of gambling in these parts," the woman said, her forehead wrinkling under her bonnet.

"Oh, no ma'am," I said quickly. "Not that much," I said authoritatively, then added, "And Mr. Melvin Saunders would-of bought a stack of those factory-made shirts, if he knew about 'em. He wears ties most every day and never gambles, as far as I know."

"Only rich folks can afford to wear ties every day," the woman said.

"City folk," the man said.

I told them where Mama and Papa and Lucy and Julia lived, in the house off to the side of the road on the eastern edge of Town Creek, where Bynum Road turned south, and told them that if they traveled that far, Mama and Papa'd take them in for the night, especially if they told about meeting me on the road. I allowed as how they'd probably like to hear that I'd made it this far without a serious hitch.

"Well, reckon we better get going," the man said. "If we expect to make it by night, we better move on."

Kicking Jed, I said, "Yeah, you'll have to go at a pretty good clip to make it by sundown."

I heard the sound of their wagon's squeaking wheels as it disappeared behind me. I figured they wouldn't make Town Creek by nightfall. I figured they'd be lucky to make four or five miles before one or more of those worn wheels gave way and dropped to the wayside. Then they'd sure enough have trouble, out there alone on the road. But at least they had two horses, tired and worn-out as they appeared. They'd have transportation to get them to Mama and Papa's by late night, then Papa'd lend them a hand tomorrow morning. He was always good at helping strangers in trouble. He'd taught me to stop and give people help when they needed it. Years ago he told me the story about the good Samaritan, and he believed in carrying it out in everyday life. "If we don't help our fellow man," he said, "we can never expect help when we need it. That's the way this old world keeps from going totally crazy, what with all these new-fangled ideas people keep coming up with, like the automobile and the airplane. Whoever heard . . ."

As we moved along, I heard his voice in my head. A stern man with a hard look. Nevertheless, he was good and strong and helpful, strong in his beliefs but gentle and generous by his very nature. I hoped that I could be half as good. If I could, I'd become much more than I ever thought possible, when I was shining shoes or cutting hair. My mind was always swimming off in wild directions. I liked listening to Paul "Simple" Simon talk about betting on horses at a track north of the river, where a full-blooded Cherokee Indian operated a tourist attraction for visitors from as far away as Nashville, Memphis, and New Orleans on a flat piece of land he'd quit farming when he discovered that some people love to gamble more than anything else in the world.

"Simple" Simon, who had bought several of the Pontotoc salesman's factory-made shirts and dressed in city-slicker clothes with multicolored bow-ties, said you could gamble on more than horse races up at Mad Dog McGhee's Plantation Club. He said fancy women from big cities came and spent weeks on end in their stagecoach-styled rolling bordellos. Sometimes, when I was idle, I'd conjure up pictures of such women in my mind. They played there, strutting and posing provocatively, sending evil messages. According to "Simple" Simon, sportsmen from Kentucky and Ohio brought cages filled with fighting cocks to McGhee's and staged their own recreation. "And the finest sour mash whiskey made in the United States can be bought from a distiller who brings his wares down from Lynchburg, Tennessee," Simon recollected.

It was times like that, when I delighted in the colorful tales of another life beyond Town Creek, that I wondered if I'd ever grow up to be anything near as good as Papa. A fine and honorable man, he filled a shoe too big for me to imagine at times.

As we moved across the rolling landscape, acre after acre of rich red fields already plowed, waiting for the spring rains to come and feed the cotton seeds and begin the new growth for another season, the loneliness of the first day of travel was settling down on me with a tired weariness that put me in a thoughtful mood. I found myself talking to Jed and Jenny, telling them about the fast-talking gambler, "Simple" Simon, a man who wore his sinful life on his store-bought shirt sleeve, and about my boss, Carl Guyton, a good, honest, hard-working man, a good husband whose wife, Mary Elizabeth, was the God-fearing mother of two little boys and a girl, and about Caleb Andrews, who had fought in the Spanish-American war in Cuba as a Rough Rider alongside Teddy Roosevelt, who later became President. I found myself recollecting the couple from Aiken, South Carolina, and hoped aloud that they'd make it as far as Papa and Mama's before their wagon met with disaster.

The sun was falling behind me when I spotted something ahead of us near the highway. It looked like a Fourth of July parade out here in the middle of nowhere. It was purely a colorful sight: a huge balloon colored green and yellow and orange with stripes of blue. At first I thought it was an illusion. Surely my weary mind was playing tricks on me. I was seeing things, like the time I played football too long on an early September afternoon and got too hot and near-about fainted from the heat.

After I blinked my eyes a time or two, I looked again to see the colorful balloon floating at least fifty feet up in the air with a large straw basket hanging under a round mouth. I reined Jed to a halt. "Well, I'll be . . ." It was the first time a word of profanity had entered my mind since leaving home.

In the basket was a man wearing a cowboy hat. He had gray-speckled hair that flowed back like wings on each side of his head. Seeing me, he lifted the hat in a wave.

I raised my hand.

Jed whinnied.

Jenny pulled back, jerking her head, but I held tightly to her rope.

"I swear," I said aloud.

I held to the animals while the balloon floated down in our direction.

I patted Jed's sweat-soaked neck, trying to calm him, telling myself that there was nothing to fear from this apparition.

Jenny jerked her head and pawed her hooves against the dirt, but I clutched tightly to her rope. Both of the animals, as scared as I, looked wild-eyed and nervous. Their hooves pawed at the hard dirt. None of us had ever seen anything to match this sight.

Suddenly, the balloon swooped quickly down toward us, barely missing Jed's head. "Damn!" I swore, trying to keep control of both animals' reins.

But the large basket swept straight toward my body. I twisted and turned in the saddle to keep from being slammed.

As I turned, the reins slipped from my fingers.

Jed's head rose. His nostrils flared. His eyes bulged wilder than before.

In fighting to hold Jed, I released Jenny, who rared up and threw her head sideways and made a strange, frightened sound that made me shiver. Behind me, her hooves stomped against the ground.

As the basket raked against my shoulder, knocking me backwards, my boots slipped from the wooden stirrups. My body off-balance, I tumbled toward the ground. Jed whinnied again, a wild, uncontrolled sound, not unlike Jenny's mad mule sound.

My shoulder hit the ground with a thud. My head shook, then settled on the dirt, stunned. I tasted blood where I'd bitten my tongue. I spat.

When I raised up, the horse and mule galloped away from the collision and disappeared into the curtain of woods to the south.

Hurting, my teeth raking against my sore tongue, I cursed again.

Behind me, the balloon dropped to the middle of the road, silhouetted against the orange-and-blue-streaked sunset, matching last night's dramatic beauty. The basket bounced, then settled onto a cloud of dust.

The man in the cowboy hat grabbed for the ropes holding the basket under the balloon. He wrapped the ropes around his wrists as he struggled to hold the bucking balloon in his grip.

He climbed out of the waist-high basket and began pulling, trying to settle the balloon to the ground.

I sat up, gazed toward the woods, looking for a sign of the horse and mule, feeling helpless in my sudden predicament.

Soon the man in the cowboy hat had his balloon under control. It was laid out in a half-deflated state. The man tied the ropes securely to a tree.

In a rolling gait, he loped over to me and once again swept the big white hat from his head. Dark hair speckled with gray swept back on the sides of his large head. He had a big hawk's nose and a generous mouth filled with big yellowed teeth. "I'm sorry about that," he said. "It just got away from me." He glanced toward the woods. "Your horses run?"

I nodded. "Hell yeah, they ran," I said. "Your crazy damned balloon spooked 'em. They probably won't stop running 'til day after tomorrow."

When he grinned, showing all of his teeth, I clamped my sore mouth shut and tried to think of more good strong curse words to throw at him. I didn't see any humor at all in this situation.

"A balloon does that to animals sometimes," he said.

"Why in the hell did you fly toward us like that?" I asked incredulously.

"I didn't do it on purpose," he said apologetically. "I lost control. Sometimes, especially at sunset, when the air pressure drops and grows suddenly heavy, it happens like that. I just lose control and can't guide it."

"Knowing that, why'd you aim at us?" I asked, my anger building each time my tongue raked against my teeth. "Looks to me like you could-a stayed down the road, away from us."

"I thought maybe you'd like a little show," he said. For the first time, I noticed he had an accent foreign to north Alabama. But at a time like this, I couldn't bring myself to ask about his heritage. All I could think about was myself and Jed and Jenny.

"Everything I own in the world is with those animals," I said, feeling a quick empty feeling in the middle of my chest, hurting worse than my tongue.

"Well, I didn't mean anything by my action," he said. "I was doing everything I could to lower the balloon nice and easy. I wanted you to see how a balloon looks in the sunset. When the light's just right, a balloon can be a pretty piece of drama."

"Did I say anything about wanting to see a balloon?" I asked.

"I don't reckon we had a conversation," the man said.

"And I didn't ask you to interrupt my trip, did I?"

"I don't even know you," the man said.

"That's the whole point," I said. "Me and Jed and Jenny were out here on the road, minding our own business, then you came soaring in."

"I didn't mean to harm you or them," he said. "I only wanted . . ." He cut off his own words.

All I could do was stare at him. I wanted to hit him, but I knew that wouldn't help matters.

"We'll find 'em," he said.

In the last light of day, I asked, "How?"

"In the morning," he said, like it was an everyday occurrence. "We'll go up in the balloon . . ."

"And scare 'em again?"

"No, no, we'll be up high enough to see 'em, and I can let you out nearby. You'll see. You can see forever when you're up there. We'll find them."

I did not move from my sitting place. I hadn't been gone from home a full day, and I'd already failed. Jed and Jenny were probably already halfway back to Mama and Papa's.

All of a sudden I wished I had not brought everything with me. What I told the stranger was true: everything I owned had scampered away. Not only was my shoeshine stand packed aboard Jenny, so were my prized barbering tools that I'd saved

42

to buy. Wrapped in a leather case: hand-clippers, two pairs of scissors, a razor made of prewar German steel, and a leather strap for honing. Mr. Guyton had picked out the tools from a traveling salesman and told me they were all I needed to earn my living as a barber. He'd let me pay him a quarter every week for two years and two months. I had made the final payment on the last Saturday in February, less than two months ago. And now they were gone.

"They'll run all the way home to Town Creek," I said, thinking about Jed and Jenny following the road. I could see Papa now: out in the field checking the cotton tomorrow morning, looking up and seeing the horse and mule, shaking his head sadly.

The man said, "Don't fret. They won't go far."

"They've got supper, and tomorrow's breakfast and dinner." I felt a quick heavy push just behind my eyes. A knot clamped in my throat.

"Don't worry," he tried to reassure me. "I've got enough supper for both of us."

"They've got my shoeshine box, my . . ."

"We'll find 'em in the morning. I'll show you. I promise."

I stared at the half-withered balloon in the darkness. I shivered, wishing I had my heavy coat that was packed in Jenny's saddlebags. I was not at all sure I could climb into that basket with this crazy man and soar across the sky. The very thought of it sickened me.

I ran my fingers over the bib of my overalls. At least I had my knife.

Four

His name was Anthony Katanzakis, a Greek born on the Isle of Andros. His father was a goat farmer. As he spoke to me in his accent-thickened words, I stared at him in disbelief. If I ever thought I could talk, I was mistaken. Here was a *talker*. He learned about balloons in Europe, where he traveled with a French circus until all the shooting of the Great War started a few years ago. "Then I had to leave, or be imprisoned, or killed," he said matter-of-factly.

As he spoke his foreign-frayed words I listened intently.

He shook his large head in an impassioned gesture. "I am not looking for tragedy!" he announced as though on stage. He grinned, his thick lips and his long teeth expanding. "I seek the experience of life. It is *so* wonderful! Life itself throbs to a beat that is here!" He pointed to his heart.

"I'm going to Decatur to fetch my brother who's been in the army in France," I said. I looked around. "Or I was, until you came floating in." My voice pierced him.

He winced. "I didn't mean to hurt you, or spook your horses. I wouldn't have done it for anything in this world. I wanted to give you a thrill, to excite you with a new wonder." His voice sounded totally sincere. His coal-black eyes sparkled with dampness, reflecting the flame of the fire he had built from dried twigs gathered in the woods where Jed and Jenny had disappeared.

"What the hell were you doing, floating around up there in the sky over north Alabama?" I asked.

"I am a world traveler," he said, his voice unique to my ears. I had to listen hard to understand every word. "I've traveled through most of the countries of the world in many different ways. Today, yesterday, and tomorrow are days for the balloon. Air travel will become extraordinarily popular among the gentry of this country and Europe. This is one of Katanzakis's great predictions. I am far ahead of my time. I will teach you Americans about this new way to travel. It is so easy, so smooth, so thrilling, so beautiful! It is not boring, like when you're riding along on a horse. What is traveling, if you can't experience the natural beauty of geography? If you can't be swept along with the rhythm of the road?"

I hugged my arms to my body, shivering, moving closer to the fire.

"Tomorrow at daybreak we will go aloft and search for your runaway beasts," he said. "From up there, we can see for a long, long distance."

When I told him I didn't give a whit about going up in his balloon, he looked at me like I had slapped him. "It is a great way to travel," he insisted.

"I don't like heights," I admitted.

He shook his head. "I will explain it to you. You will not be afraid."

"I hate to climb a ladder," I said. "When I reach a height higher than my head, I grow dizzy. My balance is upset."

"It is a new world, up there," he said, his eyes looking toward the moon.

He draped a wool blanket around my shoulders, then he went about fixing supper. He worked handily, quickly. Like Papa in the gin-house, there was no wasted movement.

Later, over warmed sourdough bread and salt-cured ham and a soup he called gumbo, the man told me about the place where he was born, in the hill country of Andros, where his father tended to a herd of goats. "He wanted me to continue his

46

duties, but I was not made for that kind of regular work. I stood on the rocky hillside and looked out over the sea every day. I longed to board a ship and sail off across the horizon. The sea was so beautiful. It thrilled me. It was blue-green, like the eyes of a gorgeous woman, and as appealing. Have you ever been to sea?" he asked.

"I've never even seen the sea," I said, but I would love to see such a sight. I had read about the sea and stared at pictures in books at school. I'd even flipped through pages of Ida Mae's literature she'd brought home from college.

"There is something seductive about the sea," he said. "The Aegean particularly. Have you ever read Homer?"

I shook my head. I felt enormously ignorant.

"You must. It's about a man who goes to sea. Homer writes about it as it is. The sea beckons to the wanderlust, teases the imagination. Not just the look of it, the beauty, the feel of its texture, like the richest velvet you have ever stroked." His voice sang a lilting song. "It calls to you, its sound haunting, tantalizing. At land's end there is water. The sea has an undulating rhythm unlike anything you've ever experienced—until you've been aloft in the belly-bottom of a balloon or ridden abed with an adorable lady."

Each of his words grew in volume. I gazed at him as though he were an actor, presenting a performance for an audience of one.

I listened eagerly as he told about joining the crew of a sailing ship. "Captain Aristotle Xides was crazier than Ahab in his search for the white whale," Katanzakis said. "But I enjoyed every minute's ride with him. We sailed the Mediterranean, the Atlantic, the North Sea, the Indian Ocean and the Bay of Bengal. We even pulled into dock at Calcutta." As he pulled a deep breath, I waited anxiously for more words. Momentarily, my thoughts had been lifted from my worries. "Of course you've heard about the back-alleys of Calcutta." Although I nodded, I had no idea where or what he was talking about. "Now, don't say nothing!" he declared.

I had no intention of saying a word.

"Talking about cutthroats! In the back-alleys of Calcutta live the most awful hellions you'll ever come across, black as death, sick as pneumonia. You've got to watch your front, your sides, your back, and overhead. They'll come at you from every direction, surrounding you like cold night air, and you dare not drop off to sleep in one of them dens where opium is smoked like it was Prince Albert, or you'll wake up with your private parts sliced into little bitty pieces. I had Captain Xides and my fellow crew members, so I did not feel totally alone. But it was a frightening time, I'll tell you. But then, I'll tell you that story on a different day. It's a long and involved story that'd keep us both awake the entire night.

"For now, don't say nothing! When we were back on the ship and out on the water, everything was great and wonderful. We rolled over the water like it was a washtub, a fine sailing, smooth as ice. But we had our hard times too. We hit a storm north of Scotland once, where the winds out of the north tore at us, sending us rolling, forty-foot waves like a stone thrown into a lake. It was so foggy you couldn't see your hand in front of your face. You stood at the helm, feet wide apart." He rose and stood opposite me with the flames of our fire between us. He acted out the part, holding his calloused fists sturdy, each extended from his thick wide body.

"You held to the wheel, not giving an inch, afraid you'd rock to the side and be thrown onto rocks bigger than many mountains. It was three days into a storm like that. We were tossed side to side, but we made it. And once again, down in the Atlantic, dark as the devil's breath, the wind and the water bounced us up and down, throwing us into a hellhole. For a week, morning, noon, and all night every night, never seeing the sun or the moon or stars or any other light, we fought a hurricane that lifted us up and threw us down like we were a piece of kindling wood, ready to break in two any moment. That's the kind of power God has, my lad; it's awesome!"

I found my heart beating to the tune of his words. His own rhythms were like that of the weather he described, rolling and rocking, rising and falling.

"After years aboard a sailing ship with Captain Aristotle Xides, ballooning is a gentle transportation. At the end of a long sail, the water dumps you onto the earth like you're Jonah himself," he said. He raised his hands, palms toward me. "Now, don't say nothing! I'll tell you all about the world I've come to know." Then he began describing his travels through Greece and Italy, France and Spain. "Hannibal's got nothing on me: crossing the Alps in a balloon beats the hell out of an elephant's back.

"Now, don't say nothing! I've ridden an elephant's back. In India on the flat plains south of the Taj Mahal, Maharajah Rihajandi became my personal friend when he begged me to take him aloft. With the sweetest of voices, he begged like he was pleading with Buddha. He was a little short brown man with big black eyes and tiny hands. And his voice was squeaky high, like a child's. In the short run, he offered me half of his harem to take him on a trip through the sky. I smiled and shook my head. I think he thought I was playing with him. I was not. I told him, 'Sure, I'll take you up. You don't have to give up your loved ones.' And after I took him on a flight, he was forever grateful. Any time I wish to go back to that vast and fanciful country, his temples are open to me. They are mine. That, my young friend, is the power of the balloon."

Looking at the foreigner and hearing him, I wondered how he could have dropped out of the sky onto me, spooking my animals, ruining my chance at success. Of all the places in all of his world travels, here he was in the middle of the wilderness, finding me. The odds were so terribly huge, yet here we were in the middle of north Alabama, huddled around a fire, the Greek standing and talking.

"Travel is a wondrous thing," Anthony Katanzakis said. "It is even more delightful when you float across the sky. It is like being on a ship in the middle of an ocean, floating up and down with the waves. But it is even more enchanting, exciting, because you are part of nature, up there." He pointed toward the heavens, where thousands of stars twinkled down upon us in the darkness. "It is most remarkable."

His eyes grew wide, his expression expansive. "Have you ever flown through a night?"

I shook my head. "I've never flown," I said incredulously. "I told you, I don't like heights."

"You mean, you're afraid of being way up high."

"Well . . ."

He looked at me wide-eyed, like he had neither heard my previous words nor had paid any attention to me whatsoever, like he had been talking to the night. I wondered if he put on such a performance for himself and the night animals when he bedded down alone in the countryside.

Suddenly it came to me again that Jed and Jenny had been frightened out of their wits, running off without knowing which direction they were heading, now lost in the middle of strange woods. With the thoughts, I once again felt like crying. Instead, I jerked at the meat that was tough as boot leather. And I drank from the man's canteen, which he'd filled at a spring, miles back at the Walker house. "You'll enjoy that place," he said. I told him shortly that I'd been there before, when I was a child, traveling with my father and brother and sister. Tomorrow, I might make it by nightfall, even if I didn't have Jed and Jenny. I'd be walking, alone and hurt, throughout tomorrow. Every step of the way, I'd think about my lost shoeshine stand and my tools. I'd have no way in this world to pay my way, if I had to stay in Decatur any length of time. I wondered about Papa's friend, Mrs. Prudence Longshore, and I thought about having to tell her what happened. Then I told myself that I would formulate my plea on the long road east tomorrow. I would have plenty of time. And during all that time, I would never think this man's words were magical. Never.

As the night grew long, the moon bright and full, my lids felt weighted as I listened to Anthony Katanzakis. "Now, don't say nothing!" he said for the umpteenth time. I started to interrupt, but I kept my already bitten and swollen tongue stuck against my lower teeth. I wanted to break through to him and explode his stories. I wanted to say: *Look, old man, you're as full of shit as a Christmas turkey, and I know it; you're crazy as a stir-mad fool, flying across north Alabama in a damn balloon, acting a fool.* I stared through the blazing fire at him, now sitting on his bedroll with a blanket around his shoulders. "I've got a world of stuff to tell you about, Harold Reed, a world of stuff."

I yawned and closed my eyes, then was awakened abruptly with a new explosion of words.

He talked. "I worked with a magician in southeast Asia. It was a wonderful trip through the valleys of the rice fields, bordered by purple mountains. You've never seen anything until you've traveled by balloon through India, viewing the temples of Buddha that rise out of the flatland like trees growing tall in this country. Think about stacking ten of the largest oaks you've ever seen one on top of the other: that's how high those stone temples are. They were built by man in the worship of a god. Can you imagine?"

I couldn't. I shook my head. *When does he ever stop talking?* I asked myself. I tried not to be angry, but I found it impossible. I had only *thought* that I could talk. I was nothing compared to Anthony Katanzakis.

He didn't stop long enough to allow me to think, but soon I felt my eyelids closed, my body relaxing, my head drooping.

"I was a magician's assistant," he said again. "I truly believe in magic. You have to have faith, believe that the magic will lift you and carry you, will make you disappear and reappear, that it can transport you across space and time. It will carry you to a place that previously existed only in your imagination. It's not simply a trick. It is truly magic. It is!" He pointed at his head. "It's here." Then he pointed to his heart. "And here."

He chewed as he glanced up into the stars and regarded the full moon.

"That balloon over there is magic. I heat the air. Then it lifts you high, up into the sky, and it carries you across hill and dale. It shows you sights you never thought possible to see. It makes the world a more glorious place. I've soared high above the snow-covered Alps and I crossed the great Rhine River from Germany into France, before those countries became overrun with war.

"Oh!" he exclaimed. "When you give yourself the thrill of flying at night, it's like you're in a dream. When you're sailing below the stars, feeling the cool breeze of night against your cheeks, unable to see the floor of the earth, it's as if you're floating up into the sky forever. It's endless. The stars and the moon become your focus. They take you into another world." He slowed, breathing deeply. "It's marvelous," he added, an afterthought.

Marvelous, I thought.

I stretched out a few feet from the fire. My body, covered by the blanket that he said had been woven by his mother from goat's hair, was worn out with the day's journey. Katanzakis was still talking when I drifted off into a deep sleep, dreaming about my down-soft bed in the little back room of the house on the edge of Town Creek.

Five

I awakened with a start. It was dark and the remains of a fire crackled. Beyond the fire, less than six feet away, a man with shaggy dark hair speckled in gray, and a dark-splotched face featuring a strong nose and dark-shadowed eye sockets, lay wrapped in a bear's fur. Behind him, something big and odd-shaped moved awkwardly in the darkness. I raised up, blinking.

A moment later, it came to me: the movement was the balloon shifting in the breeze. The man was the Greek who'd dropped out of the sky and scared away Jed and Jenny.

Who will ever believe me? I asked myself. It was all too unbelievable. Things like this didn't happen in north Alabama. My friends in Town Creek would think I'd gone looney. *A Greek? Traveling in a balloon?*

I shut my eyes and soon fell back into a deep, restful sleep. I had never had a problem going to sleep, no matter where I was. Often, coming back from the river after a day of frolicking in the sunshine, I'd fall asleep in the bed of Papa's wagon that bumped across the washboard road.

The next time I awakened, a twinkle of sunlight touched my eye and the fragrance of brewing coffee filled the air that was warm with a new blazing fire.

Anthony Katanzakis squatted, lifting a tin coffee pot.

"You're a sleeper," he declared.

I rubbed my eyes and accepted a cup of steaming black coffee. Bringing it to my lips, I tasted a strange aroma.

"Chicory," Anthony Katanzakis said, watching my eyes alight. "It's a grand ingredient I found among the cajuns in the bayou country of southern Louisiana."

"Cajuns?" I said. I knew about the Louisiana purchase. I'd traced the outline of the boot-shaped state on the atlas in geography class. And I'd read about General Andrew Jackson and the battle of New Orleans. History was my favorite subject.

"They're French people who settled first on the island of Nova Scotia off eastern Canada, then migrated south to the Louisiana bayou country, where they've lived ever since. They developed this coffee with chicory, a bittersweet herb that's quite worth the trouble, don't you think?"

I tasted it again and nodded. It was delicious. I'd never been a big coffee drinker. But this was different.

He said that he'd gotten the recipe for the gumbo we'd had last night from the cajuns, and I remarked that they definitely knew how to cook, those people who'd settled in Louisiana.

I regarded Anthony Katanzakis in the broad-open daylight. The morning sunshine poured onto his face, showing it burning red, his large hook-nose lined with veins, his high, broad forehead like that I imagined belonging to a king, his hands big as a bear's paws. His skin was burned a swarthy brown, rough as boot leather. He was definitely unlike any person I'd ever come across in my almost seventeen years.

In a pan over the fire, he cooked chopped potatoes laced with onions, and it smelled like Mama's best Sunday dinner. When he raked half into a plate and handed it over, I shoveled it into my mouth like a starving urchin. After I finished, I took the plate down and frowned and said, "Please excuse me, Mr. Katanzakis, my manners have apparently failed me."

He laughed lightly. "You're a hungry young 'un."

"My Mama would disown me," I admitted.

He laughed again. It was throaty, full, hearty laughter, coming up and out of his chest, filtering through his large mouth.

"Out here, son, in the middle of nature, it's just me and thee." His smile held, and he winked. "And we'll not tell on each other. Okay?"

I nodded.

The man whom I had considered a demon in yesterday's twilight appeared to be a great rugged clown in the light of day. His eyes, dark and shiny, had a twinkle of foolishness in them, and I wondered if they did not mirror my own.

I looked all around us, up and down the long road, through the trees into the darkness of the forest, a meadow filled with golden sedge up ahead. It hit me afresh that Jed and Jenny were gone. My heart turned heavy before it had gotten its full steam of mirth from this stranger whom I thought would never stop talking last night.

As he stored away his utensils, his wide-brimmed white western-style hat square on his head, Anthony Katanzakis said, "You ready to go aloft to find your beasts of burden?"

I regarded the large basket, where he packed away his things. Looking at it and the balloon behind, my heart sank. My belly, filled with the potato mixture and coffee, turned slightly. "My Lord," I uttered.

"You've never been in a balloon?" he asked.

"You know what I told you last night," I said.

He might as well have asked if I'd been to the moon or New York City or London town. Of course I'd never been in a balloon. It had never truly crossed my mind. I'd seen pictures in magazines and books. I'd heard stories from a writer named Jules Verne about traveling around the world in eighty days. But I had never actually seen a balloon, until yesterday.

"I know who the Wright brothers are," I said, "but I've never been in an airplane."

He laughed again. His wide chest shook. "That's good," he said. "You're a lad with a sense of humor."

I looked at him with eyes as solemn as Papa's.

"I like a sense of humor, especially in the young. When there's nothing but sadness, it drains life. And the way you talked last night, I wondered about you."

As he spoke his last sentence, he began unfolding an attachment from within the basket. With his long-handled tool and its shovel end, he scooped up coals from the fire. He lifted it over the basket and held the heat beneath the bottom of the balloon. He said, "Help me with these ropes. I'll need the balloon to float up above the basket."

I moved around to the far side, grabbed a handful of rope, began pulling, following his instructions.

"I'll tend to these gizmos," he said as he continued his process.

Within moments, a gaseous substance was blowing up through the large hole in the bottom of the balloon. It hissed and vibrated, and I thought that there was no way Jed and Jenny would ever come to such a sound. It would frighten most men, much less the ignorant animals.

Within minutes, the balloon filled and stood upright over the basket, bucking like a horse raring to go. The hissing lowered to a bare whisper.

He instructed me to cover the remaining coals with dirt. "Always leave your campsite as you found it," he said. "Nature is meant to stay fresh and unhampered by man's sorry ways."

I rushed to do the appropriate work.

"Now, hop in," Anthony Katanzakis commanded.

I hesitated, looking at him and at the bright-colored balloon. My stomach rumbled queasily again. My eyes wandered over the large straw basket that looked downright unsubstantial to me.

"What's wrong?" he asked.

"I . . ." I started. *What could I do? What would I do?* I knew that if I got sick climbing to the top of the tower at Saunders Castle, I'd surely die if I went straight up into the air in this straw basket with this crazy Greek.

"It won't hurt you," Katanzakis insisted.

"You nearly crashed yesterday," I said. Once again, I felt as though I could hit the man, if I were bigger and taller and older. Before last night, I considered myself lighthearted, a joker, filled with good times and frivolous words. But now I had a mission to accomplish, and I was as serious as Papa about fulfilling my duty.

"I can't go flying off with you, end up no-telling where," I said quickly. "I've got to meet my brother Bosworth at the train in Decatur," I said to him, like I was informing him for the first time. As I spoke, my voice broke. A nervous twitter tickled my throat.

"What kind of name is Bosworth?" he asked playfully.

I didn't feel like playing. I clamped my lips together and swallowed. Then I said, "A damn good name!"

He chuckled.

"It's not a funny name," I said. "Unlike you, he's not a clown."

"I'm not making light of a man's name," he said.

"He's a fine, upstanding man," I said. "He was on his way to being a businessman when the war . . ."

"I am sure he is a very fine man," Katanzakis said.

I glared into his grizzly face. I could not tell if he was funning me or not. Usually it was me who made fun of others. "He's been off fighting for his country. He was injured in France," I put in. Of course, I had no idea whether Bosworth had been wounded or not. I just thought it a good point to make, so I added, "And he's a decorated hero, a very brave soldier."

"He sounds like a very fine brother."

"He is. He is." I repeated my words as if to reinforce my thoughts. "I was going after him . . ." My voice broke again. "I was going after him. Then you came down out of the sky like a madman, slamming into me and spooking my livestock. You interrupted my journey with your foolish dipping down onto us, like . . . like . . ." I gulped a quick breath.

"I'd say this balloon travel is a dangerous way to go," I said, looking over the mode of transportation.

"That was at twilight. I was blinded by the brilliant colors of the sun as it splashed down in the west. When a person sees something like that, he knows that God is the only artist that can create such a magical moment—such an absolutely glorious picture. And it *is* for only a moment, I can assure you. Those moments are not repeated very often. When you've lived to my ripe old age, you grab every moment like that and enjoy it to its fullest. You grab it and hold it in your mind for all the rest of your days. An absolutely breathtaking sunset is better than a Rembrandt or even a Van Gogh."

Listening to him, I heard and saw his sincerity. I knew he was talking from the heart. He had been engrossed in the pink and orange sunset, which I had to admit was truly breathtaking.

Just about the time I was making up my mind to climb into the basket with him, he said, "Now, don't say nothing—I'm going to tell you about the joy of flying."

"No!" I said.

"What?" he said, looking as though I had hurt him with my words.

"I don't want to hear a whole bunch of bullshit about your flying all over Europe in a balloon."

"But, I have," he said simply.

For an instant, I thought that I had actually hurt him.

"Please allow me to assist you," he said.

"What?" I asked.

"I'll take you up and show you the beauty of the world, and together we will find your animals."

"Well . . ." I said. He sounded so completely sincere.

He reached out toward me, imploring. "Come up with me, and we'll find your horses. I bet they're no more than fifty or a hundred feet away. Probably eating some spring clover in another man's pasture."

He was so convincing, I found myself agreeing that his was the only way to go. I grabbed a-hold on the top edge of the basket.

"Just throw your leg over, like you're mounting a horse."

I picked my foot up and placed it on the rail, then I pulled my body after, rolling over into the basket.

As he released the gas up into the open bottom of the balloon, turning his metal-handle gizmo, I clenched my eyes shut.

"Afraid?" Katanzakis asked.

I nodded.

"No need to be," he said. "Believe." He touched my shoulder lightly, like his hand was a fairy's wand.

I opened my eyes and stared into his face that looked as though it had been carved from rough-hewn brown marble.

"As I told you last night, to make life interesting, you must believe in the impossible. You must have faith in magic. Life without magic is horribly monotonous and even boring. One must never allow life to become boring. It's such a waste."

I told myself that everything was all right, but my stomach still jumped like a quivering rattlesnake, which I hated worse than heights. I held my breath and kept my eyes closed.

"Have faith," Katanzakis said to me. "Faith is not simply biblical. It is a primary support of everyday life. If you have faith, you can make every minute of every day count; make it amount to more than it is; breathe life into it. Make it vibrate with excitement.

"Now, don't say . . ." He stopped before he finished his refrain.

I opened my eyes and stared into his. His eyes were bright as cat-eye marbles—like onyx. They were dark but clear as a mountain stream. "When you've lived as long as I have and traveled half as many miles, you know that every minute must count for something besides just meandering across the earth. Look down yonder!" He pointed. "Behold a vision!"

A herd of five deer broke from a bramble bush and leaped over a small stream. They ran fast across the landscape. Beyond them was a team of red foxes scampering through the underbrush. A raccoon tiptoed away from the water, stopped, turned, tilted its head to gaze up at us, then disappeared into nearby woods.

We rose high. I held tightly to the edge of the basket and prayed for safety. We looked down onto the tallest tree. My eyes scanned the territory: through the woods, over the meadow, down the road a mile or farther. My stomach settled. I forgot where I was or the simple fact that my feet were not resting on solid ground.

As the sun rose, it brightened and spread splashes of color across the world. It raced across hills and hollows below us.

Through the sky no more than twenty-some-odd feet away flew a falcon, wings outstretched, head steady, small black eyes regarding us with fright or wonder. He was so close I could see the spots dotting his broad breast. He flicked his wings and angled away from us, dropping lower and lower toward earth.

My heart beat anxiously, trying to take in everything at once. The vast countryside resembled the gigantic patchwork quilt Mawma had given Mama two Christmases ago. It had taken her three winters, she said, to fit it all together and stitch each piece in tiny intricate needlework to form the perfect pattern. Below us, God's own perfect pattern fit together in squares of brown and red, triangles of rich greens, rectangles of golden yellow, all stretching as far as the eye could see, glittering and gleaming, exquisitely put together in a random pattern.

I'd never been so thrilled. Even after the time the harness broke and the wagon got loose and rolled wildly down Penitentiary Mountain between Town Creek and The Forest, where Mama's folks, Mawma and Pawpa, lived. When the wagon rocked up and down, almost flinging me out, then smashed against a tree at the bottom of the incline, I jerked back against the pallet in the bed of the wagon where I'd been sleeping. Frightened and sick, my breath was sucked away. My chest felt caved in. But I had had a total thrill, careening downward at such a fast rate of speed, completely and totally out of control. When it was over, I was exhilarated, my heart pounding in my chest.

"This is magnificent," I said, ogling the picturesque panorama: the deep greens of the trees, the spotted colors and whites against the backdrop of the woods, the golden glades of the sedge-field meadows, the ribbon of a creek running north and south.

In the distance to the north thick dark trees formed a straight line. Beyond that lay the wide brown water of the big river. My eyes followed the expanse of the river toward the east, thinking that if I looked hard enough I would be able to see the city of Decatur. Instead, my eyes wondered at the sight of a half-dozen flat-topped hills covered with small wooden block-style houses. I pointed toward them, but Katanzakis said he had no idea what they were. I figured they could not possibly be Decatur. Papa had said nothing about Decatur being built on flat-topped hills. And I didn't remember such from my one trip there.

In the far distance due east was the very tip-top of a great house. In its crown was the square white railing of a widow's walk, high above the trees that surrounded the place. It had to be the old Walker place, Home Sweet Home, where General Joseph Walker lived with his daughter Annie.

Then I followed the twin pathways of the road leading toward us, and in the distance I could make out a figure astride a gray donkey.

I pointed.

Anthony Katanzakis guided the balloon in that direction.

As we neared, Katanzakis said, "If I didn't know better, I'd say . . ."

"That old man's got Jed and Jenny," I announced, my heart skipping. In my excitement with flying through the sky, I'd almost forgotten that I had lost them. And now, from down the road, came a man who looked like drawings I'd seen of Kris Kringle, a small fat man with hair as white as Mr. Saunders's cotton and a beard that fell to his chest.

As we neared, I made out the man's costume. On his head he wore a small Confederate cap. Over his shoulders was draped a gray woolen cape, and his britches were the same color. He looked like a shrunken, elderly version of General Nathan Bedford Forrest. I almost laughed.

When Anthony Katanzakis brought us down, both Jed and Jenny stopped dead in their tracks. Another encounter with the wild balloon was too much for them to behold. If the old man didn't hold them tight, they'd be off on another stampede through the forest. "Bring us down slow," I urged Katanzakis, who seemed to be fighting the controls.

We landed with a bump about thirty feet from the Confederate Santa Claus and the animals.

I jumped from the basket and rushed toward the old man. Seeing that he was almost as frightened as the animals, I slowed to a walk, threw up my hands and shouted, "I'm Harold Reed, a friendly traveler. I see that you found my horse and mule."

The old man, whose eyes were bulging almost as bad as Jed's, stammered, "These are your'n?"

I nodded, reaching for Jed's bridle and Jenny's halter. "They're mine," I declared, just as I viewed the disarray of the packing across Jenny's back and the right stirrup hanging by a thread from Jed's saddle. "What on earth . . ." I started.

The old man released the reins and the rope. He raised his hands in a gesture of hopelessness and said, "I found 'em worse than this. The saddle was torn. The mule's belongings were strewn across the countryside. I followed their path through the wilderness to find what I could. Looks like you'd planned to do some shoeshine work."

I allowed as I had, while I checked over what was left of the package Papa had intricately balanced onto Jenny's backside. I had to admit that the old man had put it back as best he could. Still, some of the goods were missing. My shoeshine equipment looked like it had been torn apart piece by piece before being put back together and tied down.

I patted the necks of both Jed and Jenny, who'd been as frightened as I about the prospects of being out in this territory alone. I talked softly to them and told them everything was fine now. There was no need to be frightened. Both seemed pleased to have the weight of my hands on their backs and the ease of my words in their ears. The old man, who said he was not what was left of the Johnny Reb army but an Irish fiddler looking for work, said he'd like to travel along with us, if we didn't mind— although it was apparent that he regarded the balloon with strong apprehension.

I looked into the craggy face of Katanzakis. "I reckon you'll be on your way west," I said to him.

"I've no destination," the Greek said.

"Then you'll be backtracking?" I asked.

He shrugged. "One direction is good as another, when you're a drifter. Besides, I got lots of things to talk about, and two sets of strange ears would be right pleasing for me to talk to."

I grinned. His attitude was contagious. I knew that I could use some cheering up along the way. If he would keep his stories halfway down to earth and if he didn't repeat *Now don't say nothing* so often. But I knew I couldn't rightly put any restrictions on such a free spirit.

Katanzakis dropped a rope that I tied to the saddle horn. It stabilized him up above, pulling him along with us, while he watched out for any sign of danger on the road ahead.

The short, fat man with the fluffy white beard and curly long white hair said his name was Sean O'Donohue. "I'm second-cousin to leprechauns of County Cork," he said in a rolling brogue.

I wondered how an Irishman and a Greek would fit together traveling. They shook hands, although Katanzakis's big hand swallowed O'Donohue's tiny fingers, and their eyes sparkled when they looked each other face-to-face.

However, once Katanzakis had ascended to fifty feet, I got the distinct impression that O'Donohue was much more comfortable. He said that he was on his way east, having traveled the countryside from Memphis. "I liked Memphis fine, but it's a rowdy town without much money. I'm told Mooresville is where the action and the cash is at."

"That right?" I asked, trying to be conversational, after Jed and Jenny had been calmed down and properly fed and watered. We were on our way at a slow but steady pace.

"That's correct," O'Donohue said. "There's a world of commerce there, I'm told, where riverboats dock and cotton's loaded, and sailors come ashore with pockets lined with gold."

I had not heard such tales. I told him I was under the impression that Decatur was the most prosperous town on the lower Tennessee, unless a body went as far northeast as Chattanooga.

"Well, perhaps its reputation has not spread as far as Memphis," he said. Then he told about the honky tonks of Memphis, filled with colored musicians playing something called the blues. "It's a low-down sad music, doesn't mix too good with my fiddle, which is more accustomed to jigs and jollies." His small forefinger touched the black leather case that slapped against his donkey's flank. "I make my music for the enjoyment of the crowd, not to burden 'em down with so much weight from sorrow and sadness. Oh, I can play a funeral that'll bring tears to a mother's eyes, mind you. But it's not my natural inclination to mirror the low-down dingy horrors of broken hearts and damaged personalities. What I aim to do is bring a smile to the face of a dear sweet girl whose lover's run off with another beat-down soul, and to show her there's other menfolk out there in the world worth tons more than her grief at the moment."

Suddenly, he raised his voice to a lilting cry, *"Heaven forbid, child, there's a sea of tears over yonder hill. Dry your eyes and dance a number with me, and we'll go off into the night, holding hands and finding love. You always have to remember: tomorrow's another day."*

Jed lowered and raised his head. He blew his breath against the morning's crisp breeze, making a joyful sound. Then Jenny answered him.

O'Donohue howled a bright laughter that crackled against the brisk air. "These animals know of what I sing," he said.

From above, Katanzakis hollered, "What's that old fart singing about?"

O'Donohue hushed and looked upward.

"The old bastard hasn't hushed since he took up with us," Katanzakis shouted.

In a half-whisper, I said to O'Donohue, pointing upward, "You've got competition in the talking department."

Moments later, Katanzakis began singing a song in his native language.

Jed and Jenny whinnied in the breeze but otherwise paid him no more attention.

I asked O'Donohue where in all this world he found his Confederate outfit, and he laughed again, his cackling sound cutting the air with happiness. "A seamstress girl in Nashville was making clothes for figures in a wax museum," he explained. "She overdid her work, making too many of the gray. 'Tis a good thing she didn't overdo the blue, or else I'd have been tarred and feathered by some crazy Southerners who might mistake me for the enemy." He glanced down. "But neither can I travel north of the Mason-Dixon." And he laughed again.

He went on to tell the story of his life, having been born on a farm in the south of Ireland, poor and contrary to the rocky soil, winning himself passage on a ship out of a harbor called Dungarvan, entertaining with his fiddle and happy voice and throwing in with some deckhand work. "It was a long voyage, but one well worth it, I'll tell you. And since I've been in this country, now unto thirty-some-odd year, I've traveled a number of mile from Charleston town up to Boston and down again to St. Augustine. Now *there's* a town . . ."

And he told about the back alleys of the former Spanish port in Florida where, he said, gypsy ladies with long legs and happy feet danced to the tunes that he played for them. "It was a sight, I'll tell. We made 'em jump for joy."

In late morning we stopped at a spring, hauled in Anthony Katanzakis, who gazed into my face, worked his wind-beaten features into a frown and wondered, "Does that old geezer ever hush?"

O'Donohue, who was watering his donkey, turned and said, "I heard that disparaging remark."

"It was meant for your ears," Katanzakis allowed.

"Now, what's this with the two of you?" I said. I looked into Jed's face and saw a look of wonder even in his eyes. I'd been with them less than a few hours, and I was already picking up pieces of their way of talking. *Oh, no,* I thought. *If I keep on like this Mama won't recognize me when I return.*

I passed around what was left of the sandwiches Mama had packed for me. I gave Jed and Jenny a handful of oats, which they lapped up without hesitation.

The spring water tasted sweet as I sucked it down my dry throat. I thought I'd ask Katanzakis if he'd mind if I rode up in the basket for some of the afternoon. I'd like to view the countryside once again from that vantage. And I thought I'd give the Greek a chance to take in some of the Irishman's talk. Or maybe they could have a talking contest between the two of them.

So we exchanged places. I followed Katanzakis's instructions and rose up above them while Jed's eyes watched. My stomach never acted up. It was smooth as a buggy ride, until I pulled one of the gizmos too far to the left, shifting the balloon's direction abruptly. I grabbed against the edge of the basket and twisted the metal handle back a notch. Katanzakis warned not to twist and turn but just hold it steady. Once I was at the height of fifty feet, settled there, the horse seemed satisfied to have Anthony Katanzakis on his back. I settled into the seat in the corner of the basket.

Below, I heard O'Donohue begin once again the narrative of his life story. I smiled as the drone of his voice filtered up through the clear air of the brilliant blue sky.

Soon Katanzakis broke in and began his own tale, then they switched about again.

I looked out over the countryside as I had earlier in the day. As comfortable as a rocking chair, I rocked along at an easy flow, carried along with them at their leisurely gait, exploring the landscape ahead and behind.

I knew that now, without hesitation, I could climb to the top of the tower with Sarah Lynn Saunders without having the first symptom of height sickness. I would be a knight like in the days of old. Perhaps I would even be her knight. If she gave me her scarf, colorful with the hint of aroma from her perfume, I'd ride out across the distant lands to fight battles for her. And when I returned . . .

Six

I awakened with a jolt. The ride had been so smooth, the view so pleasing, my eyes had closed and I was dreaming that I was floating over Persia on a magical carpet when a force tugged at the basket, jerking me awake.

At first I thought I'd done something wrong again. I grabbed the rail at the edge of the basket, leaned over, and looked down. A gunshot zinged through the air, and I prayed no one was shooting at the balloon, not knowing what might happen if a bullet broke through the colorful sphere. It might send us sailing in every which direction.

Someone dressed in buckskin and carrying a long-barrel rifle stood in front of Katanzakis and O'Donohue. "Pull him in!" a woman commanded, motioning the gun toward me.

If I'd had the forethought to carry a gun, I'd shoot the highway robber before she had a chance to take all our worldly possessions.

Without arguing, Anthony Katanzakis started reeling me in, hand over fist. I tried to think fast, looking around my feet for some kind of weapon, knowing Katanzakis carried his tools and goods in the box he had fashioned under the seat. Standing at the edge of the basket, I lifted the top of the cushioned seat and began searching.

"Put your arms over the side of that apparatus," she hollered. "I'll have no commotion out of you up there."

I found a half-dozen gallon-sized canvas sacks filled with sand and raised several to seat level.

By the time she repeated her command a second time, I had the bags in both hands.

As I was being lowered, I held the bags hidden behind the wall of the basket, cocked, ready to throw.

From less than ten feet over their heads, I lifted the bags. I heaved the first one toward her.

It caught the woman squarely against the side of her head, knocking her off of her sorrel mare.

When she fell, O'Donohue leaped from astride his donkey and rushed to her before she could gain her footing.

"That was quite a toss," judged Katanzakis as he dismounted Jed and took hold of the basket and guided it to a smooth landing.

Jumping from the basket, I hurried to O'Donohue's aid, where he had the woman pinned against the ground.

I picked up the rifle, pointed it at her, and said, "Don't move!"

She squirmed beneath O'Donohue's weight, pushing up and off with little effort. She rubbed the side of her head. Frowning, she cried, "What in the world did you do that for? I wasn't planning on hurting anyone."

"It was you who was trying to rob us," I said. "We were on the lookout for a highwayman when you came riding up, shooting."

"I'm no highwayman and I wasn't trying to rob you," she said.

"It looked like robbery to me," I said.

She shook her head, her stiff oily hair shivering. It looked like tiny birds had been nesting in her black hair, and she was not pretty at all, the way I judged girls. She was rough-looking. Her skin was swarthy brown from the sun and the wind, resembling Katanzakis's Mediterranean complexion.

"I wasn't trying to rob you," she said again, rubbing her ear where the bag had hit full-force. "If I had-a been, I'd-a shot you out of the air before saying anything or asking questions. That's for sure."

"What do you call it?" Anthony Katanzakis asked.

"What?" she asked.

"What you were doing? Seems to me, you were robbing us, the way you ran up on us, shooting that firearm."

O'Donohue, embarrassed that a woman could wrestle out from under him and throw him aside, slapped the dirt from his Confederate uniform and cursed.

"I was scared," the woman said.

"Of what?" O'Donohue asked.

"Of y'all, and that apparition."

"That's no apparition," Katanzakis said. "That's a circus balloon. It's performed in Switzerland and France. We're circus performers from Greece. This boy here is my favored assistant."

She looked at each of us and appeared doubtful. "Well, I ain't ever seen anything like that in north Alabama," the woman said. "I've lived up here in the Indian nation all my life and ain't ever seen nothing to compare with that thing." Then she looked at O'Donohue and started to say something else.

"This is not the Indian nation," I said.

"Tell that to the Cherokees and Choctaws who ventured back here after the removal nearly a hundred years ago. We number well over a hundred, and then some. And we don't take kindly to signs of evil spirits being paraded through our land. It upsets our peaceful nature. We're farm people who live on mounds over close to the river. It was our land before the federals came in and hauled our ancestors off to Oklahoma."

"I've heard about some renegade Indians in these parts," I said.

The woman laughed. "You're a fool, boy," she said.

73

I urged the gun barrel toward her.

"And you don't even know how to fire that thing," she said.

"Try me," I said.

She laughed again.

Suddenly I felt foolish, thinking I could outsmart someone who smelled like a polecat and dressed in skins and looked like she'd been ridden longer and harder than Jed or Jenny. I'd always heard Indians could sneak up on a herd of buffalo and get so close they could kill one barehanded with a knife, but I knew if this person tried to sneak up on anything, the prey better be upwind or totally without the sense of smell. She was about as rank as I'd ever smelled.

I figured the only way she slipped up on us was that O'Donohue had been so engrossed in one of his stories that he paid no attention to the smell and Anthony Katanzakis was so bored with his story that he'd fallen asleep, like me, or he was so mad because he couldn't get a word in edgewise between all of the Irishman's words.

One thing for sure: Powtawee, who said her Choctaw name meant Little Squirrel, could never sneak up on anyone if they were downwind of her. Not as long as she wore the clothes that were on her back this afternoon.

As she fell in with us, I turned her rifle butt away from me, and she took it, saying she could offer us free passage through Indian territory. Indians in this area were not particularly dangerous. Not since nearly a hundred years ago, when General Andrew Jackson came down from Nashville with a band of his Tennessee volunteers. With the help of a number of Choctaw, they wiped out the Muskogee Creek nation at the battle of Horseshoe Bend. Then, after Jackson became President, he got Congress to pass the Removal Act, which allowed the white people to round up all the Indians, including the Choctaw who'd been friendly with the white settlers, collect them into forts, and then drive them west like a herd of unruly cattle on what became known in history as the Trail of Tears. I'd heard my Pawpa tell about his father, my great-grandfather, being sickened by the way the Indians were treated—captured in their camps, men, women, and children corralled into forts where they were kept like animals, until they were forced to march with little food and no shelter across the southland to the far west.

I asked Powtawee how she and her people got back to Alabama, and she threw her head up proudly and said, "We're free, just like you," and then she recounted the story, telling about her great-great-grandparents being captured and made to walk all the way to Oklahoma, where they were put on a reservation. "But now we are here, back on our homeland, and we plan to stay." She looked sharply at all three of us. "My people were here long before the Europeans set foot on this soil. Some day we will take control again. We will drive the white man to the sea. He will remember what he did to us. Then he will know our wrath."

"You're a feisty little thing, for somebody that stinks like a skunk," the Irishman said.

Powtawee glared at him with dark eyes. "You some kind of Confederate?" she asked. "Or what?"

O'Donohue began telling her the story, but she glared at him with a hateful look.

"Don't look at me like that," O'Donohue said. "You try some of that Indian voodoo shit on me, I'll put a leprechauns' spell on you."

Up above in the balloon, where he'd already escaped while we talked, Anthony Katanzakis bellowed a belly laugh.

The woman turned her head skyward. She raised her gun.

Katanzakis threw up his hands. "No, no!" he shouted.

"Put the gun down, Miss Powtawee," I said. "He don't mean no harm."

"And you need to watch your double negatives," Powtawee snapped.

"My what?"

"Don't you know anything about the English language?"

I shrugged. I hated having my use of the language being called by an Indian, much less one that smelled like an overripe outhouse.

"Mr. O'Donohue," she said, "you need to teach this youngster a thing or two about the language. You seem to speak it quite well—for a foreigner."

"Where'd you learn?" I asked her.

"At Indian school," she said. "We have perfectly wonderful teachers."

"They didn't teach you much about hygiene, did they?" Katanzakis hollered down from his perch.

She put her hand back on her gun, which she had slipped into its saddle scabbard.

O'Donohue said he'd teach me some Irish poetry, something that would allow the vowels to roll off my tongue like Blarney. "It'll be a grand day when the lad returns home, quoting a ballad from County Cork."

She laughed lightly and said I was probably full enough of Blarney as it was, without help from him.

I listened to their banter as we eased along through the afternoon.

We stopped at the next spring and ate what was left of Mama's fixings, then continued onward. O'Donohue once again told about the Nashville seamstress making his uniform. "I got it for a mere pittance," the Irishman said.

"It's a wonder you haven't been shot for impersonating a Confederate soldier," she said.

He glanced at her with a twinkling eye, saw that she was just funning, and laughed at himself.

At a wide place in the trail we slowed and looked southward up an oak-shaded hill to a large white house that rose above the trees.

"Home Sweet Home," Powtawee said.

"What?" O'Donohue asked.

"The Walker house. Home of Miss Annie and the general. It's called Home Sweet Home. They're fine people."

"Maybe we ought to stop and pay our respects," Anthony Katanzakis hollered down.

She glanced toward me. "I'm sure Miss Annie'd be mighty happy to see us," she said. "She's an old acquaintance of mine. She's one of the finest white people I know."

"We're making this journey a long one," I remarked. "What should-a taken me two days will now take three—unless y'all find a way to stretch it to four."

Powtawee glanced toward O'Donohue. "And the old general will probably weep bitter tears, seeing what his army has come to."

I chuckled.

"If your brother arrives on tomorrow's train, surely he'll have sense enough to wait for you," O'Donohue said.

"Bosworth's very smart," I said. I resented his implying otherwise.

"I'm not saying he's not smart," O'Donohue started. He shot an eye toward Powtawee. "That is not a double negative, Missy."

She smiled almost pleasantly.

"If he does start home without you, we'll pass him on the road, won't we?"

"Unless he takes the trail north of the river," Powtawee said.

"Only an Indian would go north of the river to a town that's south of the river," Katanzakis commented.

"I ought to shoot you and be done with it," Powtawee said.

"Go ahead and try," the old foreigner said smartly. "I'll have your Indian butt flat on the ground before you can turn around good."

When I looked, he had two of the bags of sand raised shoulder-high. "Hey, Anthony," I shouted. "Put those things down. Miss Powtawee's our friend."

Katanzakis pouted as he pulled the balloon down to earth. "If she's our friend, why does she keep saying these derogatory things about us? It's plumb embarrassing, the accusations we're allowing her to make. Downright character assassination, I'd call it."

"It's just her way," I said, knowing we didn't need further dissension and wondering why she didn't cool her words, at least until we got to where we were going. Once in Decatur, they could duke it out, as far as I cared. By then, I'd be home free and looking for Bosworth.

"You keep trying me, I'm going to shoot you for sure," Powtawee said.

"Now . . ." I started.

Just then, a lady in a bonnet and a long gingham dress rode a horse out of the shaded drive and reined up in front of us. "Powtawee, are you still causing trouble among the white people?" she asked.

Powtawee nodded. "Miss Annie, these are my friends." She introduced each of us.

Miss Annie Walker nodded toward me. "I know the boy. You're John Reed's son, aren't you?"

I said I was.

"You and your Papa, sister Ida Mae, and brother Martin stayed with us some years ago."

I told her that was correct and said she had a splendid memory.

She said it looked like I'd grown quite a bit since then. "You were just a little sprout that night me and your sister Ida Mae tucked you in."

I nodded, feeling my face grow hot, but still I thanked her.

Then Miss Annie commented, "If y'all aren't a sight for sore eyes, I've never seen one. What with that rainbow-colored balloon, it's a wonder you haven't frightened off all the livestock from here to wherever you came from." She turned to O'Donohue with a smile. "And who are you, Sergeant? Still looking for some Union jackass to shoot?"

Seven

Miss Annie was a formidable woman. With tufts of auburn hair pushing from the edges of her sunbonnet, she sat high on her horse that would have been a fair match with Mr. Melvin Saunders's Midnight Blue. Hers too was a Tennessee walker standing at least fourteen hands, holding his head as regally as his mistress. My little roan gelding regarded the stallion with what I thought surely was a look of envy. I reached down and patted Jed on the neck, knowing the feeling.

I argued halfheartedly for forging ahead in order to arrive at Decatur shortly after sundown.

"Nonsense," Miss Annie said. "You're John and Elizabeth Reed's son, aren't you?"

"I am," I said.

"You're Ida Mae and Lucy's little brother, the one they call Brother, aren't you?"

Again, I admitted I was.

"I've known Ida Mae and Lucy for years. They're two of the smartest women in the Tennessee River valley. Too bad Ida Mae had to go to Nashville to school, but that's the way it is when you don't have a forward-thinking educational institution nearby to fill the needs of the community. If she'd stayed here, she'd be teaching the third grade forever."

I started to say that wasn't such a terribly bad idea, knowing how much Lucy loved teaching little children, but I kept my lips clamped shut.

Miss Annie tossed her head back, holding her spirited horse steady. "I've heard the girls speak of 'Brother,' like you're some kind of natural-born gentleman, or something. I'd take offense if you didn't stay with us.

"You can stay here in a free bed, have a good supper, and become an audience for Father, who loves to regale strangers with his battlefield adventures. And I'm sure he'd like to talk with the Sergeant here." She guided her look toward O'Donohue. Then she turned to Powtawee and added, "And some of you may wish to avail yourself of our bathing facilities."

"That sounds like a splendid idea to me," Anthony Katanzakis said.

"I'll vote to make ourselves at home with Miss Annie's invitation," put in O'Donohue, who had not stopped grinning since the woman had ridden into our midst and started calling him Sergeant.

I didn't argue further. As far as I was concerned, I could have traveled on alone, leaving all of them behind. I didn't see any need for a vote. Was this not my trip? They had joined me along the way. But just like that, they had each become equal partners without being polled.

I shrugged and nodded. Katanzakis tethered his balloon to a post, then followed behind as we trailed after Miss Annie and her big horse.

I took extra time to take care of Jed and Jenny, both of whom were happy to be unloaded, rubbed down, and put into a stall with sweet dry hay. As I forked the food to them, Jed nuzzled his nose next to my side for a quick, adequate thank-you.

By the time I got to the kitchen, O'Donohue and Katanzakis were sitting in the parlor with drinks in their hands, listening to a white-haired old man propped in a corner chair with a shawl around his shoulders. As I washed, from a room out back I heard the sound of splashing water and a sigh, then more splashing.

I strode into the parlor and introduced myself to the elderly general.

"Glad to make your acquaintance," said the old man.

Miss Annie, freshened with her hair combed out, brought me a thimble of wine. "We make it on the place. From the finest cut of scuppernongs in the valley."

"Always like a touch of wine before supper," the old man said, raising his glass to sun-speckled lips. He sipped.

"You were a general?" Katanzakis asked. I had a feeling he knew exactly what he was saying. As soon as he said it, he leaned back, breathed deep, relaxing for a long story. I followed his example.

"I was a general when I was not much older'n this lad," he said, nodding toward me.

I smiled, waiting.

"It was not an easy task, leaving Home Sweet Home and my lovely bride, Amelia, God bless her soul. But I left the place with a heavy heart, although I tried my best to hide my sorrow from my boys. I led the Alabama Fifth north to Shiloh in the spring of 1862. After I huddled with Albert Sidney Johnston, we headed directly into the heat of battle. It was our job to cut off the Army of the Ohio, keeping it from splitting up and attacking us from both flanks. We managed to do that—but I'm afraid only with partial success. When the Yanks did turn on us, coming up from our tail, my boys managed to slip away and come back from the north. Then we headed off across north Mississippi to find Grant's boys over near Vicksburg. It was not long, during the western campaign, that I became known as General Fighting Joe Walker, an honor bestowed upon me by my old friend and fellow cavalryman, General Nathan Bedford Forrest, of whom I am sure you are all acquainted."

We nodded.

"We won many a-battle. But, of course, we lost the war," he said in his distinctive low-pitched drawl.

His rheumy old eyes blinked and focused on O'Donohue for a long moment. "What outfit did you serve with, Sergeant?" he asked.

O'Donohue, whose face had flushed red as a ripe beet after the second sip of wine, said, "Oh, General, I'm not a Confederate soldier." Then he began telling his story.

Katanzakis interrupted, "It's a long story, General."

O'Donohue shot an offended glare toward Katanzakis, then shrugged.

General Walker started, "After the war, I came back here to Home Sweet Home and my darling Amelia. Together with our sweet Annie we began the business of rebuilding the plantation. It was difficult, but we did our best to cope with what the Yankees called Reconstruction. I call it Hell, because that's exactly what it was. It was a damned hell on this earth!" His voice grew louder. His veins popped red in his neck and along his temples. He choked.

"Father," Miss Annie said. She rose and went to him and bent him forward and slapped his back. "You don't need to get so excited," she said evenly.

He took another sip of wine as the sun fell and lanterns dappled the room with flickering light and long shadows. When I looked at the faded portraits on the high walls I felt the presence of Walker ghosts from years past. There was an overwhelming feeling of age in the air, as though we were living in a time long past, never to be forgotten.

The old man would not be quieted. He cleared his throat, looked around as though first encountering our presence. "The War had been bad enough, but the aftermath was too much for my dear wife. She had been weakened to fragility by the worry and the weariness of long days and nights of not knowing. At least I was out there in the field, doing something, defending our land from being taken by the aggression of our greedy neighbors. Alas, my darling Amelia succumbed in the bed where I now lay my own weary head. She just could not cope. But Annie and I, somehow we made it through the hell." Like an aged actor on the last stage, realizing the drama of repetition, he spoke louder, with emphasis, "Somehow! We made it. We created quite a world here. It's a beautiful paradise, don't you think?" He glanced toward his daughter, who smiled and nodded and sipped.

"At least I did not buckle under to the negative Reconstruction forces like my old fighting pal, General Forrest."

I glared into the old man's pale face, wondering his meaning.

As soon as questions formed in my mind, he answered them. "Forrest became so distraught that he founded the Ku Klux Klan up in Pulaski, Tennessee. I don't think he realized that putting hoods on men turned them to evil hate mongers. But that's exactly what he did." The old man's eyes bored into mine. "When a man hides behind a hood he becomes a low-down sorry coward, he can hate without being seen, and that hate spreads across a nation like wildfire. Here at Home Sweet Home, some of the finest people I ever knew in my life were the slaves who stayed with us after they were freed. They helped us rebuild our home and our land. And Annie has done everything she can to make their lives more abundant."

Miss Annie said, "Now, Father, you mustn't allow your emotions to overwhelm you."

I was wondering how our old neighbor Louisa Dot, herself a former slave, could have such a high regard for a man who actually founded the Ku Klux Klan. I wondered if she even knew this fact about Forrest. I knew one thing for sure: I'd never think of Nathan Bedford Forrest as a hero again.

The old man took a sip of his drink, cleared his throat, and continued. "When we got our government back, I ran for Congress and was elected by an overwhelming majority." His voice lilted.

"That so?" said O'Donohue.

Walker nodded. "In my third term I was voted Chairman of Ways and Means. That was no small feat for a man who had fought with distinction but had known defeat—for a man who had to overcome such overpowering odds as an entire nation opposed to his way of life—the Grand Cause for which I fought and for which I never gave up hope. It was no small task either, when it came to wielding power. Then, along came another war, in 1898, when a reluctant President McKinley called for military action against Spain to allow Cuba to become a free country. When our nation's leader called, Alabama responded. We did not hesitate. We never hesitated when it came to fighting. We sent several regiments of volunteers. And I became the first general to have served in both the Confederate and the U.S. armies. And I did so proudly . . . proudly, I tell you." Again, his voice rose. His chest expanded. His head lifted a scant higher, turning his chin upward, even though it wrinkled and quivered.

"Let me tell you something that few people remember—or don't *choose* to remember." He gazed straight into my eyes, like I might be guilty of some terrible sin of oversight. "We had colored troops from Alabama that sailed to Cuba and fought side by side with white soldiers at San Juan Hill. They did themselves proud down there, I'll tell you. And so did the redskins . . ." He hesitated, looking over our heads.

We turned and watched as Powtawee entered, her head not as haughty, her demeanor not as challenging. She was dressed in what I presumed correctly to be one of Miss Annie's skirts

and blouses. She was scrubbed clean and her hair shone even in
the lantern light. Her face was almost pretty.

"Why, my goodness, Miss Powtawee," O'Donohue exclaimed.

She shifted her head slightly to glare at Anthony Katanzakis.
"Don't you dare say one word, Greek!"

Katanzakis smiled.

"Not a word!"

"Now . . ." Katanzakis started.

"Not a word!"

"Have a sip of wine, Powtawee?" Miss Annie asked.

She took the tiny glass from Miss Annie's fingers.

General Walker's speech continued, "The native Americans of
north Alabama—including this girl's uncle, Pantatow
Abernathy of the River Clan in the Choctaw nation—fought
with great skill and courage. They fought like Cuba was their
own land. And Pantatow was killed in a small skirmish outside
Havana trying to save the lives of three white boys from
Anniston.

"When we all came home, when I was well over sixty, I might
add, I marched proudly with all of our Alabama men down
Dexter Avenue in Montgomery, straight up to the capitol steps
to the same spot where forty years earlier Jefferson Davis had
stood and declared the independence of the Confederate states.
It all goes to show you how a people and a country can change.
We stood there proudly while the band played 'The Battle
Hymn of the Republic.' By damn, it was a helluva day."

After he took another sip, he looked steadily at me again.
"Young boys who grow up in the South need to understand the
complexity of the character of our region," he said. "There's
nothing simple about it, I tell you. And that complexity lives on,
even now."

I frowned, trying to comprehend exactly what he was saying.

"You sure have lived to see a lot," Katanzakis said.

The old man did not shift his vision from my eyes. I knew he was talking straight at me, and I listened to every word. "We fought hard—long and hard and mercilessly—to preserve the pride of our region, which had declared that we were an independent country. That was our cause. We considered it a grand and noble cause.

"But once we were defeated—and after we suffered our punishment at the hands of a bunch of scalawagging, carpetbagging, tariff-levying sonsofbitches—most of us once again became loyal Americans. We understood our duty. After we were given our citizenship, our rights, our dignity, we stood as hard and fast and strong for the American way as any other American—maybe even more so, because of our humiliating defeat. We know that we are the only defeated nation that has ever—and I hope will ever—be a part of the United States of America. One thing about us: we're a fightin' bunch of bastards, us Southerners."

"Father," Miss Annie said softly. "Supper's ready."

We waited until Miss Annie helped her father into the dining room and had him seated at the head of the long table beneath the twinkling of the oil-burning chandelier, then we filed in and sat where she directed.

Over plates heaped with squirrel stew, tenderloin of venison wrapped in bacon and smoked over hickory coals, green beans cooked soft and sweet with fatback seasoning, tender turnips and greens, and biscuits the size of Katanzakis's fists, the general continued to extol the virtues of the Southern soldier. We even had iced tea with chocolate mint.

Katanzakis sat on the old general's right, O'Donohue to his left. The Greek plied him with questions about the details of his military experiences, and the old man filled the air with audacious colorful meanderings about the army of the west as it sought to keep the Mississippi River out of the hands of General Grant's Union troops.

"In retrospect, Lee had it easy in the east. All he had to do was move his men from one location to another through the Carolinas, Virginia, and finally into Pennsylvania, where he was finally out-manned and out-maneuvered at Gettysburg," he said with an air of unrelenting pomposity. "At Shiloh, Chickamauga, across northern Alabama, into Mississippi, and down at Vicksburg, we were constantly having to double back across hills and hollows, Grant's shifting to the flanks putting us in precarious positions that we had to defend or lose. Our great leader was General Forrest, although I must say that I planned as many battles—perhaps even more—as he. He was more a hit-and-run guerrilla than a tactician. And we had to make our plans swiftly, without the benefit of time and circumstance. It was no easy matter, I tell you."

Katanzakis allowed as how he'd studied Hannibal's military tactics in southern Europe. "It must have been the same kind of trying circumstances for you and your men," he added. The general nodded between bites, then made another comment about the genius of Nathan Bedford Forrest's guerrilla warfare.

"Papa was considered the finest wartime engineer in the Southern army," Miss Annie commented.

General Walker patted his thin, colorless lips with his cloth napkin and nodded. "Daughter loves to quote the military historians and their generous adjectives, describing my contributions to the effort on behalf of The Cause. I tend to be more humble about my own genius."

Katanzakis nodded and contributed his own benevolent assessment of the general's valiant career, both in the Civil War and the Spanish-American War.

I glanced up into the sensitive eyes in a portrait of a navy officer whom Miss Annie had described as her devoted first cousin, her mother's sister's oldest son, lost at sea during the battle of Havana harbor—a cadet only two years older than I when he died. I was sure I saw a smile playing at his lips, amused at the old man's generous remembrances of his own military talent.

By the time apple cobbler was served, General Walker's voice slowed to a barely audible sound, like the words on a Victrola that needed winding. His eyes snapped shut after each drawn-out word, pronounced with considerable exertion in his soft twang.

After his grizzled head fell forward, his chin resting against the top of his chest, Miss Annie slid her chair from the table and rose. Katanzakis, O'Donohue, and I helped the old man from the table, through the kitchen, and up the narrow rear stairs to his bedroom. We undressed the old man and draped his nightgown over his head and let it fall to his sides. His daughter settled him into bed while the Greek and the Irishman tiptoed to their bedroom.

I followed Miss Annie back down to the kitchen, where she and I and Powtawee sat at the lamp-lighted table. "It was wonderful of you to bring your new friends for a visit, Powtawee. They're very interesting. And they provided Father with a new and attentive audience."

Powtawee nodded silently.

"Father had a wonderful time. He doesn't get too many visitors. And when they come, he tries to shine for them. Each is his last performance, you know, and that's very important to a man who has lived such an exciting, often uncompromising life."

I nodded, trying to encompass the entire meaning of her words. *Perhaps some day,* I thought.

She extended her dappled hand, unashamed of its calloused knots, and took a-hold of Powtawee's own darkly ridged hands. She turned the Indian's palms up toward the light and studied the surface. "You have lived hard," Miss Annie said, gazing into Powtawee's sun-toughened face.

Powtawee nodded. "But not as hard as my people who came before me," she said.

Miss Annie said, "It is good that you want to get an education. Learning is the best thing you can do at this stage of life. Then you'll be able to repay your ancestors for their suffering."

As she looked back down at Powtawee's palm, Miss Annie's face hardened into a frown.

"I want to give to the generations ahead," Powtawee said.

Miss Annie dropped her hand, then turned to me. "Are you going on to college, Harold? Like your brothers and sisters?"

"No, ma'am," I said, almost apologetically.

Powtawee looked at me like she didn't believe my answer.

"I'm a barber in Town Creek," I said.

"And you want to be a barber the rest of your life?" she asked.

"I also shine shoes," I said.

"That's not a life's career, is it?"

I felt myself wondering, questioning, thinking. "I like working in a barber shop," I said. "I like making people look better than they did when they came in the front door."

She nodded thoughtfully.

"I will become a teacher," Powtawee said simply.

Her eyes stared into mine. Her face was set with determination. I felt the strength of her words.

I didn't feel the necessity of continuing my explanation of my future. That would have to come later, I knew, to others who were near and dear to me. But most of all, I had to decide for myself whatever direction I would travel. It would be my decision to make, no matter what anyone else might say.

"Are you tired?" Miss Annie asked.

When neither of us argued for bed, Miss Annie showed us the icehouse out back, where ice cut from the frozen river last December was kept in a deep rock-lined cavern beneath a low-roofed log structure. In the middle was a shallow well that kept the room cool. Outside, low-hanging oak limbs guarded the sun from shining directly onto the roof. It was the first ice-house I'd ever seen, and I marveled at the ingenuity of the General's paradise.

In the moonlight, Miss Annie led me and Powtawee down a path between several other outbuildings, one a blacksmith's shed. We followed her through an arched latticed gateway laced with a flowering vine. We stepped through to find a small cemetery dotted with stones. Miss Annie showed us the graves of her mother, her aunts and uncles, and the cousin who had died at age eighteen while serving in the navy during the Spanish-American war. "I was the same age when I went down to Cuba," she said without the bragging quality her father had displayed.

"You?" I said. "You fought in the army?"

"I served in the Red Cross. I was in the middle of battle, but I didn't carry a gun. I tended to the men who were wounded. They needed us as much as they needed more guns and ammunition. We ministered to their wounded limbs and their broken hearts."

It was difficult to imagine this Southern belle in the middle of a blood-letting battlefield, and I said so.

Miss Annie smiled softly. "I'm not a little ol' honeysuckle-scented Southern belle, Harold," she said in her exaggerated north Alabama nasal drawl. "Not many of us are."

Powtawee shook her head. "If I'd been there, I would have had a gun. I'd welcome the opportunity to kill the people who killed my uncle. They must have been some sure-enough bad characters. I know he was a fine man."

Her voice rang in my head even when I finally put it down on the soft pillow in the upstairs bedroom where Miss Annie led me. I thought about all of my new friends for only a moment. I'd never met so many strangers in such a short span of time. Then I closed my eyes and slept.

Eight

We were on the road early. Miss Annie's cook, Ella, a fat squatty woman who looked O'Donohue over like he was a clothing display, fed us a whopping breakfast. When I first saw it spread across the long table, I thought there was no way I could eat such a feast, after the fine supper of the night before. But once I sat down, I filled my plate with grits and scrambled eggs and biscuits and bacon smoked with pecan wood. Thank goodness, there was no porridge in sight. Anthony Katanzakis shared his chicory with Ella and gave her the address of a company in Louisiana where she could order a package of the special coffee.

We moved along at a pretty good clip. All the animals were rested and raring to go. Even O'Donohue's donkey brayed sassily and picked up her feet as we stepped out from the Walker front yard onto the road.

Idle conversation took a friendly turn, especially after Katanzakis offered Powtawee a ride in the basket under his balloon, letting me pull her sorrel mare alongside Jenny. I think the horse and mule liked one another. I caught them rubbing noses when we slowed to a creep.

Overhead, Katanzakis showed Powtawee the compartments where he kept all of his goods packed, and he explained how the hot air in his compact apparatus filled the balloon to capacity, and how the various levers worked to lower it to the ground, then made it rise high above the tree tops. He showed her how he could turn it in one direction and then the other.

After they settled into a steady altitude, we traveled faster.

As we moved, I listened to their talk. At first Katanzakis rambled on and on about his multitude of adventures in Europe and India, how he'd been to the top of the highest mountain in the world, which I suspected was a stretch, even for his overactive imagination. About the time I began to tire of his speech, he asked, "How'd you come about receiving a name like Little Squirrel?"

"My mother said I squirmed around in her belly like a little squirrel," Powtawee answered. "And after I was born, she said I crawled all over the floor, scampering here and there, just like a little squirrel. So that was it, my father and mother agreed. I've been Powtawee ever since." Her voice was light and happy, a far cry from the tight sharpness of yesterday. She seemed to enjoy the flight as much as I had grown to delight in it.

As a slight breeze rustled through blackberry bushes in the shallows between us and the fields, O'Donohue called up to the balloon, "Y'all live in a *tee-pee*?"

I could have choked him, thinking that he was once again reverting to his annoying ways.

"We're mound people. We build our houses, made of logs, timber, wood from the forest, high on mounds."

"Why's that?" Katanzakis asked.

"We live north of here, near the river, and every spring and fall, when the river floods, it never rises to the top of our mound."

"I'll be," I said. I knew how the river rose over the bottomlands in the spring and fall, when the rains came.

"What?" asked Powtawee, shouting down to me.

"Anthony and I saw your house yesterday from the balloon," I hollered up.

"You did?" she asked anxiously, twisting her head to look in a northerly direction toward the river.

"Take her up higher and let her see," I suggested to Katanzakis.

"The wind's beginning to blow, but I think it'll be safe enough," he said, then turned his heating apparatus to full blast.

Jed and Jenny and the sorrel mare quick-stepped nervously. O'Donohue's donkey brayed.

As Katanzakis and Powtawee rose above us, I released the rope from my saddle horn, letting them float free.

We moved along between the plowed fields that spread out on both sides of the road. Above, we heard Powtawee exclaiming the beauty and the majesty of the view. When she spotted her village next to the river she pointed and laughed. "That's my cousin's house. On the first mound. It sits higher than the two on each side."

"You'd think we just discovered the Blarney stone," O'Donohue declared.

"I imagine it's just as good," I said.

"You've never seen the Blarney stone, and sure as goodness haven't kissed it, I'll wager."

I nodded in agreement.

"Looks like you would have shown off a bit for the general and Miss Annie last night," I said. "I was hoping you'd play your fiddle for us."

"You never mentioned it," O'Donohue said.

"I didn't want to bother you."

The man whose hair had been in tangles until Miss Annie combed it out after his bath last night rubbed his miniature hand over the fiddle case that bounced against his donkey's neck. "I was tired plumb out last night," he said. "And the vittles were so good and plentiful I could think of nothing but my belly. Besides, the old man was so full of himself, it would-a been a pity to spoil his fine speeches."

Again I agreed.

"I promise you one thing: I'll play up a storm tonight, when we've got us a paying crowd in the town."

"They'll pay you?" I asked.

"How do you think I earn my keep? By my sweet unstoppable charm?"

I laughed.

"My old Mama used to say, 'That Sean's got the wit of a leprechaun, he has,' but she knew it was the fiddle that made me what I am. Without it, I'd be just another lost Irishman on his way to nowhere in particular." His round cheeks shone rosy in the sunlight.

Then, no quicker than he'd said the sentence, the wind picked up and a black cloud blew in from the northwest.

Jed quick-stepped nervously, just as he had when the hot wind rushed up into the balloon. Jenny jerked her head. I glanced toward her, seeing her eyes flare, giving her a scared look.

A hot wind covered us like a blanket, going damp, almost wet. Then it cooled quickly, like a flash, bringing on a chill.

Jenny brayed and O'Donohue's donkey answered.

Before I could grab the rope that dangled from Katanzakis's balloon, it whipped sideways and accelerated through the air. Katanzakis hollered, "Hold on!" Powtawee grabbed the basket's rail with both hands while Katanzakis worked his levers, working as fast as he could move, twisting and turning one way, then the other.

I kicked Jed in the sides. As he jumped forward, I reached toward the rope that was bouncing away from us.

Thunder clapped overhead.

Jed whinnied nervously, kicking at the dirt of the road.

Lightning streaked, flashed through the sky that had darkened, cracked through the nearby woods, and hit something in the distance.

Jed threw back his head and jerked at the reins. I held tight, trying to keep him steady.

Thunder rumbled through clouds that rolled over us, like more than a thousand wild horses galloping over our heads.

The balloon swept past us, Powtawee screaming like a banshee. The wind was carrying them in a southeasterly direction. Katanzakis worked at his metal apparatus but nothing responded to his efforts.

I followed O'Donohue, who was kicking his donkey's ribs to make him trot. I held to Jenny and the mare, letting their lines out as far behind as possible to give them space to trot along at their own speed.

Clouds streaked darkly across the sky, covering the sunlight completely. Within minutes, sheets of rain slashed, sweeping in from the west, drenching us as I tried to keep my eyes on the balloon as well as the road.

Again, thunder roared its ominous growl and I felt Jed quiver uneasily.

When the rain caught up with Katanzakis, the balloon became half-hidden in the downpour. I could only imagine what it was like, riding fast and furious, wild as the wind, over the fields in the basket swinging back and forth, being dumped with water, speeding through the darkened sky. The thought of it caused my heart to sputter, hoping that Powtawee was managing to hang on to the rail as the basket spun like a top under the opening in the balloon, as the wind from the northwest blew down in a whistling gale.

With my hat soaked, the brim guarded my eyes from all but the strongest gusts. I caught glimpses as the balloon grew smaller and smaller, as it traveled higher and farther away from us.

I said a quick prayer but didn't have time for much of a conversation with the Lord.

I kept pushing, as did O'Donohue.

The rain slackened, then I saw in the far distance a hummock covered with a thick growth of hardwoods toward which the balloon was traveling at full speed.

Something fell from the basket before the balloon dipped quickly and dropped like a stone, disappearing. My heart grabbed. My breath gasped. I clenched my teeth.

"My God!" I uttered.

"Praise be unto heaven!" O'Donohue prayed.

We pulled off the road at the edge of a long field.

As quickly as it had started, the rain slackened to a drizzle.

We found a pathway along high ground. We dismounted and led the animals through a narrow gap in the thick bushes. Then we rode down the path, our eyes alert to whatever lay ahead.

We searched through the first rows of tall oaks, ash, hickory, and gum, thickened with a mishmash of underbrush, briars, and vines, and tromped through a sprinkling of dainty yellow trillium, sprigs of red-blossomed Little Sweet Betsy, and stalks of white hyacinth.

As soon as the rain stopped, humidity covered us like a thick blanket. I was not sure whether I was wet with the rain or the sweat that suddenly rushed to my brow. My soaked pants rubbed against the rough leather of the saddle's flaps. My soaked brogans slid against the slippery wooden stirrups.

O'Donohue pointed to a tall pine.

As we neared, a piece of cloth dangled from a limb, possibly blown there by another storm. It did not resemble anything about Katanzakis, Powtawee, or the balloon.

We kept looking, searching.

Now and then O'Donohue shouted their names.

Then he was silent.

We heard no answer.

High in a thick grouping of trees something glinted in sunlight that suddenly broke through a crack in the clouds. A piece of material the size of a small tent flapped in the branches. It slapped loudly, slowly rhythmical, like a dull drum, against the tree trunk. Then it was quiet. A yellow and green triangle from the balloon hung like a flag at dusk, the wind ceasing. I saw nothing else, nothing but limbs and young buds preparing to flower into leaves.

Behind me, O'Donohue called out again, his voice high-pitched, plaintive, almost desperate.

I listened. I heard no reply. I dismounted and tied the horses and mule to a sapling, where they leaned down and plucked fresh grass that grew in clumps at the edge of the woods.

Without hesitating, I stomped into the woods, pushing back bushes as thick as curtains, shoving myself forward, keeping my eyes peeled, hoping against hope that whatever had fallen from the balloon was one of Katanzakis's gizmos. With each step, I felt a hard emptiness in my stomach and chest. I gazed through the woods between the trees and saw something high in the branches. I moved closer, pushing into an opening. Above me was Katanzakis's body hanging limply in a pine, not moving. Without further thought, something stirred inside me. I bent forward and vomited.

Behind me, O'Donohue called out.

After I wiped my mouth on my sleeve and spat bile, I turned toward the little Irishman and said, "Sean," my voice barely more than a whisper. The sound raked against my sour throat as I spoke.

He stood about ten feet behind me. His eyes followed mine as I nodded in the direction of the tree that held Katanzakis.

"My heavenly Christ!" O'Donohue uttered, his eyes popping from his head with the pressure of sudden remorse.

A limb of the pine stuck straight through the middle of Katanzakis's body, entering at the top of his stomach and exiting through his back. His arms and legs hung out and down. His large head drooped as though in prayer. His open eyes stared down toward the ground, unseeing.

I was about to be sick again, but I managed to swallow, then I hollered as loud as I could shout, "Powtawee! Powtawee!" over and over.

I stepped around the spot where Katanzakis's blood had poured into a pool on a carpet of old leaves. It now dripped, steady drops that ran down his chest, to his chin, then onto the earth.

Beyond him, past another layer of thick trees, the flutter of something flapped against wood, limbs slapping in the newly strengthened wind. In the low-hanging branches of a gum tree, a large section of the colorful balloon was caught while another section dangled free.

I pushed my way forward. A stream of sunlight shone onto a portion of the balloon caught in the wedge of two giant oak limbs.

"Powtawee!" I called out again while I rushed toward the mangled large section of the straw basket.

Still hearing no reply, I reached up to the first limb, grabbed a good hold, pulled myself up, pushing against the bark with my feet. I slipped back, almost fell, then steadied myself.

I retreated momentarily, reached down and untied my heavy wet shoes, kicked them off, then started again to climb.

"Let me help," said O'Donohue, who came up behind, anchored his hands at my waist, and heaved.

I grabbed a new hold, pushed up, and pulled to the first limb, throwing my leg over and steadying my body.

I stood on the limb and called her name again.

This time, from somewhere overhead, a moaning sound grunted like an injured animal.

"I think she's here," I called down to O'Donohue.

Then I heard her cry out and saw the section of basket teeter.

"Don't move, Powtawee. Stay where you are. I'm coming."

I called down to Sean to fetch Jed and bring him into the woods. We'd need him to move her out of the forest. If she was hurt badly, we'd have to find a way to transport her.

Then I climbed upward, pulling and pushing, until I was directly beneath the basket.

"Powtawee?"

"I . . . I hurt!" she managed.

"Don't move. I'm right under you. Let me try to find a way."

I surveyed the limbs, especially the two large ones between which she was balanced. Holding to the branch overhead, I stepped gingerly out, away from the trunk. As I stepped, the basket moved.

"Harold!" her voice cried.

"I won't hurt you," I said.

I looked at the tree from a different angle, trying to determine how I could go about the business of getting her down without further harm to her and without allowing her to fall. Such a fall would probably be fatal.

I moved around the trunk, found a thicker, steadier limb, stepped onto it and pulled myself up again.

As my head raised above the floor of the basket, I saw her. I winced. Her body lay crumbled, twisted like a square knot, the skin of her leg ripped open, the bone bare, protruding, extended and torn like a snapped twig, blood seeping over the skin.

For another moment, I thought I was going to be sick again. I swallowed and told myself: *No, you can't! You've got to help this girl. It's up to you.*

Powtawee stared into my face. Lying there, she looked like a little squirrel, injured and frightened and helpless. Tears seeped from her large dark eyes, her lips quivering, she said, "Harold?"

"Be still. Don't move. We'll get you out of here and to a doctor. But you have to cooperate." For a moment, I sounded like Papa; I growled.

Below, O'Donohue returned with Jed.

Again, I explored the layout of the tree, how each limb turned at different angles, each having its own strength, each angle and thickness determining that strength.

I worked my way around the basket, talking to Powtawee all the while, telling her to relax, not move, be careful, and we would have her down before she knew it. While I spoke to her, I was also talking to myself, calming and easing myself, knowing that I was a jumbled bunch of nerves that could easily fall out of this high tree and kill myself any moment, if I made a fool mistake.

Before I realized what I was doing, I had climbed way above any height I had ever climbed in my life. Now that I was up here, I felt a heaviness in my body like never before. It was like those first few moments in the balloon. It was like reaching the top of the tower at Saunders Castle and looking down. But I knew now that the heaviness and queasiness and dizziness had gone away when I had looked out of the basket and viewed the great scenery that surrounded me.

Now there was no such scenery. But I knew that I had to do what must be done to lower Powtawee and take her to safety. That was far more important than my own feelings.

I climbed higher and higher.

Pushing my back against the thickest limb, I slid my right hand into the bib of my overalls and took out the knife. I opened it and began sawing at the closest rope that remained attached to the basket below.

I cut the ropes and secured each at the top of the basket and around the tree. The knife was the perfect tool.

Within five minutes, I had fashioned a pulley through a V-shaped fork. I told O'Donohue what I had in mind.

"You be prepared to ease her fall, if the rope slips or breaks," I said.

"Oh, God, Harold, my boy!" Sean O'Donohue said, his voice shaking.

"Try to stay still," I told Powtawee. "Hold to something inside the basket."

"What?" she whined.

"Anything!" I said. "Hold on tight. We're going to lower you as easily as we can. But you may slip. You may turn. If you do, I know it'll hurt. If you hold steady, we'll get you down out of this tree as quickly as we can."

I scurried around the basket. My foot slipped against a patch of moss on the trunk. I grabbed for a branch. It snapped.

"Dammit!" I said under my breath.

"Harold?"

"I'm okay."

I managed to wrap a broken piece of rope around the far side of the basket that had broken and ripped during the fall. I tied it securely, pulled, and made sure it would hold.

"Now," I said. "You ready?"

She made a positive sound.

I hollered down to O'Donohue, who said he was ready.

Several minutes later I worked the basket loose and it was hanging free. It hung precariously, a long way between it and the ground, making me wonder fearfully.

Overhead, I began lowering, feeling the weight tug at my shoulders. I pushed my back against the trunk, trying to steady my position.

After I let it down a few feet, something slipped. The rope gave in my grip. I whispered, "Oh no," hoping I was the only one hearing myself, feeling muscles tighten in my arms.

"Aaaiii!" Powtawee cried.

"Hold tight, Powtawee," I called, trying to sound confident.

I steadied my hold. Then I began again, letting the heavy basket down inch by inch, feeling my muscles burn with each movement.

At the halfway point, my shoulders gave. The tendons between my shoulderblades pulled tight. It burned like fire. But I didn't let go. I held, even though the ropes rubbed my palms until they too stung with the weight. I tightened my grip.

"Just a little way to go," O'Donohue urged me.

I lowered her inch by inch. The rope gave between my fingers. The pull pained my fingers to the bone. I knew the skin was pulling away, cutting into my hands. Although I tried to keep it anchored to the trunk, my back bent forward. The rope gave, slipping through my fingers, burning even more intensely.

"Damn!" I said.

"Hold tight!" O'Donohue said.

"I am."

"Aaaiii!" Powtawee cried.

"You'll be down in a minute," I promised.

As the blood oozed between my fingers, I clenched my teeth and tightened my grip.

I closed my eyes to keep from looking at the ground. If I looked down again, I thought I would surely grow dizzy, like in the tower at Saunders Castle. This was not the time for dizziness. Not now.

I eased the ropes through my fingers where the skin was torn, where the pain ached to the bone. But I couldn't let go. I couldn't.

Feeling my back give with the weight, I allowed the rope to slide down, down, down.

Just when the pain was about to overcome me and pull me away from the tree, O'Donohue shouted, "I've got her. Let go, Harold. Let go! Release the ropes and climb down."

I threw the ropes away from my body. I opened my eyes and stared at my palms covered with blood. The skin was torn from my fingers. The meat of my flesh lay open and bare. I wiped my hands against the sides of my overalls. I hurt all the way down my back from my neck to my butt. But I smiled and began climbing down.

By the time I lowered myself, O'Donohue had fixed the basket between two long poles he had attached to the sides of the saddle on Jed's back. "I saw this in a William Hart movie," the Irishman said. I didn't know what he was talking about. Of course, I knew that Hart was the most famous cowboy movie star in America, but I'd never seen one of his movies. In fact, the only motion picture I'd ever seen was a comedy about the Keystone Kops chasing some criminal all through a town, around buildings, until he finally fell into a great huge watering trough, nearly drowning. I laughed. I thought it was the funniest thing in the world, the way those cops kept falling over each other, knocking into doors, hitting each other over the head with bats and clubs and even their guns. But it set Papa off to damning the movies. All the way home from Sheffield he ranted about it being the silliest thing he'd ever seen. "If I let myself be taken by some sharp-talking Hollywood shyster, selling a ticket to pure nonsense, then I've got only myself to blame," he said. Mama chided him, making Papa madder. He fumed late into the night, hiding in the pages of his Bible in the parlor.

"In one of his best movies, William Hart helped a damsel in distress," said O'Donohue. "Using his innate ingenuity as a hero-star, he built a similar piece of equipment for her transportation." He took hold of the end of the poles and jerked them back to test their strength. When he did, Jed pulled forward with a jerk, nearly knocking the Irishman off his feet. He gave Jed a look and said, "Hold it, horse!" roughly.

"What'd you expect?" I asked. "You pulled on him, he'll pull you back. It's his nature."

"I usually kick old Nelly if she's ornery toward me," he admitted.

I shook my head. "Well, Jed's my horse, and you're not kicking him. You can kick your jackass, if you want."

He glared into my face for a moment, then remembered our task at hand. He moved to the side of the basket and looked down at poor Powtawee, who writhed in agony. "You take the other side and help me pick her up," O'Donohue said.

I started to protest, then decided to go along with his plan. I could not think of a better way to haul her out of the thick woods. Wiping my hands again on my overalls, I grasped the railing on my side of the basket. Together, we heaved it up and lifted it into place in the makeshift sheath O'Donohue had built behind Jed. As we lifted, Powtawee groaned and shifted her body and cried out again.

After we strapped her into place, O'Donohue began looking around for pieces of wood to use for a splint. The least we could do, he said, was try to secure her leg to keep it from moving.

With my knife, I stripped limbs from two pieces of green gum, each about three-and-a-half feet long. Then I cut a half-dozen pieces of rope, each about a foot long. Then I tied the rope around her leg at several points along her calf and on her thigh, ripping back the tattered cloth of the dress given to her by Miss Annie Walker, securing the wood. When I pulled the ropes tight, she cried out. A spasm jerked through her body. I reached out and touched her shoulder and stared into her face that was twisted with the pain that ravaged her. "Try to stay still," I said. "We're going to get you out of here and to a doctor." Silent, she stared back, unbelieving and unknowing, her big-eyed face showing suddenly an unusual calm where only moments earlier tears had flowed down her cheeks and her mouth had quivered. Now, she waited for the inevitable.

I stepped to Jed's side and began guiding him out of the forest.

As the basket jerked and bounced, I heard an imperceptible moan, a sound that started deep within her throat, caught in her mouth, quietened by her set jaw and pursed lips.

I wondered how much more pain she could endure, but I couldn't dwell on such a thought. I had to get her out of this place.

She had to have a doctor soon.

BOOK TWO
Into the Darkness

Nine

Between the woods and the road, Powtawee lost consciousness. The pain was too much for her. She breathed deeply, her chest heaving, her eyes closed.

After most of the goods Mama had packed on the mule's back were secured around Powtawee's prone body, using the baggage as a protective nest to keep her body from jerking about, I rode Jenny bareback and led Jed, dragging Powtawee behind. O'Donohue followed on Powtawee's sorrel mare, leading his donkey.

When we bounced across the narrow plank bridge over an almost dry creek, Powtawee awakened. She raised her head and opened her mouth. She did not cry out. As quickly as she had awakened, she fell back.

From a half mile away, I saw the first houses of a town. There were a few trees and a yard. We moved toward them so slowly that the town appeared to be receding away from us. I swallowed a gulp of air. In the still, humid afternoon, nobody would have had the notion that several hours earlier the wind had blown so fast and hard that it killed a man and tortured this woman.

We were within hollering distance of the house when a buggy appeared out of nowhere. A man in a frock coat and a wide-brimmed black hat snapped long leather reins across the backs of an identical pair of white horses that pulled his well-greased buggy, its spring-bottom seat covered by a black canvas canopy.

The buggy sped past us before I could shout, "Hey! Hey, mister, stop!"

Ahead, the man reined in his horses. He pulled to the side of the road and looked back with a scowl of distrust across his rugged face. "What is it?" he asked in an unfriendly manner.

"Well, sir," I started.

Harried and short of temper, he said, "Go on! Spit it out! I don't have all day. I'm hot and tired and need to get home."

"We've got a young woman who was injured in a fall," I explained.

"Whyn't you say so?" he said shortly. He stepped from his buggy and moved toward us. Seeing Powtawee, he leaned over the side of the basket and shook his head. "Good God almighty!" he stated. He turned and hastened back to his buggy.

Thinking he was preparing to abandon us, I let go of Jed's bridle and guided Jenny toward the buggy. If necessary, I'd take over the man's buggy, put Powtawee on the rear axle, speed her off to a doctor somewhere, then return his property to him later.

Just as I rode to the buggy, the man reached into the short bed behind the seat. From it, he took a black leather bag.

Instantly, my heartbeat lowered.

"Doctor?" I said.

The man nodded as I slid down Jenny's back and dropped to the road.

He walked past me toward the basket. While he moved, he unfastened the lock on his bag. From it, he extracted a vial of pills. "You got any water?" he asked.

O'Donohue was on the other side of the stranger with a canteen already open and extended.

The doctor slid his fingers beneath Powtawee's head, stuck the pill between her lips, then raised the canteen, pouring the water into her mouth. She coughed and swallowed. Excess water spilled around her lips and ran down her chin.

Moving down to her leg, the doctor exclaimed, "God, it's a wonder . . ."

With the tips of his fingers, he touched the splint we had built.

Then he straightened his body, stretched his neck, and studied the situation. "Leave her where she is," he said. "That pill should relieve some of the pain—even if only slightly." A pained expression covered his face as he looked over the basket and the poles again. "If we try to move her to my buggy, it might destroy her leg or even . . ." He had a way of not completing his sentences.

Then he looked into my face. "Y'all did the best you could. Now, follow me."

We rode past the first clump of houses, all within fifty to a hundred feet of each other. Then we crossed over another bridge. A big building on our right looked shut-down. Sitting high on a knoll above other business-style buildings, it had five large columns down the front. It was two-storied and very imposing, bigger than any structure in Town Creek.

Down the packed-dirt street, other buildings, two-and-three-storied, made the first one look smaller and more natural. One after another with second-floor balconies and wide porticoes and square columns, and doors that made the front entrance of Saunders Castle appear small, came into my fleeting sight.

We followed the doctor to a large house with a wide porch. Over the front was a sign with CLINIC in large letters.

When the doctor jumped from his buggy, he called, "Y'all stay right here. I'll get someone with a stretcher." He rushed up the steps and disappeared inside.

Momentarily, two young men with a long canvas stretcher between them rushed out the door and down the steps. With expert hands, they lifted Powtawee and laid her onto it gently. She grunted once as they took her into the building.

A tall and broad man in a long white smock and a shapeless hat pulled to his ears stepped briskly to the stretcher. He moved with unusual grace for a man so large. His hands looked the size of a catcher's mitt with long piano-player's fingers. He leaned over and stared down into Powtawee's face. Then he shook his head in a slow, sad movement.

"What?" I asked.

He looked up into my face. A flicker of the bright lantern hanging in the middle of the room blinded me for a moment, then he shook his head again.

"What?!" I asked louder.

"We can't treat her here." He looked over at the other doctor. "We can't treat Indians. You've got to take her to a colored clinic."

"Colored clinic?" I asked.

"On the other side of town," he said.

I looked toward the man we'd found with the buggy. "Doc?" I asked. "Isn't there something . . ."

"The girl's hurt," the doctor said.

The man in the hat raised his huge hands. "There's no discussing it," he said. He stared into the other doctor's face. "We cannot do it here. That is not only the policy, it's the law. Besides, if the Ku Klux hears of it, they'll burn us out."

"The Ku Kluxers are nothing but a bunch of bullies hiding behind masks," the doctor said.

"They're mean sonsofbitches," the man said. "They could close us down or burn us out. They beat a woman in Danville the other night for running around on her husband. Beat her damn near to death. If we treat a Indian, it's the same thing, far as they're concerned."

"Powtawee's lost a lot of blood," I said. "What if she dies?"

"She will die there. Not here. Now, get her out!" The big man ordered the young men who had brought Powtawee into the clinic.

The man's words stabbed me in the stomach with their sharpness. His expression twisted the knife against my innards. As the two men lifted her, I stepped in front of them.

"Move, son," the first doctor said. He moved to me and touched my shoulder.

I stepped aside.

They lifted the stretcher again and headed outside, where O'Donohue and the animals waited.

I stepped in front of them, but they kept moving, pushing me aside.

I turned to the first doctor. "Can't you do something?" I asked.

The man shrugged. "I deliver babies. That's where I'd been all day when I found y'all. I delivered three babies since six this morning. I'm about as tired as a man can get."

Staring down at Powtawee with her eyes closed, the sun bathing her face, I asked, "Do you think . . ."

"I think we need to do something as soon as possible," he said. "Put her in the back end of my buggy."

The men followed the doctor's instructions and placed her gently onto the rear of the buggy. O'Donohue and I rode behind. At the doctor's house, we picked her up with clumsy hands, waking her instantly. "Ohhh," she cried and tried to pull up.

But the pain knocked her back. She clenched her teeth and fought the tears that seeped from her eyes.

I touched her shoulder. "Stay down," I said. I had to fight my own tears through clenched teeth.

We took her into the house through the back door. The doctor cleared his kitchen table with a sweeping motion of his arm.

"Put her here," he said, and put a boiler of water onto the hot wood stove.

His wife appeared from within the house, her eyes wild, asking what was going on.

"I've got to care for a poor girl."

"But you're . . ."

"I know what I am," the doctor said shortly. "But the girl's injured. I've got to help her."

"The clinic's . . ."

"Hush, woman! I've got water on to boil. Bring the strips of cloth and my instruments." He already had his black bag open on the cabinet.

"I've got to have both of you men hold her when I start working," he said to us. "It won't be easy, I'll tell you that."

"Won't you give her something?" I said.

"I'll give her another pill, but that won't keep her anesthetized."

I went to her head and placed my hands onto her shoulders. I stared down into her face. Somewhere deep inside, I began to pray. I asked the Lord God to please step into the room and do whatever had to be done, work with this man's hands, that which had brought life to three babies in the morning hours, please allow him to keep life within the body of Powtawee.

I didn't want to lose two friends in one day. *I can't!* I told myself. *He won't let it happen. Not now. Not today.*

When he ripped away the cloth of her tattered dress, I gazed through a foggy mist into reality: blood bubbling, a bone turned up, another twisted out, away from her leg, the meat torn as though gnawed by a hungry animal's teeth. When he clamped a pair of silver-shiny pliers around the end of the bone, my brain began to swim. I closed my eyes. I fought hard. I held to Powtawee, feeling her squirm beneath my weight. I squeezed, my fingers like a vise. When I heard her cry out I thought my stomach would turn. I clamped my teeth harder and prayed.

When she reached down toward the doctor, I grabbed her upper arms and pulled her back.

The doctor looked up at me without expression. He nodded. Powtawee's head knocked back against my sternum.

I held her wrists in the grip of one hand while I caressed her damp cheek and chin with my other palm. "It'll be all right," I whispered. "It'll be all right."

On the other end, O'Donohue held her feet clamped in his hands.

The doctor took a saw from boiling water and wiped it clean with a sterile rag. When he leaned forward and touched the metal to Powtawee's leg, she shuddered. She opened her mouth. I felt her throat vibrate beneath the light touch of my fingers as she screamed an animal-like shriek.

I would have fainted long before that moment if I had not fought it with all of my strength. Every conscious thought was geared to holding her, helping her, keeping her from hurting any more than absolutely necessary. The fog in my brain thickened before it cleared. It clouded, heavy and gray, settling in front of my vision. It kept me from seeing everything. It kept me suspended from myself long enough to block the pain that I was feeling through her writhing body.

I stood there holding her, never relinquishing the steadfast grip, until the doctor touched my shoulder and told me to release her. It could have been hours. It seemed like hours. My whole body was numb, like my mind.

I blinked. "Is she . . ."

"She's resting now, son," he said. He led me and O'Donohue into the dark house where the man's wife silently gave us cups of steaming tea. Putting it to my lips, I sipped the sweetest, most refreshing liquid I'd known up to that point in my life.

"Thank you," I said, and she patted the same shoulder her husband had touched.

O'Donohue was also grateful.

We lingered there into the night, when the doctor lit lanterns. "If I hadn't taken the leg, she would have surely died."

"All because she's an Indian?" I asked.

"It's the way folks are," he said.

I swallowed hard. My mind wheeled back through the day, the afternoon, the movement beginning with morning. I shut my eyes. When I opened them, I gazed at Sean O'Donohue and said, "It's my fault."

"Oh, no, laddie, not your fault at all."

I nodded. "I'm the one who told 'em to go up. I told Powtawee that she ought to go on up high in the balloon, where she could see her home near the river. I told her it was fun."

"It wasn't your fault," the doctor said.

"She was joyful about the experience," I said. Then, I remembered, "And Katanzakis."

"Who?" the doctor asked.

"He's a Greek guy, flew the balloon, a helluva man, a head full of gray hair, wore a white cowboy hat, talked with a thick accent. He loved the world, made fun of it, made fun *in* it. He's gone, just because . . ."

"It's not your fault, Harold Reed," O'Donohue said again.

"If I'd only felt the wind, seen the clouds, known what was about to happen. If I'd just listened to Katanzakis, neither of them would be dead right now."

"You are not a weather prognosticator," the Irishman said.

"There's no way to tell about the weather up here in this country," said Dr. Jedediah Daves, who also introduced his wife, Irene, both of whom had been born and raised in the twin cities of Decatur and Albany.

120

"That was Albany where we were at the clinic. It's the first town to the west. Now you're in Decatur."

"Ah," O'Donohue said. "It's good to be in Decatur."

"We're the bigger of the two towns," Irene Daves said. It was then, after the first cup of tea, that she asked her husband about the morning's work.

"Three babies," he said. "All delivered with bright red bottoms, screaming at the world, freshly spanked and hearty." He smiled for the first time in hours. "Two boys and a girl," he said. "Eight dollars each for the boys, seven-fifty for the girl."

"I declare," said O'Donohue.

After a while, we looked in on Powtawee, whom Dr. and Mrs. Daves had moved to a bed. She was sleeping soundly, Dr. Daves having given her another sedative.

"She's not out of the woods yet," Daves told us.

I said nothing, just stared questioningly into his drawn face.

"There are many complications that could occur. Like you said, she's lost a lot of blood. She's running a fever now, but that's not unexpected. At any time, pneumonia could set in. If it does, we'll have to take her to the colored clinic immediately. If she takes a turn . . ." His voice trailed off. "We don't have facilities here. Irene can't . . ."

I stared into his tired face.

He said, "If we can pull her through the next few days, then she'll have a lot of recuperating ahead of her. It's going to be a hard life."

I nodded. "More than just recuperation, I suspect," I said.

"A lot more," he said. "When you lose a limb, the first thing after you get your health back is depression—deep-down hard depression, knowing you are not as good as everybody else. And I imagine, for an Indian, that might be twice as hard. Lord knows what it'd be like if you're an Indian woman with only one leg. Sometimes, I think, they expect more out of their own people."

The Daveses offered their living room floor for our pallets, but we declined. "We've got to see the sheriff, tell him about what happened, see about getting Katanzakis out of the tree," I said. "We'll come by tomorrow."

One of the doctor's helpers had taken care of Jed, Jenny, O'Donohue's donkey, and Powtawee's sorrel mare. We paid him a dollar, which he tried to refuse, but we were insistent. We left the mare and rode away to find Market Street and the sheriff's office.

Ten

After talking with the sheriff, explaining the afternoon's happenings, we found the boardinghouse, a tall gingerbread-style Victorian home with a wide porch skirting the first floor, a portico on the second, and a high gabled roof, all bordered with fancy woodwork.

Although O'Donohue said we might get shot, ringing a door bell in the dark of night at a strange house, I told him my father had insisted that I come here.

When I twisted the bell at the front door, we were met by a woman who was almost as tall as Papa. She was wrapped in a long robe with a scarf tied around her head and white goo smeared over her forehead, cheeks, and her neck, which seemed too long for her head. As she opened the door, I reached out and introduced myself immediately. "My goodness," she said, straightening the ash-blonde hair that was tufting from beneath the scarf. "You're John Reed's boy," she said, taking a bag from my hands. "You're the spittin' image."

O'Donohue and I stepped into the glow of the hall lanterns.

Mrs. Prudence Longshore put my bag on an ornately carved chair next to a tall grandfather clock that showed the time a quarter past eight.

"Let me apologize for my appearance," she started. "After dark I don't look for more boarders," she said, putting her open hands up to her face. "I'd just prepared for bed when I heard the bell, and I didn't want my guests to be alarmed."

"If we're imposing," O'Donohue said, "we'll leave." He turned back to the door.

"No, no, no," she said. "Y'all come right in and make yourself to home, if you don't mind how I look, that is. Of course, you are not simply boarders. You're like family. I've known Harold's father for years." She took my hat and O'Donohue's and hung them both on a rack in the entrance hall.

"A son of John Reed's is certainly welcome in this house at any time of day or night," she said, moving into the interior of the hallway. She glanced toward O'Donohue without comment. "How is your father, Harold?"

I began telling her that Mama and Papa were fine, that I was here to fetch my oldest brother Bosworth, who was due home from the war, where he had become a hero; then she interrupted me. "You do have your mount outside?"

I told her about the stock and she told us to turn them over to Roscoe at the barn behind the house while she warmed up some supper.

"You don't have to go to the trouble," I started.

"Nonsense, I do and I will. John Reed will come down here and scold me if I don't take care of his boy," she said, playing with her hair again as she disappeared into the kitchen in the rear of the house. While she was obviously dressed for bed, there was the faint air of playfulness about her, a sheen in her eyes that signaled a youthful heart, and a touch of gay delight in her voice. Although her face was fairly covered with the thick white cream and her eyes looked like deep dark caverns, I had seldom seen grownup women move with such a happy cadence. I was used to a houseful of young women putting mud-like stuff on their faces at night and cleaning out the sockets of their eyes. But all three of my sisters had been slow-moving and deliberate, except that time when the young man from Moulton called on Lucy and she awakened earlier and worked happily at fixing herself up for him. But that had ended one weekend when he failed to show up and follow through.

O'Donohue and I backtracked, something we'd become accustomed to, and took care of the animals, speaking with Roscoe, the colored man who was in charge of Miss Prudence's stables.

Back inside, she had cleaned the cream from her face and had touched up with a slight sprinkling of makeup. I smelled a hint of perfume and saw that she had run a pencil over her brows to arch them beneath a high forehead. She had put out some bowls on one of the dozen tables in her large dining room. She'd lighted one of the wall lanterns to make enough light. "Most of my guests are already upstairs or in the parlor. I allow smoking only in the parlor."

We nodded. The food smelled scrumptious. O'Donohue and I were both ravenously hungry. It had been a long day. Since the breakfast Ella had fed us this morning, we'd had nothing but a taste of biscuit on the run. And we'd been doing some running, especially after the breeze had taken the balloon for its wild ride.

While we stuffed ourselves, we told Mrs. Prudence about the tragic day. "I *swan*," she said, after I described the balloon's careening through the air and Anthony Katanzakis's fall.

"Poor, dear man!" she said. No wonder my father had a fond remembrance of Mrs. Prudence. In the new light, she had the bluest eyes I'd ever seen. Bluer even than Sarah Lynn Saunders's eyes. I remembered suddenly Katanzakis's description of the sea at his childhood home on the Isle of Andros: a deep blue-green that was hypnotizing to watch, like the eyes of a seductive woman, he'd said; that was the way her eyes were. Contrasted with her blonde, almost white, hair, and the muted-gold shade of her complexion, she was mesmerizing just to gaze at. Interestingly, Papa had never mentioned her startling, striking looks, and the creamy smooth complexion that at first had been hidden by the cream. Perhaps Papa had not seen what I saw.

"When the sheriff brings your friend Katan- . . ."

"Anthony Katanzakis," I said. "He was from Greece. The island of Andros. His folks were goat herders. His mama made blankets from the hair of the goats."

"When the sheriff brings him into town tomorrow, I will arrange to have a very nice Christian funeral," Mrs. Prudence said.

"That would be nice," I said. "He was my first friend on this journey." Then I remembered the couple from South Carolina, but I couldn't very well call them friends; I'd only met them and spoken with them. That was not a friendship.

Leaning forward at the edge of the table, she looked directly into my eyes as though she cared totally about me and my purpose.

Hypnotized by her handsome features, I rambled on about my brother Bosworth's heroic acts as a soldier, fighting valiantly for his country in Europe. Of course, all I knew was that Bosworth was in the army and had been wounded. I had no idea the extent of his injuries nor the circumstances under which he'd sustained the wound. But for her benefit, I elaborated with fancy details about how Bosworth had actually killed hundreds—perhaps even thousands—of the enemy German troops. And, I added, he saved the lives of many Americans while he was at it. He'd received decorations on the battlefield. Now it was my duty to meet his train and take him home safely to Mama and Papa.

"I know you're tired, after such a day," she said. Then she showed us to our room in a corner on the second floor. O'Donohue would sleep on a single bed in the corner. I took the larger bed that was so high off the floor I had to climb a small ladder and let myself down onto the feather-filled mattress.

Before she closed the door, Mrs. Prudence said, "Harold, there's no need for you to blame yourself for what happened today. Natural tragedies happen in this country. Weather blows up in no time. It strikes hard and without warning. Sleep well and put those horrible events out of your mind."

I looked into those eyes that gazed on me. They were eyes to dream of, to remember forever, eyes that offered hope and promise, a sweet dream. It was funny, I thought, how a person can change so quickly, just by doing a little something to themselves to alter their looks.

"It wasn't your doing," she said. "You said your friend was an adventurer. An adventurer will soar higher, longer, faster, and with more abandon than a regular traveler." She stepped inside the room and went to a small oval portrait hanging near a high chifforobe. She gestured toward the handsome young man in the picture. "This was Andrew," she said. "My husband: Andrew Dawson Longshore. He too was an adventurer. He was twenty-eight when he drowned swimming in the Tennessee River near the Indian village of Coaltaco. I was little more than ten years younger than he," she added.

"I'm afraid of water," I commented. "I have been for several years, since I almost drowned in the river. I don't go there any more. Never."

"Oh," she said.

I didn't want to talk more about it. On this of all days, I didn't want to dwell on an unhappy time in my own past.

"Well," she said. "That was a long time ago, when he drowned. I hated it more than anything. I loved that man, and I sure didn't want him to leave me a childless widow, but he did. I cussed him at first. Oh, I mourned. I mourned hard and long. I cried so much I thought my eyes were gonna fall out. I questioned my own motives about how it could have possibly happened. I relived our last moments together. Had I said some-

127

thing awful that caused him to make a mistake? I went out there to Coaltaco, where he had a sideline investment with a Choctaw fisherman who not only harvested fish but raked the shallows for mussels they'd sell as fertilizer and to street-paving companies in cities. A. D. always said it'd be a profitable venture, especially after motor cars were invented. Of course, he knew nothing about cars; didn't know the name. But he knew that sooner or later somebody'd come up with a horseless carriage." She chuckled emptily. "Well, he was before his time on that one. Very prophetic." She reached up and touched the man's cheek in the picture, like he was alive.

"He had himself a snootful of liquor that afternoon, got in an argument with some of his pals, and wagered he could swim the river across and back again. He was on his way back when a swirling undercurrent grabbed his ankles and pulled him under. He was gone before he could holler more than once." Her voice ended in a slight cry. "He was an adventurer, I told myself later. He wasn't meant to linger to old age. Some people aren't. Maybe your friend . . . What's his name?"

I repeated Anthony Katanzakis.

"What with his being a circus performer and a balloon-flyer and a magician's assistant, it sounds like Mr. Anthony Katanzakis lived a long lifetime, especially for one so adventuresome. He had fun right down to the last moment, soaring wildly through the air."

She left me with the scent of her jasmine perfume and the memory of her eyes. I wondered what that hair looked like when she let it down to hang over her shoulders. After washing, I climbed the small ladder and lowered myself onto the bed. I felt as though I were floating on a cloud. I thought of poor Katanzakis. My picture of him was the first time I saw him up close: his shaggy hair falling onto his brown burned neck, sweeping back like a bird's wings, and the white cowboy hat making him look like a western movie star. I was asleep within moments, dreaming about floating high, high above the earth.

When I started tumbling down, being blown by a disastrous wind, I woke abruptly. I looked around at the strange dark room. I surrounded the great fluffy pillow with my arms and squeezed. As I began to piece together the events of the past three days, seeing the beauty and the horror all mixed together, tears flowed. I wanted to call out for Mama, but I clenched the pillow and held it to my cheek and knew that I was all alone for the first time in my short life. Even when I was out there on the road, I had Jed and Jenny. I could talk to them freely and tell them my troubles. I could speak out, knowing that I was talking to myself, but not caring. Not so now.

I heard old O'Donohue snoring on the narrow bed in the corner. He was here but he was of little comfort to me at this very moment. Nor was he meant to be. He was just a man I had met in my travels. A good man. He and Katanzakis and Powtawee. Poor Powtawee.

My mind stayed on her, picturing her, thinking about her awful predicament. It made me feel the emptiness that had become mine to carry, to live with and remember. The journey from there to here had given me the emptiness that I now presumed I would feel forever. Even when I was happy with a joyful companion, with the sun against my face and the breeze blowing at my backside, there would be a part of me that would always feel an empty chasm, never to be filled.

Knowing that, I released the pillow and rolled over onto my back and stared up into the shadowy ceiling. Momentarily, I closed my eyes and slept soundly for the rest of the night.

I was awakened with the sunlight pouring through the window and a rooster crowing somewhere outside. I lay still and listened to movement in other parts of the big house. I heard O'Donohue's feet hit the floor. He poured water from a pitcher into a basin. He splashed water onto his face with a slight "Ugh!" sound. Then I rolled over and out of bed.

"I guess we've got plenty to do today," the Irishman said as he finished dressing.

"I have to meet the morning train first," I said.

"Do you know which one he'll be on?" he asked.

I shrugged, pulling the straps of my overalls over my shoulders, then sliding my feet into my brogans. "This morning, I hope," I said.

"But you're prepared for tomorrow? Or the day after?"

"Or next week, if need be," I said.

We had our breakfast in the large dining room. At other tables were two salesmen from Memphis who sold farm implements, a hardware salesman who called on stores in three states, a timber broker, and a representative from the railroad company who told me the first train from Louisville and Nashville was due into the depot here at eight-fifteen. Another, coming up from Mobile and Birmingham, stopped in Decatur at four-fifteen in the afternoon. I thanked him for the information. I knew Bosworth would be traveling south from Kentucky through Tennessee. He'd been shipped from France to a hospital in New Jersey last November and for the past three months he'd been hospitalized near Baltimore. Papa said he would travel by train from Maryland to Louisville, then south to Decatur. "He'll be arriving on the morning train then," the representative said, tipping his hat as he excused himself.

Looking even more radiant than she had last night, Mrs. Prudence Longshore swept into the room in a long white dress, a blouse with a wide collar and fluffed sleeves, and a pale pink sash around her slender waist. Her gleaming hair was combed out to her shoulders. "I hope you men slept well," she said pleasantly.

We said we did.

"I've already spoken with my minister, Dr. Alfred Summerall, and he is arranging for a fine Christian send-off for Mr. Katanzakis tomorrow morning at ten, if that meets with your approval."

I nodded. If Bosworth was on today's train, we'd just have to stay over until tomorrow. And her schedule for the funeral tomorrow allowed me ample time to meet the train and then attend the funeral. I thanked her for her generous thoughtfulness.

"He is also arranging for Father Grady Murphy from Hartselle to deliver a prayer, just in case the poor man was a Catholic," she said.

"Praise you, ma'am," said O'Donohue.

"We have no idea what his religion was," I said.

"Chances are he was Catholic, being from a Greek island," O'Donohue said.

Mrs. Prudence said there were no Greek Orthodox churches in the valley, so far as she knew.

When we stood I caught her giving O'Donohue more than a once-over look. As we turned, she said, "Pardon me, Mr. O'Donohue, but would you be offended if I found you something else to wear to the funeral?"

O'Donohue's face flushed as he looked down over his miniature Confederate uniform.

"I couldn't help but . . ."

"It's hard to fit me, ma'am," O'Donohue confessed. "I'm rather small with short arms and legs."

"I'll have one of my girls work on something with her sewing machine," Mrs. Prudence said.

"I'd be obliged if you'd do that," he said.

I told her I thought it was wonderful of her, doing what she had done and helping O'Donohue with his dress. I thanked her again.

"I could do no less for the son of John Reed," she said. With the morning sunshine glistening through the high windows facing east, looking out onto a rose garden, Prudence Longshore literally glowed with the backlight. The brightness shone in her hair like crystal chips glittering in sparkles. Her eyes were as deep blue as I remembered from the lantern light in the night. Staring into them, perhaps more intently than I should have, having just met her, I saw flecks of green floating in the pools of blue, giving the appearance once again of the colors of the sea that Katanzakis had described. I had never looked so closely at a female's face, with the possible exception of Mama's, when she was leaning over my bed to say good-night.

"What's wrong?" Mrs. Prudence asked, suddenly aware of my steady stare.

I shook my head. "Please forgive me," I said. A quick embarrassment came over me. I stammered, "I . . . I was staring at your eyes." Then, hastily and nervously, I tried to explain how Anthony Katanzakis had described his island home and the Mediterranean sea. "I thought I saw the same shade of blue-green in your eyes," I said.

She cast her eyes downward. A quick flush spread across her cheeks. "That's very complimentary," she said.

"It is meant so," I said.

"You are your father's son, aren't you?"

I did not answer, thinking she did not intend to ask a true question. But her words stayed with me, even as I rode to the sheriff's office with O'Donohue, then on to the depot after I'd spoken with the lawman.

Riding down the widest street between buildings two and three stories tall, I was overcome by the immensity of the city. Its life burst around us with an exuberance. Strangers crossed streets. Men nodded to men. Horses pulling buggies and wagons clopped down the hard-dirt thoroughfare. I looked from one to the other. The whole view sent excitement soaring through me. I'd never seen so many vehicles or people. It made me feel weird, thinking that I didn't even know the name of one person in this huge place.

Then I heard a growling, grinding sound, the bump of metal and rubber against the road, and recognized it as a Ford automobile.

Jed jerked sideways as it rolled and coughed toward us, looking exactly like the tin lizzie owned by Mr. Melvin Saunders, with wide-set wheels on dirt-coated axles and two headlights like gigantic eyes in front of the engine. A man wearing a flat-topped straw hat and a three-piece suit and a gray silk tie sat behind the wheel under a canvas top. As he passed, he nodded and tipped his hat.

I nodded back to him and kicked Jed in the ribs and jerked easily on Jenny's rope to urge her along.

From high on a bluff I looked north down a winding narrow road toward the river. I wondered if that was the way to Moccasin Alley. Beyond a half-dozen frame buildings sitting in a row I saw the railroad trestle that a man at the boardinghouse had told us was rebuilt after being destroyed by Union troops in the Civil War nearly sixty years ago. I didn't ask how he knew such history, but I took him at his word. And when I saw the train roll onto the track to cross the water, I pushed Jed past the intersection.

A boy about my age, only thicker through the middle, was swinging a broom from side to side along the wooden walkway in front of a grouping of buildings. As far as I could see, his sweeping was doing little or no good, just stirring up the dust.

I spoke a greeting, but he kept his face bowed, staring down at the cloud of dust at his feet.

"Hey," I hollered louder.

Still, he didn't look up.

I guided Jed closer.

When he lifted his head, that had been shaved up above his ears and high on his neck like someone had used a bowl to guide the razor, he gazed at me with small eyes that didn't focus.

"Is the depot in this direction?" I asked, pointing east.

He stared into my face, showing no sign of recognition or understanding, like I was speaking in a foreign tongue.

"Is the depot in this direction?" I asked again, louder.

Still, he simply stared at me and then looked at Jed. He gazed straight through me without responding to my question.

"Hey!" I shouted, exasperated, wondering how he could look at me and not answer my question.

A tall man wearing a gray felt fedora-style hat stepped onto the wooden walkway from inside the hardware store. He looked from the boy to me and shook his head. He put his hand on the boy's shoulder, turning him. "Come on, Pete," he said. To me, he said, "There's no need to shout."

"I'm looking for the depot," I said.

"He can't tell you," he said. "Pete's deaf and dumb."

I swallowed hard, feeling stupid.

"It's down yonder," he said, pointing.

As I rode away, I glanced back, seeing the man and the boy disappear into the store. I wanted to go back and say, "I'm sorry," but I had business to tend to. Perhaps I'd come back later, when I had more time.

I tied the animals to a post between two twin-seated Fords as I heard the whistle blow in the distance, then I rushed into the crowded station.

A group of a half-dozen well-dressed businessmen were clustered in the middle of the waiting area. Two women in long everyday dresses sat together on a bench that resembled pews at the Town Creek Presbyterian church. Several small children dressed in hats and bonnets, frills and laces for the girls, blue jackets and short pants for the boys, scampered around the ends of the benches and in the aisles between them. I craned my neck to look for a sign of the arriving train.

At a barred window, a man in a dark blue cap with a golden insignia and a matching coat pointed toward gate number one. "The passenger train from Louisville, Nashville, and points between will be arriving in . . ." He checked his fobbed pocketwatch. ". . . in three minutes."

I nodded and strode across the tiled floor toward gate number one.

Outside, under a massive shed, more than a dozen people stood on an elevated ramp staring anxiously northward.

In the distance, the same train I had seen rumbling along on the trestle made its appearance. The gigantic black engine was clacking toward us, moving from the bridge across the river onto the incline to head in our direction.

As it drew closer, it rumbled louder. The click-clack of the huge iron wheels on the tracks slowed. The puffing of the steam engine breathed steadily, huffing and puffing, grunting loudly. The jerking motion of the long iron arms on each side of the black soot-coated engine slid back and forth, slower, back and forth, until the last puff choked down within a few feet of the platform where we waited.

A woman with a baby in her arms was the first to squeal with delight as a man in a three-piece suit stepped down from his place between two cars.

Another woman sounded joyful when an elderly man and woman were helped down black metal steps by a Negro man wearing a red cap with a golden insignia, similar to the one worn by the agent behind the barred window.

Others met their loved ones, business partners, mothers and fathers, and other family members, friends.

I stood on the edge of the crowd that was growing thinner and thinner as the people stepped off the train, met those waiting, and walked off together into the depot, talking excitedly.

I waited, but Bosworth did not show.

After the last person stepped off, climbing down the small metal steps into someone's waiting arms, I went to the man in the red cap and asked if he'd seen a soldier aboard. He said he had not.

I turned away, feeling low and disappointed.

"Maybe he'll be here tomorrow," he called.

I turned and nodded and thanked him. I didn't know why I was thanking him. It just seemed like the thing to do. He'd only answered my question, then had added his own extra wish, being neighborly.

By the time I got to the doors leading into the depot, the people boarding the train to travel south were coming out. I stepped aside to let them pass.

Before going through the doors, I looked back at the train one more time, thinking that perhaps Bosworth had been napping and hadn't awakened in time to get off with the others.

But I saw no one else getting off. All of the people were walking toward the train.

Maybe tomorrow, I told myself.

Eleven

Later in the morning we found Katanzakis's body still hanging in the tree. I lost all of my breakfast on the floor of the woods and didn't care if the deputies were staring at me. The only dead person I'd ever seen was old man Rivers, the retired pharmacist, and I didn't really know him except when I saw him at church on Sundays.

The sheriff's men chopped down the tree and quickly covered Katanzakis's deteriorating body with a canvas. After he was taken into town to the undertaker, we visited the house of Dr. Daves and his wife and discovered Powtawee missing. O'Donohue and I followed the doctor's directions and found her at the colored infirmary where she was being treated for pneumonia. We were told she might die soon.

"POWTAWEE JUST LAY there in the bed and stared up at us," I told Mrs. Prudence Longshore. She and O'Donohue and I sat at the kitchen table, where she'd poured tall glasses of sweetened iced tea that had been brewing in the sunlight in the kitchen window all afternoon. "I don't know what to do," I admitted.

"I know those people at the infirmary," she said. "They're good folks but terribly underfunded. Nobody in the community seems to care whether Negroes or Indians receive adequate medical help. But that young doctor, Dr. Albritton—he's from down around Cullman—is a fine man with a dedicated heart. Although he doesn't have the equipment he needs, he'll work overtime to take care of his patients."

Her assurance made me feel better about Powtawee's situation. But I still worried about her.

That evening, Mrs. Prudence's cook made a great beef stew that was succulent. Mrs. Prudence herself sat at the table with me and O'Donohue. Looking freshly washed with her cheeks aglow, pink and shining, she told us the big chunks of fresh beef came from her cousin's cattle farm in Limestone County. The stew was also packed with whole new potatoes, butterbeans, carrots, onions, and cabbage directly from her garden out back. She said her man Roscoe made the garden early every spring, picked the vegetables, and she and C. Q., the chief cook, put them up in jars where they'd be fresh-tasting all year. Looking at it and smelling the aroma, I knew I was famished. Even in my heavy sadness, I felt the urge to stuff my stomach. I went to bed full and tired.

I lay awake on the soft mattress, staring up into the shadows of the ceiling, thinking about the day. It had moved so fast, yet so much had happened. The quick rhythm of life in downtown Decatur made my small-town brain swim. The last thought to cross my mind was the picture of Powtawee's falsely calm face and her tortured, heavy breathing with raspy sounds in her throat as she rested in a drugged sleep.

I awakened several times to look around in the darkness, each time wondering where I was, what I was doing here.

I thought about Papa, Mama, Lucy and Sister. I thought about poor old Katanzakis and Powtawee.

I felt so alone.

I closed my eyes and wished for good dreams.

I got up early, put on my Sunday-go-to-meeting trousers Mama had packed, buttoned my collared shirt to the neck, slipped on my barber-shop shoes, and took my shoeshine stand with me to the depot. After my visit yesterday, I judged it a good place to do some active commerce. I shined eight pairs of shoes before the eight-thirty whistle sounded by the train from the north. As I walked out to the shed, my pockets jingled with the new money. I felt good and lucky as I waited and watched. This was my morning, I felt sure. When two soldiers appeared in the opening between cars, my heart skipped. I stretched up onto my toes. My vision cleared. But neither was my brother. Both walked past me with broad smiles across their faces as two happy young women rushed into their arms, kissing and hugging.

Beyond the women was the well-scrubbed smiling face of a little boy in a suit and a floppy bow tie. One of the soldiers released his woman and bent down and picked up the boy and hugged him close. Sides rubbing together, they moved into the depot.

I was turning away when a passenger shouted, "Hey, boy! You want to shine some shoes?"

I wheeled around on the balls of my feet, halfway expecting to see Bosworth standing there with a grin on his face.

A dark-haired man in a three-piece suit lifted the leg of his trousers to reveal a dust-laden shoe.

My smile vanished as I nodded, bent down, and started to work. I put a good spit shine on his wingtips and gave my rag an extra pop as I finished.

Looking over the work, he nodded. "That's a fine shine," he said. He gave me a quarter.

I reached into my pocket for change, but he held up his hand and said, "That's yours. You earned it."

After three more shines, I went off to find Mrs. Prudence Longshore's First Methodist Church.

O'Donohue had gotten spiffed up with the new clothes Mrs. Prudence's housekeeper had fixed for him. She had found a store-bought shirt one of her boarders had left behind, and the seamstress had cut the sleeves and taken up the waist. She had also fashioned some small pants to fit him. I sat between him and Mrs. Prudence, who halfway through the service reached out and took my hand in hers. I thought it was a mighty kind gesture from someone I'd known little more than a day. I squeezed her fingers lightly to show my appreciation.

I sat and listened to the words of the blank-faced Dr. Summerall, who worked his words carefully not to lionize nor to demonize the man who lay in the plain wooden coffin. He spoke the scripture on a higher plane than I'd heard it before. When he said a few words about Katanzakis, he obviously knew nothing of his character. And the priest, a rosy-cheeked man with a bulbous red-streaked nose, read passages from the Holy Bible, "Verily, verily, I say unto you, He that heareth my word, and believeth on Him that sent me, hath everlasting life, and shall not come into condemnation; but is passed from death into life."

Later we stood next to the hole in the earth into which four suited men from the funeral home lowered old Katanzakis. Just as I felt the dam behind my eyes about to break, the fat little Catholic priest, Father Murphy, read: "Thus saith the Lord: Refrain thy voice from weeping, and thine eyes from tears: for thy work shall be rewarded, saith the Lord; and they shall come again from the land of the enemy."

I swallowed hard. I guess I swallowed my tears, because I could hear Katanzakis saying, "Harold, now, don't say nothing! You've got to fly high to have a great time in this life. If you don't fly as high as possible, you'll never see the rainbow." His words and his balloon had taken me higher than I'd ever been in my life. The remembered lift of his voice chased away my fear and relieved me of that burden. He took Powtawee up and showed her the world as she had never seen it. For all that he had shown me and had given me through his words, I was proud and glad. I swallowed hard. Still, it was painful.

140

We walked slowly to Mrs. Prudence's buggy. On the way she pointed out the hundreds of graves from the year 1888, when most of the town died in a yellow fever epidemic. She said a traveler named Livingston came to town and got sick with a cough and fever, was nursed through several nights by the kind, good Christian woman with whom he was staying, then he moved on west without a word. Within days, the woman who had shown kindness to the stranger came down with chills and headaches, followed by the black vomit, and she became the first to die in the epidemic. "Hooded Ku Klux Klansmen searched high and low for the traveler, Mr. Livingston, but they couldn't find him anywhere. It was said they rode all the way across the Tennessee River valley to Florence, trying to find him."

"What would they do with the poor sick man, if they'd found him?" I asked.

Mrs. Prudence said, "Kill him, I suppose. Hang him." Then she added, "The men who ride under the cloak of the Ku Klux Klan show no mercy."

Looking at all the graves, rows stretching almost as far as the eye could see, I shivered and thought it must have been a sad, sad August in 1888, only thirty-one years ago.

After we climbed into the buggy, Mrs. Prudence said, "Since we're all dressed up, I'll take y'all to The Tavern for dinner. It'll do us all good. I know I'd like to eat some food that C. Q. hadn't cooked, for a change. We've had enough sadness for one day."

I said I thought C. Q. was a very good cook.

"Oh, she is!" Mrs. Prudence said. "But a change is good for the soul now and then."

"The treat will be on me," O'Donohue said.

"I've got a little money," I offered.

"I insist," Mrs. Prudence said. "You gentlemen keep your money. You'll probably need it." She chuckled. "Besides, I'm a rich widow."

She took us down Bank Street, over to Grant, and east to Sixth Avenue, where a three-story red-brick building with cut-stone arches covered an entire block, with a second-floor balcony all the way across the front, extending onto the Grant Street side.

"It's a big one," O'Donohue commented.

I agreed. "It's magnificent," I said, remembering how Katanzakis used that word to its fullest.

As we entered the wide double front doors, I looked up into the brilliant curlicue designs in colorful stained glass over the doorways. "Those are frescoes by the artist Tiffany from New York," Mrs. Prudence said. "They're very famous. Artists and architects from as far away as New Orleans and Charleston come here to admire the elaborate, intricate work."

Above a mahogany registration desk curved a circular stairway with heavy carved woodwork for banisters. Similar carving followed the wainscoting along the walls.

Mrs. Prudence said the thick carpeting over which we walked was actually woven in Brussels, Belgium, by artisans who'd been trained in a king's palace.

She led us through a wide opening. Behind a wooden podium stood a gentleman dressed in a black formal coat and a tight bow tie. When she asked for a window table for three, he snapped his heels, spun around, and led us into a huge dining room. I had been impressed by Mrs. Prudence's large dining room at her place, but it was tiny compared to this enormous, elegant space. The ceilings, more than twenty feet high, showed off complex, extravagant carvings. Large green leafy plants grew from vases that came chest-high on me. They were placed strategically to separate the larger tables from clusters of small tables.

I squeezed my elbows against my bony ribcage as I followed behind Mrs. Prudence. My eyes darted from one sign of elegance to another, overwhelmed by the sights. I had stared at pictures in *The Saturday Evening Post* and *Collier's* and other magazines that found their way into the barber shop at Town Creek, but I had never truly believed that such luxury actually existed. And here it was in a town in north Alabama.

As we wove our way through the room, Mrs. Prudence nodded and smiled and spoke to most of the people in the place. Now and then a man would raise his cloth napkin and stand, bowing toward her. I felt as though I were following a queen.

In her shadow, I squared my shoulders and kept my head high, knowing that I was here with someone who belonged. I took a deep breath and tried to relax in the rich atmosphere of the place. A person had to learn to live in comfort in such a place as this.

We were seated next to a window with a view of the avenue, where buggies and automobiles and wagons and men on horses moved in a kind of magical rhythm. I had never seen so many people in one place. It was all indeed a sight to behold and almost too much for my mind to comprehend.

"I'd suggest the trout," Mrs. Prudence said, when the waiter brought the menu. "If you like fish, it's excellent here. Carl the chef bakes it in lemon butter, then browns it quickly in a sauté pan."

I followed her advice, but O'Donohue spotted calf's liver and said that was his favorite and he had not enjoyed it in ages.

"By all means, order it," she said.

I had discovered straightaway that Mrs. Prudence was not only an attractive woman when her face was not smeared from ear to ear with cream and her hair was not tucked under a sleeping cap, she was a person filled with facts about the place where she lived. While we waited, she told us the history of the

143

building where we were having lunch. It had been constructed the same year all of the people had died, 1888, and, because its opening was so ill-fated, experts predicted a disastrous failure for such a luxurious experiment. But the owner had deep pockets, able to weather the initial misfortune of apprehension caused by the epidemic, and by the following year The Tavern flourished and became the most popular hotel and eating establishment in the Tennessee River valley, described as "a grandiose palace that rivals the Peabody in elegance" in the *Memphis Commercial-Appeal* and as "a superb place to visit" in *The Charlotte Observer*. Even *Harper's* had given it a glowing review.

"That's quite a report, considering the Peabody," O'Donohue stated. "I've been to Memphis and know the Peabody. It's the grandest hotel in the South, I'd say."

"It's where the Mississippi Delta starts," Mrs. Prudence said. "In the lobby of the Peabody Hotel." She smiled softly, her eyes sparkling in the noonday sunlight that angled through the beveled glass of the high windows.

"I'm looking forward to seeing this entire area, after I move on to the town of Mooresville tomorrow," O'Donohue said. He added that it was awful to have his travels interrupted by such a tragedy as the balloon accident. He shook his head sadly.

The Irishman told us he had been praying steadily ever since that first whiff of wind had blown down on us from the northwest. "As a man blessed with the magic of the leprechauns, I was of very little help," he said. "While we were following the Greek to his terrible fate, I was asking for divine intervention to save both him and the Indian girl."

"Oh, Mr. O'Donohue, you did all that you could," Mrs. Prudence said. "Anyone can see that both of you did everything in your power to save the girl. As for poor Mr. Katanzakis, his time had arrived, I'm afraid."

"But it was not enough, was it?" he said.

I tried to reassure him. Then the plates heaping with food were brought to the table and placed before us.

Even in our sorrow, O'Donohue and I ate as ravenously as we had last night. Our appetites seemed endless. And the food was delicious. I had to agree with Mrs. Prudence: this place was terrific. I was already becoming spoiled. I knew Papa and Mama would think I was living way too high on the hog and far beyond my means. They would not have approved of my spending money or time in a place such as this. But I did not allow my thoughts to interfere with my appetite for this glorious food and the surroundings.

As we finished our entrees, a thick-bodied planter from Athens with an iron-gray mustache and neatly trimmed matching hair stepped to our table and bowed gracefully. "Mrs. Prudence," he said, "you look particularly ravishing today, if I may be so bold." I glanced down to see that his two-tone brown-and-tan shoes were polished perfectly beneath cuffed, pleated brown trousers.

Our hostess smiled generously, her lips red as cherries, her cheeks the blush of a pale rose, her eyes clear and bright. "Boys, this is John D. Lawrence," she said. Both O'Donohue and I shoved our chairs back and rose.

Mr. Lawrence put up his palms. "Don't stand," he said. But we already were standing with our hands extended.

"John D. is an old friend," she explained. "He's a controlling influence in Limestone County and in the state legislature, I might add."

With his own smile holding, Mr. Lawrence said that she overstated his importance, but he appreciated it nevertheless. "We're old friends," he said. "We go *way* back."

"Every other year, John D. travels to Montgomery, where he sits as a member of the House of Representatives. He's a very powerful man, knows the governor, has influence in the state offices as well as the county courthouse," she added.

"You exaggerate, ma'am," he said. Then he added, "But if I can ever be of service to you, Mrs. Prudence, all you have to do is send word. I hope you know that."

Still smiling cordially, Mrs. Prudence nodded and said she appreciated his concern for her well-being.

Somehow, I felt they were speaking in a shorthand designed only for the two of them. It seemed to me that a spark flashed from his eyes to hers, and vice versa. I had witnessed similar exchanges only rarely, then in a church vestibule or on the side-walk outside Mr. Guyton's barber shop or at a table in Maggie's Cafe, a half-block north of the shop, where I sometimes splurged with tea and apple pie. It was not your everyday kind of conversation.

As he moved away from our table, I did not inquire further into their relationship. I preferred to hold it in my imagination, just as the thoughts about her personal remarks about Papa— whom she always referred to as John Reed, using his full name, pronouncing it with a special gentle quality, holding the long *e*'s an instant longer than usual—made me wonder.

After John D. Lawrence had left our presence, I asked Mrs. Prudence about the deaf and dumb boy, Pete, whom I'd encountered on my first trip to the depot.

"It's a sad story," she said. "Pete's father, Joseph Powers, came here from up in Tennessee, opened the hardware store, and met a young woman, Laura Wilson, whose father was also a local merchant. Joseph and Laura fell in love, got married, and she became pregnant with their first child. Laura was a frail little thing, had never been a picture of health, and she suffered many complications during the pregnancy, including a fever that simply overtook her. During the premature birth, Laura died. Their child was Pete, born without words or the ability to

hear. The doctors immediately recommended he be institution-
alized, but Joseph would not agree to put his son away in an
asylum. Pete's eighteen now, and Joseph takes care of him like
he was a baby. He's very protective of the boy, and I guess a-
body can see why."

I shook my head, remembering the absent look in the boy's
eyes, his round face colored the complexion of kneaded dough,
his purely innocent appearance. "I wish I hadn't spoken so loud
and gruff," I said.

"You didn't know," Mrs. Prudence stated.

"I'm afraid Mr. Powers took an instant dislike to me," I said.

Mrs. Prudence smiled. "I can assure you, he's heard much
worse. He knows you didn't know."

"I hope so," I said.

Moments later I felt a pressure against my left hand. I glanced
down to see her pressing a ten-dollar bill into my palm. She
leaned toward me and whispered, "Take care of the bill, Harold,
and leave the change for our waiter, please."

"Yes, ma'am," I said. After I paid, the waiter brought back
three dollars and some change. I started to leave only a dollar,
keeping the rest to return to Mrs. Prudence after we returned to
the boardinghouse. I remembered her words. Still, my strict
Scottish Presbyterian upbringing urged me to follow my own
conscience.

Outside, Mrs. Prudence offered, "Let's go by the clinic to see
the Indian girl. I'll say hello to Dr. Albritton and make sure he
gives her his fullest attention." Her words alone made me feel
better than I had since leaving the depot this morning, after the
train arrived without Bosworth.

At the colored clinic, a tall uniformed nurse led us through a
maze of halls to the rear of the building. On our way we passed
a room where two colored men were holding a white woman
on the bed while a doctor was pressing a syringe into the flesh

147

of her upper arm. I felt a little queasy at my stomach, seeing the woman's face swollen and bruised black and blue. While the men were holding her, she was fighting, trying to pull away from the poised needle.

At the room at the end of the hall we found Powtawee in a bed, behind bars raised high on the sides, like an oversized baby's crib.

We looked down on her as she breathed deeply in her sleep, now and then mouthing painful sounds that tore at me like yesterday's thorns. I still blamed myself for the accident. I could still hear my words echoing, "Take her up and show her." If I had not made such a suggestion, Katanzakis would be alive and Powtawee would have both of her legs. But I had said it, and now we had buried the Greek and were now looking down on a piece of a girl.

When she opened her dark eyes, I reached out to her between the bars. She stared into my face. Her own face showed no sign of recognition.

Before my fingers touched her, she turned from me. "No," she uttered. She cried out weakly.

I looked toward Mrs. Prudence, whose high forehead wrinkled, then she glanced toward me and shook her head.

I withdrew my hand. I wanted badly to touch Powtawee, hold her, tell her I was sorry. I wanted to rock her and comfort her. I wanted her to treat me like Sister and Lucy and even Ida Mae, my sisters who always forgave me if I made a foolish mistake, if I dropped the morning's milking, if I soiled their new dress or did something else that was stupid and childish. They were always forgiving. They always came to me and touched me gently.

But Powtawee did not look at me. She turned away. She stared at the far wall.

Then I saw her shoulder that was pointing toward the ceiling. It began to shiver. She moaned deep in her throat. I could not understand the painful words. I smelled the harsh odor of strong medication. All of the senses mixed to stir nausea within me. I turned away.

Mrs. Prudence wrapped her arm around my shoulders. She held me close and whispered through a hint of perfume, "Leave her alone for now, Harold. She'll need you later. Let her rest."

I shook loose from her hold, turned back to the bed, and knelt beside the girl and said, "Powtawee, I'm sorry."

Through tears, still not looking at me, she said, "Go away! Go home! Get out of here! Leave me alone!"

I reached out again, trying to touch her.

As the tips of my fingers touched her arm, she cried out, "No!" loud enough to puncture my ears.

I rose from the bed, backed away from it, and followed the others from the room. Shuffling down the hallway behind them, tears poured from my eyes, my grief for all that had happened overflowing, the dam breaking.

Mrs. Prudence glanced back, as did O'Donohue, but neither came to me. They let me drift into a corner, where I faced the walls and cried. I heard someone behind me, but they were guided away by my friends, leaving me to cry alone. I did not think any one emotion. In my mind I heard the thunder and saw the lightning. I felt the rain that came down in sheets. I was blinded by the sorrow.

Twelve

In the buggy, after my tears flowed unrelenting for a long while, Mrs. Prudence told me that Dr. Albritton had promised to take special care of Powtawee. He said she still had a touch of pneumonia in her lungs but he felt she would recover soon. Still, he would watch her and give her medication. The mental recovery would take a long time, even after her physical ailments were cured.

At the boardinghouse, after O'Donohue went upstairs for his belongings, I followed Mrs. Prudence into the parlor. I thanked her for the lunch and handed over her two dollars and coins. She looked down at the money and frowned. "I told you . . ." A touch of anger sharpened her voice.

"I knew you didn't want to leave the waiter more than a dollar," I said. "Three dollars is more than an entire meal."

"I said, 'Leave the waiter the change,'" she said sharply.

"But I . . ."

She glared into my face, her blue-green eyes flashing like flames of fire. "When I say something, Harold, I mean it. I am not a person accustomed to idle, false conversation. I do not talk simply to hear my words."

"Yes, ma'am."

"When a person is accustomed to the finest service, he or she pays for it," she said. "I am accustomed to the very best." Then she turned and stepped away from me, her footfalls heavy against the hardwood floor.

Watching her leave, regret filled me. I wanted to say more. I wanted to explain my actions. I had disappointed her, which made the entire experience of the luxurious meal lay sour in memory. On another occasion, I promised myself, I will prove my worthiness to her. It was all I could think at the moment.

In the dining room, Mrs. Prudence's chief cook, C. Q., almost as tall as her boss, poured a cup of coffee while I waited. With a strong, stone-hard face and big black eyes, C. Q. held me in her stare.

"Is something wrong?" I asked.

"You upset Madame," she said.

"I didn't mean to," I said.

"She's a strong woman, but I think she's taken with you."

"Oh," I said.

She started to turn away and leave with the pot.

"C. Q.?"

She turned to face me, brows arched.

"Do you know how Mrs. Prudence knew my father?"

"They were friends long many years ago."

"That's all?"

"That's all I know." She started to turn away again, but she stopped. "Madame is a lady, Mr. Harold. She is a lady who is strong. But she has many sides to her personality. Many sides. Don't ever forget that."

I said nothing. I looked into C. Q.'s own face, at the African features chiseled hard against her bones like a princess from some distant culture.

"She's a lady who doesn't allow too much of herself to be seen or known. There are things about her nobody—no man or woman—will ever know. And she ain't about to tell you, or anybody else."

She floated away, her legs shuffling beneath the long flower-covered skirt, leaving me with that thought.

I looked around the dining room that had seemed so large on my first night here. After the experience of The Tavern, it appeared smaller but no less unique. There was something about this house and about its owner that both mystified and thrilled me. It was a big house with many nooks, strange turns, and hidden alcoves. It was like its owner: a place with many sides. The more I knew about her, whether I felt her warmth or her wrath, I found her fascinating: from the look of her eyes set in the Mediterranean smoothness of her olive complexion to the jingling sound of her voice to the last sharpness of her sound, warning me.

The more I saw here, the more I knew that every piece of furniture, every knickknack, every photograph was placed at an exact place for an exact effect, calculated by a fascinating personality. This morning, after I'd finished washing and brushing my teeth, I found myself staring into the face of her late husband and wondering why he would do something foolish like swimming in the waters of the Tennessee River. I knew it was the last thing I would ever do. Especially after my childhood summer Saturday afternoon when I was swimming to Sand Island where Ida Mae and Sister and Lucy were sitting in the sunshine, and I went down with a gulp of lukewarm water wedged in my throat, choking me. When I got to the island, Lucy jerked me out of the water, shoved her palms onto my chest, and sucked the water out of my mouth. I lay there breathing hard and swore I'd never swim again.

In the afternoon O'Donohue left for his destination of Mooresville. I rode with him to the bank of the river, where he and the donkey boarded the ferry behind three Ford automobiles. I shook his hand and thanked him for his help and his friendship. "You will be in my thoughts, laddie," he said. He clasped my shoulder briefly. "The accident was not your fault, Harold, and you shouldn't let it burden you," he said again. "You're a young man and there will be many days ahead, many good times." I nodded and thanked him. "I hope your brother arrives soon and that he's fine and healthy."

I stood on the shore and watched as the paddlewheel on the rear of the thirty-foot-long wooden flat-bottom boat pushed it slowly across the water. He waved his gray Confederate cap and I returned the gesture with my old worn wide-brimmed hat. I thought it especially sad that in the midst of all of our tragedy of the past two days he'd never once played his fiddle. I'd wanted to hear his music and see him dance a jig. It would have been a fine sight and a sprightly sound, but not appropriate for a funeral or the aftermath of a funeral. I pulled myself aboard Jed and we climbed the hill up toward Market Street.

As we maneuvered away from the river, my mind was not on Mrs. Prudence's boardinghouse but a place where I had seen a sign pointing toward Moccasin Alley.

As we passed Powers Hardware Store I slowed Jed to a creep and looked up and down the street for Pete, the boy who couldn't hear or talk. If I saw him, I wanted to smile and call out to him. But I didn't see him, and thought it best not to stop and inquire.

Moving on, I figured the best way I could escape the torture of my conscience would be to find a forbidden place and hide there. Papa had warned me to stay away from Moccasin Alley. The way I figured it, he really wasn't thinking about the reality of my being nearly seventeen years old and able to take care of myself. I was a tall boy. Skinny but tall.

Papa didn't know I'd gotten into a fight with a boy almost twice my size one Saturday afternoon at Bynum, he saying Thomas Riley couldn't pitch a baseball ninety miles an hour and I saying he could throw it faster. Before I knew it, the big guy was shoving me in the chest. I wouldn't take his insolence, so I popped him in the jaw with my fist. Then we went at it, and I came out on top. I had a knot on my head and my jaw ached, but he was the one with the bloody nose and the skin't place over his right eye. Another time, when Jeffrey Stokes jumped on my friend Raiford Bradford, Jeffrey being three years older and twenty pounds heavier, I pulled him off Raiford and took care of him then and there by my own self. I didn't tell Papa about my fights, so he wouldn't know that I had already grown into a man, especially in the past year. Besides, Papa was barely older than I when he married Mama, which I figured surely made him a man at the same age.

From the ridge of Market Street, Moccasin Alley curled north toward the river, snaking between two buildings like an afterthought, not advertising itself, attached to the rest of the town by this thin piece of packed red clay that dropped off and twisted between rubble and garbage and waste dispensed by the commercial concerns facing the opposite direction.

Sitting high on Jed, I explored the territory of unpainted buildings that stretched out along the low-lying bottoms, all shaded brown and dark red with dirt and dust. It didn't look sinister, as I had imagined; it looked filthy. It was like an unwanted goiter or a diseased growth, festering. Beyond the piles of scraps, the road turned downward again at a wide frame building with red-clay streaks down the side, like it had been weeping crimson tears. Several horses and a team hitched to a wagon were fastened to a post. Over a double wooden door a sign was painted *McRae's Beer Hall* in uneven letters. A few feet beyond the door, balanced on a red-clay mound of dirt, was a small black-charred cross that teetered unsteadily, leaning one way, then shifting in the opposite direction. As I moved past it, I looked back, trying to decipher what it meant, if it was a Christian symbol of something.

Then I continued down the street that narrowed and turned to run parallel with the riverbank. A half-dozen nondescript houses without porches sat facing away from the water. As I passed I noticed each had a stoop on its backside, where the houses floated on the water. A Negro woman was washing clothes on one floating stoop. Another hung out sheets and women's undergarments on a line that hung precariously low over the water. On my right were wooden buildings with names over the doors: Cash's Saloon, Riverview Tavern, McCartney's Pub, and the Starlight Club. Each had a smattering of horses, buggies, and even a Ford or two parked on the dirt alleyway. I pulled up to the Starlight, dismounted, took a deep breath, and held it in my chest. I smelled the stench of last week's garbage, sweltering raw and rotten, about as uninviting as a place could get. I squared my hat, stepped forward, and pushed the door open.

Inside, it was like night. I stepped into the darkness. The sound of a tinkling of laughter drifted from somewhere in the rear. Feeling my heartbeat quicken, I moved through the hazy, heavy atmosphere toward a chest-high bar that started halfway down the right side and ran to the rear, where a light shone from the kitchen. Smells of turnip greens and collards boiling with fatback floated through the opening, mixed with the stale odor of tobacco being used in its many forms, and a strange flavor that wrinkled my nose, all filtered into my system and made my head swim with foreign thoughts.

I nodded toward three men who sat on stools at the bar. They nodded back. They all looked like traveling pilgrims, from the dirt caked on their brogans and britches. None sported professional haircuts or wore shined shoes. They weren't the same type of gentlemen I'd seen at The Tavern or the depot. In the dimness, I figured they weren't working men: not farmers or miners, or they'd be there and not here in the middle of the day. A balding man with thick shoulders and an apron tied around his middle strode behind the bar to the place where I straddled a stool. "What'll you have?" he asked. His hair was trimmed neat and his mustache was clipped close to his upper lip.

I looked around, seeing the stacks of whiskey bottles in front of a mirror the length of the bar. I swallowed, trying to think.

"Little beer to wet your whistle?" the barkeep suggested.

I nodded.

I reached up and pulled my hat down, stretching it, hoping it would cover my youth, disguising me as a man.

He brought a glass filled with yellow liquid with a foam on top. He placed it on the bar in front of me.

When I reached out with both hands, he said, "That'll be a nickel."

I nodded again. I reached into my overalls and felt around for my change. I pulled out a quarter. Instead of digging down again, I slid it across the bar toward the man, who picked it up and looked at it in the lantern's glow.

He took it with him and disappeared through the opening in the rear. My heart sank. I wondered if he was going to keep my quarter. I glanced at the other men, who had turned to gaze at me.

I was thinking that they were judging me a fool to pay a quarter for a glass of beer. It would serve me right if I had to pay the price.

Again I picked up my glass with both hands and put it to my lips. I raised it and swallowed.

When the bitter taste hit my throat, I thought for a moment I was going to throw it right back up. I turned away from the onlookers. I took the glass down and smacked my lips. I swallowed some stale air. I breathed through my nose and prayed I wouldn't be sick. It would be embarrassing, right here in the middle of my first saloon, to throw up in front of everybody.

I'd never tasted anything like the beer. People drank this stuff for *enjoyment*. Raiford and Peter had told me they'd sneaked some of their father's home brew last spring. They said it was good and made their heads light as a hummingbird's wings. They said it made them think like that too: fast and buzzing. Ever since I heard them talk about it, I wanted to find out for myself. *Surely their home brew must have tasted better than this,* I thought.

The bald-headed man came back and put four nickels on the bar. He studied me a moment, then asked, "Does the beer taste okay?"

I nodded. "Fine," I said. I picked up the glass again. This time I took a larger swallow. It went down a little easier. The strange bitter taste tingled my throat. When I brought the glass down, I said, "Reckon it was just that first taste," and smiled.

The bartender smiled too. "Have a pickled pig's foot?"

"A pickled pig's foot?" I repeated. I'd never heard of such a thing.

"Me and the old lady pickled 'em last winter, at hog-killing."

I shrugged. I reckoned there had never been a part of a hog I hadn't eaten, except the feet. I'd had souse or hog-head pudding, when the head and other parts were boiled together in a big black washpot, then put up to settle in squares wrapped in a gauzy cloth, all the gristle and goo sticking together in bars to be eaten later, after they'd ripened. Mama and Sister had made it at first frost, when Papa helped Mr. Saunders with hog-killing. I'd had intestines or chitlins, boiled and fried, eaten for breakfast the morning after hog-killing. If a person can eat boiled chitlins, he can eat anything.

The man brought a small plate with two fist-sized hunks of pig's feet. "Just pick 'em up and suck 'em. The goodie between the toes is the best part."

I nodded, picked one up, slid it between my lips, chomped down with my teeth, heard gristle break, and a piece of meat fell onto my tongue. I sucked the marrow between the toes, tasting something salty and sour and rich. The taste was flavorful and intense. But the best thing about it: it made the beer better. I ordered a second glass.

When the barkeep came, I ventured to ask, "Back up toward town a ways, next to that McRae's Beer Hall, I saw a black cross."

He nodded as he dried a glass with his towel. "What's left of it," he said. "A married woman was caught down there at McRae's a week or so ago. The Klan heard she was running around on her husband. They burned the cross and whipped the daylights out-a the woman."

I made a pained expression.

"They didn't give a shit that her old man was running around on her," the barkeep said. "It was *her* doing the evil, they said. They said they wanted to cure her from doing it again. If you ask me, they're a bunch of raggedy-assed cowardly sonsofbitches. They hide behind their masks and pick on poor niggers and wayward women."

Then he left me to dwell on the idea.

The other men on the other stools did not say a word, agreeing or disagreeing. They sat and drank and looked at him. He was a man with biceps that bulged against the short sleeves of his shirt. He had a square jaw and hard little eyes above a nose that had been broken a time or two.

I was having my beer, feeling good and comfortable with it, when three men entered. They were cheerful, loud, and boisterous. The biggest was double the size of the bartender, maybe even larger. His head sat on his shoulders without a neck. When he opened his mouth, which he did with great abandon, it looked as though the top of his chest was speaking. His arms were muscular, his hands like clawhammers. His fingers surrounded a big glass of beer and he sucked it down with a slurp. Like that, the beer was gone. When he caught me staring at him, his beady eyes glared and his mouth drew tight. "What you looking at, boy?"

I almost choked. "I'm sorry," I managed.

"Shit, boy," he exclaimed, "you keep looking at me like that, I'll turn you inside out." Then he laughed loudly, his chest shaking. "You ain't no sissy-boy, are you?"

"No, sir," I said.

The bald-headed bartender moved quickly to stand opposite the big man and face him with hands reaching for something under the bar. "You trying to run off my business again, Bubba?" he said.

When Bubba didn't answer, the bartender said, "You know what I've got under here. If I have to take it out, I'll use it."

"I ain't causing no trouble, Billy," Bubba said.

"See that you don't."

"He was just looking at me . . ."

"'Cause you are a sight for sore eyes," Billy said.

"Well . . ."

"I told you before. Now, tell the boy you're sorry, then you and the rest of your crew just settle down and drink your drinks."

"Well . . ."

"Tell him!"

Bubba managed to look at me and nod his head. Then he mumbled, "I'm sorry," and he stuck out his huge hand.

I slid my hand into his, and he shook it. I knew, if he wished, he could have thrown me across the room and tied me in a knot, but he shrugged and went off to a table to sit with his friends.

I thought about leaving, thinking that perhaps some other ruffians might be heading this way, since obviously Moccasin Alley was the place such men liked to congregate. But I decided it wouldn't hurt to sit where I was and have one more beer,

since they tasted better in quantities and since Billy the bartender was friendly and made me feel safe, even if I wasn't.

After Bubba and his friends started cursing somebody else—
two men down the bar that they knew and wouldn't take it
without cursing back—I introduced myself to Billy, who said
he'd come here three years ago from Mooresville, where the
religious element had chased him out of town when he opened
a honky-tonk. I told him I had a friend headed in that direction,
looking for work as a fiddler.

"I wish he'd-a come down here," Billy said. "I could-a given
him some nighttime employment. We're always in search of
good entertainment. These old boys and girls get restless when
they can't shake it to some music now and then."

About that time, two women in long dresses with big bustles
and blouses that dropped open down to the tops of their ample
breasts strolled into the darkness and searched the place with
eyes that finally settled on Bubba and his two buddies.

"Bring your sweet self over here," Bubba invited them, and
they sashayed to the table, where the men rose and found
chairs for them.

Within minutes, after the talk amplified and the atmosphere
sweetened, a girl not much older than I moved quietly through
the front door. Inside, she stopped and looked around. Several
of them called, "Lacy, baby," but she ignored them.

As her eyes settled on me, she stepped past the others and
headed my way. As she came closer, I made out her features
and her youth. She was dressed about as cheap-fancy as a body
could dress. The best I could tell, the dress must have been bor-
rowed. It did not fit properly on her slender body. It hung on
her, like clinging to a post. When she leaned against the stool
next to me, she looked pitiful. The dress, made of royal blue
false velvet, was designed for a woman with breasts much larger than hers, and her waist was too long and narrow, making

the skirt fall from her body just below her rib cage and tighten around her buttocks. Her black hair fell to shoulders the color of coffee and cream. Her eyes were chocolate brown. Her face would have been pretty, if it had not been caked with rouge and her brows and eyelids had not been painted too thick and too black. "I'm Lacy Beauchamp," she said, slurring her words in an accent.

I introduced myself, feeling ill at ease, my stomach suddenly nervous, wondering how the beer was affecting my senses. I had talked to girls. Sarah Lynn Saunders and I had had numerous conversations, but we'd known each other all our lives. I had talked with Sister and Lucy and Ida Mae, though she was seven years older and not really a girl. I didn't count sisters as girls. And I knew I'd never talked to a girl like this one.

"I've got a sister named Lucy," I said.

Her face lightened with a smile. Lips that had been painted twice their natural size with bright red lipstick parted to show crooked teeth across the front. "Not Lucy, Lacy. Don't you think I look 'lacy'?" She tried to make her voice low and sultry.

I grinned and half-nodded. "Lacy," I repeated, pronouncing it in my own way, a light, feathery word.

After he'd filled the other women's orders, Billy the bartender came to us from behind the bar. "Is she bothering you, mister?" he asked. To Lacy, he said, "You might better get your floozy butt back over to Mimi's, Lacy. You know what I told you about hanging around over here. You get the boys all stirred up."

"What about *them*?" Lacy asked. Her accent disappeared. She motioned toward the women sitting with Bubba and his crew.

I shrugged uneasily. "She's okay," I offered, not wanting to offend either of them.

"Hey, Lacy, you found a fish?" one of the men with Bubba hollered across the room.

I twisted around on my stool to look sternly in his direction across the dimly lighted room.

"Fuck off, Frank!" Lacy snapped.

"Lacy!" Billy said. "You know what I told you about profanity. One more outburst and you're gone. Understand?"

Lacy pouted. "Everybody can cuss but me."

"I don't want you starting a bunch of shit in here," Billy said.

"Those railroad workers think they own Moccasin Alley," she said.

To me, he said, "She bothers you, you let me know."

Lacy drew close to me, moved her face within inches of mine, and looked into my eyes. In a soft whisper, she asked, "Am I bothering you?" The accent returned.

The smell of her was outrageous. She must have taken a bath in perfume. I took a deep whiff and felt my head go light. I closed my eyes.

"Am I *that* seductive?" she asked.

I tried to answer. I fought to find words. My mind was jumbled. My fingers quivered as I reached for my glass. Then I placed my hands upon the bar to steady them.

She giggled flippantly.

"I didn't mean . . ." I started, then stopped.

"You're just a boy," she said.

I looked around the dark room. No one was paying any attention to us. My fingers steadied. I took another swallow of my lukewarm beer, forcing it down.

"That beer won't make you a man," she said.

Defiantly, I finished the glass, slid it away from me, the way I'd seen other drinkers do, then looked over at Billy with a little nod. I was learning my way around fast. It wouldn't be long before I'd know all the signs and signals in such a place as this.

"How old are you?" she asked.

Billy pulled another beer and extracted the cost from my change, glanced toward Lacy, then moved back down the bar toward the others.

"How old are *you*?" I asked.

"Eighteen," she said.

"I'm nineteen," I lied.

She giggled lightly. "I like boys," she said, putting her hand on my thigh, where it felt heavy and hot against my leg. For a moment I didn't think I could breathe.

I almost pulled back, but I didn't. I looked down at her hand. It didn't move. It lay heavy on my thigh.

I told her that I was from Town Creek and I wouldn't be in Decatur long. "I've come to pick up my brother Bosworth who's coming in on the train from up North," I said. "He was wounded in the war."

"What's a 'war'?" she asked.

"Huh?" I said, dumbfounded.

She giggled again. "I'm joking," she said, and squeezed her fingers against my thigh.

"My brother's a hero," I blurted. *If I could tell a whopper to Mrs. Prudence, why couldn't I elaborate on Bosworth's situation to this tan-skin girl?* "He's been fighting in the army in Europe. He and his outfit were surrounded by the enemy. Bosworth climbed out of his foxhole and ran straight at the enemy soldiers without regard for his life, killing every last one of them that got in his way."

She shook her head in all seriousness and kept her hand anchored on my leg.

I nodded to confirm my words. "He was wounded and has been confined to a hospital in Maryland. He should be arriving in a day or two, then I'll be going home to Town Creek."

I breathed deep, trying to think of something else to say, something bright, something witty, something meaningful, but I had said my say, and my brain could think about nothing but her hand and its weight.

"You . . . eh . . . live around here?" I asked.

She laughed just loud enough for me to hear. If it had been louder, I swear, I would have pushed away, stood up, and walked out of there that moment. But it wasn't loud. It wasn't taunting or mocking.

"You're a funny boy," she whispered.

I turned and leaned into the bar. I rested both of my forearms against the bar and stared into the new beer, looking away from her, trying my best to feel superior. If I didn't look at her she wouldn't see the way I felt, the way I wanted to reach out to her and take her to a bathtub and scrub her and make her clean and beautiful.

She moved her hand. She reached up and put her fingers on my forearm nearest her. "I didn't mean funny *funny*. I meant . . ."

I stared into her painted face. "What?" I asked.

"I meant funny different. You know." She raked her upper teeth down over her lower lip. "I'm not making fun of you." She squeezed my arm. "I promise."

I nodded. I thought I knew what she was trying to say. I thought that she was suddenly pretty, but I didn't say it. I held my words heavy inside, weighting me down, the same way her hand had been heavy on my leg. Maybe it was the way the shadows fell across her face.

For an instant, I could hear her breathe, and her breath too was heavy, like the smell of her perfume. I looked around again at the workers from the L&N railroad shop and the fancy-dressed women and the other men from other places. The entire interior of the Starlight Club was heavy in my mind, weighing more than I had ever imagined a place could possibly weigh on my young mind.

"You want to go over to Mimi's with me?" she asked, holding to my arm like it was her last buoy to cling to.

"Mimi's?" I said.

"Across the street. The place where I work."

My stomach tightened again. The beer rose to the top and floated there. It too was heavy, holding me down.

She did not release my arm. She pulled closer, the soft material of her dress rubbing smoothly against my skin.

I felt the softness of her small breasts inside the bodice that was too big for her. I felt the weight of her small breasts press against my arm.

"If you go with me, I'll show you a good time," she said into my ear. "I promise."

My brain bobbed like it was a float on the river, swept downstream by a strong, unyielding current. I found myself standing, being led through the twinkling light of the club, past the table where one of the women had climbed into Bubba's lap, beyond the other drinkers at the bar and Billy the bartender. Behind us, someone laughed. I stopped and looked back. The woman in Bubba's lap ran her fingers through his hair. She laughed loudly, having a good time.

Lacy led me out the door and into the street where Jed whinnied in the pending darkness of the sunset that cast many vibrant colors down on all of the ugly world. Holding Lacy Beauchamp's hand, I walked past my horse without giving him a hello. She opened the door of the unpainted plain-front batten-and-board building and I stepped into the room of eternal twilight.

Thirteen

She led me into the smoke-fogged front room where lanterns glowed dimly against faded flowered wallpaper. Two women in ankle-length gowns sat on a sofa, smoking and staring at us. One said, "You getting a jump-start on the evening, ain't you, girl?"

Lacy gave her bottom a sassy twist and pulled me toward a hallway, where she introduced Mimi, a short fat older woman with a permanent scowl on her powdered face. I could see where Lacy got her instructions in cosmetology. "It'll be a dollar," Mimi said, holding out her wrinkled palm.

"He wants all night, don't you, sugar?" Lacy said.

"Well, I . . ." I stammered.

"That'll be five," Mimi said. Her hand did not move.

I reached deep into my overalls, feeling the bulge of my money. Five dollars represented more than I made in a week of good barbering and shoeshine work back home. No telling how long it'd take me to make that much shining shoes at the depot or on the street outside The Tavern.

Lacy pushed close to me, rubbing her breasts against my arm the way she'd done at the Starlight. She whispered, "I'll show you things you ain't never dreamed of. I'll . . ." She glanced toward Mimi, then put her lips to my ear and said, "I'll take you 'round the world."

Mimi snickered.

"You'll go where few men have ever been before."

In the secrecy of my breast pocket I separated bills with my fingers and thought on her promise. I wanted to stay all night with her. I wanted to do all the things she spoke about, but I had too much of Papa in me for such an extravagance. I didn't trust a promise from a girl I just met minutes ago. I pulled out a dollar and handed it to the older woman.

"What?" Lacy Beauchamp said, disappointed, pouting, pulling away from me but still holding my hand.

Mimi's eyes wandered over the money and clenched her fist and uttered, "That'll be thirty minutes, missy." She glanced toward Lacy. "No longer."

My heart sank as Lacy pulled me down a narrow hallway toward the back of the building that swayed slightly over the slosh of the river water. The thought of being only a few feet from the river played at the edge of my mind and I tried not to think about it.

Moments later we entered a small drab room with a narrow bed covered with a cotton-knotted pale pink spread. In the corner opposite the bed was a small handtooled chest of drawers with an off-white pitcher and washbowl on top next to the colorless wall.

A Negro woman with a scowl as deeply etched on her fat face as Mimi's followed us into the room without a word, carrying a kettle. She poured steaming water into the pitcher. From her left arm, laden with a thickness of towels, she unfolded one and placed it next to the bowl. With a smirk, she glanced toward me.

When I didn't move, Lacy nudged me. "Tip her a dime," she said.

I dug a dime from my overalls and handed it to the woman, who left without a word.

"She your Mama or something?" I asked.

A smile played at Lacy Beauchamp's lips. "Naw," she said. "She ain't. She's Sissy Little, been Miss Mimi's maid for twelve years, and don't like it one bit that the old lady uses girls like me. But what the hell, that's the business. And she ain't ever turned down a tip that I know of." She poured out an inch of hot water into the bowl and dipped a washrag. While she was wringing it, she turned to me, where I was standing motionless next to the bed, and said, "Go ahead, baby, drop your drawers. We don't have all night, you know." Ever since I failed to give the woman five for all night I sensed a bitter sharpness to Lacy's voice. It had moved from a mellow softness to a flat, businesslike tone.

Looking around first, feeling embarrassed for what I was about to do, I took a deep breath and let it out. "I'm not gonna bite you, sugar," she said, her words a little softer.

I unsnapped my overalls at the bib and shucked them down over my hipless middle. I stepped out of my brogans.

Lacy stood in front of me with the washrag in her hands. She looked over me, standing there in my Union suit of underwear, sleeveless straps over my shoulders and pants clinging to my thin white thighs. "Go on and pull that off too," she said.

After hesitating another second, I did.

She pushed me back onto the bed, reached between my legs, and covered my middle with the hot rag. As soon as she touched it, it sprang upward, pointing at her.

"Down, boy," she said, teasingly, pushing it back and watching it bounce toward her again.

I tried to turn away, but her fingers wrapped around me and held me tight. "I got you," she said, smiling.

She pushed me back, until I was prone, then she jumped onto the bed.

The springs squeaked beneath us.

I tried to hold her still to keep the springs from squeaking, but she threw her leg over my body, raising her skirt in the same movement. She shimmied out of the dress, raising it over her head and tossing it onto the chair where my discarded

169

clothes lay. She wore no underclothes. She turned to me, show-ing her entire naked body from the small breasts to the triangle of black hair at the top of her legs.

When she reached down and grabbed a-hold of me, I spurted.

"Hey," she said, leaning down and examining me.

"I didn't even . . ." I started. I felt hurt and betrayed by my penis.

She rolled aside, picked the damp rag up from the floor, then wiped my belly and hers.

"I didn't . . ." I started again. I thought for a second I was going to cry. My voice caught in my throat and held there.

"Hush," she said. She put the rag back onto the floor and lay her head onto my shoulder.

When I looked into her face, she was smiling.

"It's not funny," I said.

She rolled into me, kissed my neck, and raised her head above mine. "I wasn't laughing," she said.

"But you . . ."

"Hush," she said softly. She put her finger to my lips. "Let me," she said. She reached down and wrapped her fingers around my penis that had already started to come to life again. "Ain't nothing like youth," she said, as she pumped it up and down.

On her third stroke it was once again hard as rock and stiff as steel.

She rolled, lay on her back, parted her legs, and said, "Crawl on top."

I lifted up, the bed squeaking with every shift of my weight, and elevated myself above her, looking down onto her smooth light tan body. Her tiny brown nipples pointed straight at my chin. I lowered myself, her fingers guiding me.

"Ummm," I grunted, sliding into the velvety warmth, enter-ing where I'd never been before, fulfilling her promise, my stomach muscles contracting, my thighs jerking tight, my lips surrounding her stone-tipped nipples, hearing rusted springs sing a creaking rhythmical song. And then I exploded again, and I pushed downward in a thrust, the springs creaking one long out-of-tune sound as I halted all movement and held to her slender shoulders, my cheek resting next to her own silky smooth cheek, and then my fingers cupping the firm softness of her right breast.

We lay like that for a long moment, unmoving, my heavy breath sucking in and out, she holding my shoulders, her face against mine. Then she squirmed from beneath me, rose, and soaked the washrag. With shadows from the shaded light playing over her silken body, she leaned over and washed me again.

When I sprang to life anew, Lacy giggled in her throat. "You ought-a paid the five. We'd-a gone all night long and had us a big old time."

I wished too, but I had not. I quickly covered myself.

I watched from the bed as she washed between her legs and wiped the cloth over her breasts and under her arms.

"Well," she said, coming back to me, walking nonchalantly naked in front of me. My eyes settled on the indention of her ribs, the curve of her backside, the length of her subtly tapering legs. She bent to retrieve her dress and stepped into it.

I said nothing as I pulled my Union suit up and hooked my arms through the holes.

After she slid into her dress, straightening it, she sat next to me on the side of the bed. She smiled into my face. "You gonna come back?" she asked.

I shrugged. "I reckon," I said.

"You didn't like it?"

"Sure, I did."

"Well?"

"I'll come back."

"Tomorrow?"

"I guess. Yeah. If my brother doesn't come in on the train in the morning. I'll come back."

"What if he comes?"

"I'll have to take him home." I swallowed hard, wishing I'd paid for all night and wishing I didn't have to worry with Bosworth and wishing . . . It seemed that suddenly all the heaviness, the giddiness of the beer, the atmosphere of a sinful place on Moccasin Alley, all of it had disappeared, vanished in the night. "That's what I came for—to take him home," I added. "It's why I'm here."

She put her hand on my knee. "I hope you come back," she said. "I like being with you."

"You're not worried about the Ku Klux?"

Her face twisted into a frown. "The what?"

"I saw that black cross, what's left of it, up in front of McRae's Beer Hall, and Billy said it was the Ku Klux."

"They ain't nothing."

"But . . ."

"I'm not afraid of 'em. They're nothing but a bunch of rednecks who can't get it up, even if I was to blow on it, which I ain't."

I followed her out the door and down the hall, where we had to step around a couple heading in the opposite direction. Up front, where smoke filled the dimly lighted room, several men milled about with glasses in their hands, talking to the women in low whispery voices, glancing at me as I said good-bye.

I stepped into the darkness of Moccasin Alley.

I walked across the hard-tromped dirt and looked among the dozen or so horses tied along the front of the Starlight Club where I'd left Jed, but I did not see the roan gelding among them. As a jazzy sound rocked the walls of the club, I walked up the block and then back again, inspecting each of the horses.

"Jed," I said aloud to no one. My heart sank. *What if . . .* If someone took my horse—Papa's horse—I didn't know what I'd do.

I walked all the way down to the last barroom and back again. I started to go back to Mimi's to ask Lacy, but I figured I would really look and sound stupid if I did that.

At the doorway into the Starlight I hesitated, the music inside whipping up a strong beat. I searched down the bar for Billy, then glanced into the far corner where, to my amazement, Sean O'Donohue had his fiddle cocked on his shoulder. Next to him stood a red-headed youth with a flute stuck to his mouth.

"Well, I'll be," I said to myself.

I wandered along the bar, where I found Billy, who grinned at me and drew a glass of beer without my asking. He put it in front of me as I sat. "This is on the house," he said. "The fiddle-player said he's a friend of yours."

"But how'd he know . . ."

"He saw your horse outside, came in, and offered to play—him and the whistler."

I frowned.

"My boy Joe took your horse around and gave him some oats. Hope you don't mind. O'Donohue said he didn't want you riding away without seeing him first. He said y'all'd said good-bye earlier today."

"That we did," O'Donohue said, stepping up to the bar.

"He's the one I told you about," I said to Billy, who was still grinning.

The redheaded flutist behind him was introduced as Colin McCluskey, a friend of O'Donohue's whom he'd met on the north side of the river, heading south.

"Colin had been to Mooresville and reported no action from that town, so I decided to backtrack with him, hoping we could find a gig down here in the bottoms," O'Donohue explained. "Your horse is out back."

173

I nodded and winked at Billy. "That was not a very good trick," I said. "Scared me out of my wits, finding Jed missing."

O'Donohue shrugged. "I wouldn't-a thought you had any wits left, after what you've been through the last few days."

"Starting with you stealing my horses."

"You mean running your horses down and bringing 'em back to you, like a good Samaritan," the Irishman said. "Packed with all your goods, I might add. It sure wasn't thievery, I'll say."

"I'm sure glad I ran into this Irish whiskey-head," said Colin McCluskey, who said he hailed from Edinburgh, where he'd had a misspent youth.

I told him that my own folks came from the highlands of northern Scotland. "I've heard family tales all my life," I said.

"Speaking of a misspent youth," O'Donohue said, "I reckon you were in church when we arrived at this den of iniquity."

As my face grew warm I lowered my eyes.

At that instant, Lacy Beauchamp entered through the front doors and swept past the railroad workers, who had gotten louder with the passage of time.

"And here comes the sacred minister of that church," announced Billy the bartender.

I threw him a look, then my eyes settled on Lacy, who suddenly looked as radiant as a movie star. She grinned crookedly and moved to my side. I inched away from her, pulling my beer along the bar. When she followed, I stepped away from the bar.

"Are y'all doing some kind of dance?" asked O'Donohue, who was slushing down a beer Billy had handed over the bar to him.

"A mating dance?" Colin McCluskey asked.

I glared into his face menacingly. He didn't know me well enough for such a comment. Because he was O'Donohue's friend, I let it go without affront.

"Well," Lacy said, looked around, and strolled off and stepped near a young man who was sitting alone at the opposite end of the bar.

"I guess that settles that," O'Donohue said.

"I guess," I said, feeling silly and wishing she'd come back and stand next to me. She embarrassed me one moment, then made me jealous the next. I didn't like seeing her with another man, but I knew deep down that it was none of my business where she stood or who she was with.

O'Donohue said he'd be staying for a few days or a week. He and Colin had a room on this side of town. "It's not as fancy, nor as expensive, as Mrs. Prudence's place," he explained. "But it'll do."

"Which makes me think," I said.

"You're doing a lot of thinking, aren't you?" O'Donohue asked.

Smiling, I shook my head. "I don't have time for it," I said.

I said I needed to go. I knew Mrs. Prudence would be looking for me. We all shook hands. Then I looked across the dark room toward Lacy and the other young man. She was standing as close to him as she had stood near me an hour ago. My stomach felt suddenly queasy again. I wanted to go over to her, but I forced my thoughts in another direction.

I walked out of the place, mounted Jed, and rode out of Moccasin Alley. Glancing toward the blackened cross still teetering next to McRae's Beer Hall, I was glad I made it through the night without being harmed. I breathed deeply the fresh night air.

I found Mrs. Prudence's, led Jed to the barn out back, then felt my way up the unlighted path to the porch. At the door, I fumbled with the lock. I was twisting it one way, then the other.

The door opened and I stumbled forward into the hallway.

Mrs. Prudence reached out to catch me. "Harold," she said.

"I'm okay," I said, leaning toward her.

She held to my arm, steadying me.

After she released me, I took another awkward step in the semi-darkness.

With my foot, I hit the bottom of the hat rack, which rocked sideways toward the high mirror.

As it started to fall, I reached out.

Just in time, I grabbed the C-shaped chin-high holders. I balanced it, until Mrs. Prudence, in an exuberant attempt to assist me, reached over my shoulder. When she did, she pushed her weight against my body and sent me wheeling toward the wall.

My body fell under the hat rack that toppled onto me, sending hats flying down the hallway and walking canes skittering across the floor.

Lanterns flickered at the top of the stairs.

"Mrs. Prudence?" someone inquired.

"I'm fine," Mrs. Prudence answered.

Someone else called out and she reassured them that everything was okay.

She had landed on top of me, her body draped across my legs.

"Are you all right?" I asked.

"Yes," she whispered. "Are you?"

I shifted on the floor where the bottom section of the hat rack lay across my upper body.

Mrs. Prudence pushed up, relieving the pressure against my legs, then she pulled the rack upright, freeing me to move about in the shadows of the hall, retrieving the hats and putting them back onto the stand.

Suddenly my eyes began to shift. I reached out, stumbled backward, steadied myself, felt the floor moving beneath me, and took a firm hold on the banister.

"Are you all right?" she asked me again.

I nodded. "I'm fine. I'm fine."

"You're . . ." she started, the sharpness I'd heard earlier returning to her voice.

I steadied myself for another moment.

"Are you drunk, Harold?" she asked.

I started to giggle, then I covered my mouth with my hand.

"You smell like a brewery or a . . ." She stopped and stared at me through the darkness.

She dusted off her dress, straightening it. She started to say something else, but didn't. She began picking up canes and putting them back into the rack.

I started to give an explanation, but some hidden conscience caught my words and held them.

I found my way up the stairs to my room. I lay in the bed a full minute before I realized that a stranger was sleeping in the small bed in the corner where O'Donohue had slept the night before.

Fourteen

I slept late. Whoever was sleeping in O'Donohue's bed got up and out early. I awakened when I heard him moving about the room, but I slid down under the covers and remained there until after he was gone. Then I closed my eyes and napped for a while longer, until I woke and heard no one else moving about on the floor, then I got up and cleaned myself. I stared into the mirror over the basin and knew that I looked different today. So much had happened yesterday and last night. My life had changed irrevocably. I would never be the same again. Even when I returned home to Mama and Papa, I knew they would look at me in a different perspective. Nobody in the world would ever see me the same way again. I knew now, without fail, what it was like to be a sinner. I knew that neither my sisters nor Sarah Lynn Saunders would ever have anything to do with me again. My insides felt dirty, and it was a dirt that could never be washed clean. *Never*, I thought.

Hesitantly, I walked down the stairs and entered the dining room. I sat alone in the corner. Several of the men who were finishing their breakfast spoke to me. Others nodded. I did likewise. I knew they could all tell that something was wrong with me.

I was having a tall glass of cold milk when Mrs. Prudence entered the large room and headed my way. Thinking about last night's scene in the entrance hallway, I wanted to duck under the table and escape without being seen, but her eyes fastened to mine.

She sat opposite me, the sun from the high window backlighting her head and forming a halo over her crown of ash blonde, nearly white, hair. She glowed like polished silver. "Good morning, Harold," she said cheerfully.

"Good morning, Mrs. Prudence," I said, feeling awkward, squirming in my chair, knowing that I still reeked of Moccasin Alley: beer and cheap perfume and no telling what else.

She reached out and touched my hand that was clinging to the coffee cup. "Why don't you just call me Prudence," she said.

As I squirmed again, I glanced around the room, where two maids were working to clear the tables of the used breakfast dishes. If I didn't know better, I would have sworn Mrs. Prudence was flirting with me. She was extraordinarily handsome for a woman her age. I gulped a swallow of milk, feeling it travel all the way down my throat.

"I'm sorry about last night," she said.

"No, no," I insisted. "It was I who . . ."

"You're old enough, responsible enough, mature enough to stay out as late as you wish, to come in whenever you choose. You're almost seventeen, an adult given adult responsibilities. It was I who was impertinent, to say the least. I hope you will let me make up for my . . . my intrusion into your privacy."

"It'll never happen again," I said, and immediately wondered about the veracity of my statement. In this new atmosphere of the city everything was suddenly serious with me. It seemed that my entire personality had changed overnight. I was no longer the frivolous boy I had been only days ago. I looked at life through a dark-shaded vision, no longer viewing a rose-colored world which I occasionally turned topsy-turvy.

She sat back. "I want to show you a very special place today," she said. In her voice was the hint of surprise, something magical, something enchanting, an unanswered question.

I stared into her eyes, questioning.

180

The chimes on the grandfather clock sounded seven-forty-five.

"I have to go to the railroad station. It's getting late."

The fingers of her right hand touched my wrist again. "You don't have to go today," she said. "Your brother's not coming."

"He's not?" I said.

She unfolded a paper she had been carrying in her left hand. "This came last night," she said, handing the paper to me. "It was brought late. It was not addressed to you, as you see, or I would not have opened it."

A telegraph message stated: "To Prudence Longshore: Please inform my son Harold his brother will arrive next Thursday morning. He has been suffering from a wound he received in Europe. In his condition he should require buggy or wagon transportation. If you could assist in this matter, I would be forever grateful. Thank you, your servant, John Reed."

I was still staring at the paper, reading Papa's words again, while Mrs. Prudence began telling me she had an old buggy she had instructed her livery man Roscoe to take out of storage and equip with whatever hardware necessary to have it operating by next Thursday.

"Since today is Saturday, I thought you might enjoy an outing at the Cave of the Wind."

"Sounds mysterious," I commented.

She chuckled lightly, the way a girl Lacy Beauchamp's age would laugh, tickled and playful, cute and cunning. She lifted her head to an angle, gazing at me through sea-blue eyes. "Once upon a time, when it was called Ittachoomah by the Cherokees, it was mysterious. It's now the Hotel Greerson, large enough to accommodate more than a hundred guests. Tonight we'll dine on oysters from Apalachicola and shrimp from the Gulf of Mexico, and we'll soak our bodies in the hot mineral springs that are said to be sixty feet deep and have the powers of strong medicine." She chuckled again.

"But first, I have had a few things delivered to your room. I hope you will forgive my exuberance. I hope I have not once again overstepped my bounds."

I could not imagine what she would have had delivered to my room, but soon discovered an entire wardrobe of clothes: regular pants pleated down the front with a leather belt that actually buckled, shirts with collars and buttons down the front, a pair of wing-tipped brown-and-white shoes that I'd seen advertised in a New York catalogue a traveler had left at the barber shop last year, and several pairs of socks that matched the brown and black trousers. I had never been partial to over-alls and brogans. It was simply what we wore to work around the farm, what Papa wore, and Martin. It was my everyday dress to go to school. I kept a pair of trousers, a shirt, and dress shoes at Mr. Guyton's barber shop. When I worked there, I changed in the back room when I came to work and back into the overalls and brogans when I left. I had a similar change of clothes at home, for Sundays, weddings, and funerals. In the boxes I also found a bathing suit not unlike the one Papa wore when we went picnicking at the river.

Her livery man, Roscoe, harnessed a big mare named Judy to the shiny black buggy with a spiffy surrey top. As we pulled away from the boardinghouse, the big wire-spoked, well-oiled wheels turned easily. We sat high on the black leather seat, comfortable with its cushioned back and springed underpinning. I glimpsed Jed and Jenny nibbling grass in the paddock, paying us no mind. We took the long route, leaving toward the west, passing the old Bank Building with its five thick columns down the front, sitting empty, like a Greek temple, on a hill that anchored that corner of the town.

We maneuvered southwest, then circled south of town with Prudence talking, telling me the history of the territory, when we came upon a crossroads marked by the life-sized statue of a man made of metal almost the same silver color as Prudence's hair. His arms were outstretched, pointing north and south, and he had a face on each side of his body, one looking east, the other west. His feet were held in concrete and his legs were welded together. "It's a strange statue," I said. I read aloud the legend across his belly: "Veg-a-Cal gets the bile," and I laughed. "What does that mean?" I asked. She explained that it had been erected a dozen years ago as a highway advertisement for an elixir to cure stomach ailments.

As I laughed again, she snapped her whip over Judy's back and the big horse quickened to a trot. The countryside east of Decatur was rich and lush with thick hilly woods. Hardwood trees rose around us like heavy walls that soon gave way to a pine grove, dark and foreboding beneath the dense green cover of the long needles and the layers of branches. The smell of the pines permeated the air with an oily, pungent fragrance.

There was a relaxed cadence to our trip. Unlike my journey from Town Creek, slow-moving and tight with a tension of mysterious unknowing, Prudence Longshore's horse knew the well-traveled road by which we traversed the forest. Her head high, her mane rippling against the sheen of her smooth red neck that arched with a noble presence, she was an extension of her mistress, sure of herself and her high-stepping grace.

Prudence's face held a smile, her eyes a knowledge of her sur-roundings, her voice an eager thrill. I relaxed and listened to her words narrating an Indian tale about the place, Ittachoomah, the Cave of the Wind, where a Cherokee princess was exiled by her father, the chief of the tribe, after he discov-ered she had had an affair with a young brave who had been killed in a battle with white soldiers. Pregnant from the illicit romance, the girl swam into the grotto, where she drowned. "Today, legend says, if you listen carefully, you can hear the girl's sorrowful cries as they echo through the depths of the cavern."

Chilled by her word picture, I squeezed my arms to my body. I glanced at her and smiled and nodded. For the first time in days I was totally relaxed, had lost temporarily the nightmare of the storm and its aftermath. I felt good and free and full of myself in her company.

"Do you like poetry?" she asked as we rode along.

"Not particularly," I said. I thought it was nice, the way she brought up subjects, like poetry, just right out of the blue, akin to nothing in particular, just a fleeting thought, without purpose or plan.

"Do you study poetry in school?"

"Teacher reads it to us now and then. I don't pay much attention to it. It seems to be just words to me."

"Good poetry sings to you, like the wheels of a buggy and the clip-clop of a horse's hooves."

I shut my eyes and listened to Judy's hooves clopping against the hard-packed dirt of the high road and the whir of the wheels turning around and around, a monotony that made a rhythm, not unlike a song.

"When a young man steps out onto a road, heading from one place to another, not knowing much about his destination, but looking forward to the experience of discovery, he soon finds the beauty and essence of poetry a relaxing companion in travels that might otherwise be lonely and uneventful."

Traveling like this, dropping everything at the hint of a suggestion, was unknown to my folks. In Town Creek, people planned overnight trips for weeks, if not months. You had to have a reason for going somewhere. We did not simply drop everything on the spur of the moment and take off and not look

184

back. And we never went for an overnight visit simply to see a place, experience a vista, or enjoy a bite or two of strange or unusual food. For one thing, food was for sustenance. If it tasted good, that was an extra treat. Our sweets consisted mostly of sugarcakes. At Christmas, when Uncle Alexander sent a box of dried peaches from Chilton County, Mama made fruitcake, and that was a real joy. We always took along enough food to eat on our journey. We never patronized restaurants or cafes. That was an extravagance for rich people in big cities, foreign to our country existence. Nobody, with the exception of Mr. Melvin Saunders and his family, made a habit of paying someone else for what they could do or fix themselves.

I'd once heard Caleb Andrews talk about eating barbecued goat at a place in Tuscumbia. "Simple" Simon once boasted about eating a steak dinner at a hotel cafe in Louisville when he traveled up for the Kentucky Derby several years back, and a drummer from Chattanooga bragged in the barber shop one afternoon about eating roast pheasant at a fancy inn near Huntsville. He said that once, long ago, Andrew Jackson had stayed at the same inn. After he left, Mr. Guyton said the drummer was a loudmouth who'd probably never had such an experience, only dreamed about it or read about it and figured it sounded interesting in retelling. However, riding through the woods with Prudence Longshore, I wondered about the likelihood of truthfulness in the drummer's words. Every moment now the world was growing larger for me, filled with more possibilities, while some questions were answered, more were posed.

We were now traveling south of and parallel to the river, having made our circle complete. The road broadened. It was a fine road that sat high above the flatlands that would be flooded when the spring rains came. A little after midday the woods opened like curtains being drawn to expose a new stage of nature. On the horizon to the north lay shallow water that stretched all the way to the river. A chilling breeze swept down. Prudence dug a shawl from her things and wrapped it around her shoulders. She looked at me and smiled pleasantly, asking if I needed a jacket. I said I was fine, and she slapped the reins easily onto Judy's back, then she looked out over the marshland. "Lovely, isn't it?" she asked, and I nodded. With the sun still high, its brilliant rays shone on the rippling water, dancing there, shimmering like thousands of diamonds glittering on the surface. "It's blinding," I said. She shifted on the seat, pushing closer to me, her warmth both comforting and disturbing.

Moments later, in the distance, a black cloud shadowed across the bright blue sky. It moved toward us at an amazing speed. I was suddenly reminded of the storm that had come out of the northwest as quick as a flash and had swept old Katanzakis and Powtawee away in its sudden gust. As it moved closer, I realized that it was not a cloud at all but a great gathering of geese all flying together in a flock.

"Canada geese stay here in the winter, then migrate north in the summer," she said.

"They're headed in the wrong direction," I said.

"These must be the last ones to leave, enjoying the springtime as long as they can, before heading north."

As they neared, the sound of their collective squawks grew louder and louder until it was near deafening. Judy threw back her head, her neck arching, her ears pointing skyward. She snorted the air. Prudence held tightly to the reins, keeping her under control. The giant shadow moved over us, the birds flying in a swarm so thick it darkened our world, casting us into a quick, frightening blackness. Judy's nostrils flared and she snorted louder, as though to warn us and speak out against possible danger. I felt Prudence move even closer to me.

Then, as quickly as they had appeared, the birds were gone.

I turned my head and watched as they continued to fly south-ward, dropping lower and lower, until, in the distance, they landed in another marsh, their loud chorus vanishing.

The landscape changed again as we continued east, the land pushing up out of the flatlands like there had been some great upheaval or explosion from the center of the earth. I imagined a violent happening here thousands of years ago to form hills, pushing boulders up from beneath the land, turning the world inside out, until the big rocks stood like colossal temples, smooth and rounded, like they were formed by an artist's hands, and others jagged and twisted, rough-edged, whipped by a fierce wind that had blown out of the northwest, like the vicious storm that had swept Katanzakis away. I shivered again, remembering.

Scattered between the rock formations were scrawny pines and scrub oaks, stunted by the same savage force of nature that had ravaged the surface. Then the forest took over again, its curtain closing to form an immense tapestry of greens and browns, yellows and blues, blacks and purples, covering us with its magnificence, even the smell and the feel changing from a cool lightness to a warm damp dark heavy richness.

"Have you ever had champagne?" she asked out of the blue.

"Why, no," I answered. "I haven't," I said, as though to reas-sure her. After my performance last night, she thought I was a regular drinking man. I wasn't about to tell her that yesterday had been a first for me—on several levels. In a way, it was embarrassing for me to even think about my performance. I could not possibly talk about it. When I might have joked among my peers at my silly ineptness, now my lips were sealed in silence.

Suddenly I didn't feel as good as I had earlier. I sat as ram-rod-straight as I could and tried not to think about the rumbling in my stomach. I prayed that I would not break wind and ruin this beautiful day. What with pickled pig's feet, a dozen glasses of beer, a tumble on a narrow bed with rusty springs making noise under me, and nothing of any substance for supper, no wonder my stomach was trying to act up on me now.

"We'll have some real French champagne tonight," she said.

"Along with the Apalachicola oysters?" I asked. The very thought tickled my innards.

She smiled.

I wondered how my stomach would react to such a treat of richness and decadence, such a difference from its everyday feeding of porridge and scrambled eggs, meat and vegetables, cornbread and sweet milk. In my travels I was beginning to enjoy a luxurious life the likes of which nobody in Town Creek would ever be able to imagine, much less emulate. On one hand I was embarrassed by the grand elegance of this world into which Prudence was leading me, yet on the other I felt a haughty pride swell in my breast, enjoying every moment of opulence.

Like entering a great cavern, Prudence guided Judy through the thicker, darker woods, up a long incline, then down into a long green meadow that opened onto a still, dark lake where water rippled in the brisk afternoon breeze. Overhead, the sky turned a deeper, richer royal blue. The sun's brightness glistened on the water and turned the waist-high sedge-grass a golden glow and the distant trees a buoyant shade of emerald, as though it were about to burst into the sky, like a jack-in-the-box of vivid, vibrant colors.

It was a glorious day, even with the uneasiness in my stomach that growled like a disgruntled old grizzly as we bounced up the washboard road. In the distance, beyond the lake, the first outline of the hotel appeared against the side of the hill. "You will feel much better once you've waded into the mineral water and immersed yourself in its warmth," she said. "It will tingle against your skin and give you an inner assurance."

I told her that I did not enjoy swimming.

"You said that before. I believe you. You don't have to swim. All you have to do is bathe, luxuriate in the water, let it cover your entire body, roll over you and through you."

I frowned.

"They have the water bottled for your health. Drink it and you will feel like a new person. I have been told these waters will cure rheumatism and constipation, diseases of the liver, kidneys, skin, and stomach, calm your nerves, make you sleep like a baby, drive away consumption, and appease the distress of gray hair." She laughed heartily, her hand reaching up and touching the ends of her own hair. "I'm sure you've noticed that I suffer from the latter." I glanced toward her and saw the playful sparkle in her eyes beneath the shade of her driving hat.

"Your hair is nice," I said, trying to choose the appropriate words.

She chuckled lightly. "Just nice?" Her words sparkled, like her eyes.

"Pretty," I said with a nervous twitch.

She said nothing else, holding the reins in both hands.

I knew one thing for sure: I didn't need the mineral water to cure constipation; that was the least of my problems.

Within an hour we were ensconced in our suite: a large sitting room between ample bedrooms. I had my own double bed, high and fluffy, not unlike the one at the boardinghouse. The first thing I did was tend to my toilet, taking more time than usual. When I entered the sitting room she was waiting in a long robe that covered her body. In her hands was a copy of *Ladies Home Journal*.

Self-conscious and awkward, I strolled in wearing my new bathing suit. Not wishing to show off my skinny physique and thinking that the cloth that hugged my thighs did little to cover my private parts, I let my arms hang down the front and my hands cover the area between my legs, with my towel folded there. She chuckled lightly, stood, and led the way to the stairs at the end of the east wing. Down four floors, we opened a wide double doorway that took us to the baths. We walked down an underground corridor and stepped into the large cavernous room that opened back into a rock-walled cave, the bottom of which was filled with putrid-colored green water that smelled steamy and gaseous.

Around the edge of the pool was a concrete shelf extending from the front to the rear that disappeared into darkness, looking as though it were endless.

At a pair of lounge chairs, I followed her lead, spreading my towel over the whitewashed wooden seat. Several young people and an elderly couple floated in the smelly water of the pool, beneath the cover of the cave's roof.

Prudence stood next to the chair. Slowly, she unfastened the knot at her waist. As the bow pulled loose, she peeled back the robe and stepped through the opening. Unlike her golden-tanned face and neck, full creamy white thighs appeared beneath the folds of the sky-blue skirt of her bathing suit, looking as though they had never glimpsed sunlight. Her legs tapered to slender ankles and pointed toes. I tried to look away but could not. My eyes were mesmerized by the sudden view of her rounded breasts bulging against the thin cloth that tried unsuccessfully to hide them. I gasped. I couldn't help myself. Finally, I turned away, afraid that beneath my own suit I would bulge in a way that I could not possibly hide.

I heard the faint laughter behind me as she half-whispered, "Come on," and stepped down into the water.

I followed.

As the heat caressed my skin, steamy vapors worked at my nostrils.

"Isn't it wonderful?" she asked, her voice light and airy.

"It smells," I said.

She laughed again, a bare sound of delight squeezing from her throat. "That's the sulfur, iodine, and other ingredients," she said. "It has mysterious medicinal qualities."

"You said," I said.

She moved to a place within the dark depths of the cave, where the roof lowered, the damp rocks just above our heads. She found a ledge beneath the surface of the water and sat there. "Come here," she said.

Thoughts of last night, Lacy Beauchamp, the evil yet tantalizing darkness of the Starlight Club, the smoky fog of Mimi's, the sound of Sean O'Donohue and his Scottish friend playing their music, a feeling like I'd never felt before, like something was happening to my insides, going squashy, then tight, like a knot being passed through my innards. Thoughts of that dark time, memories of that mysterious world, now terrified me. Everything had been happening too fast: first, Katanzakis and Powtawee; then, the Starlight and Lacy; now, a magical world of medicinal wonders and a woman whose beauty mystified and frightened me. I wanted to shut my eyes and open them and know that I was truly living in a dream. *What?* I thought.

I moved toward her, floating, following her command; as she called to me, I followed without question.

"Stand here," she said. "Let the water roll over you."

I moved closer. In an instant, a hot current from within the rock wall flowed into my body and its pressure pushed against me. I reached out and took her hand and held to it, trusting her, letting my body float up to the surface, feeling my skin tingle, not unlike the way it had tingled last night when Lacy touched me. "Ohhhh," I sang, without thinking, my brain floating like my body.

Prudence laughed joyfully.

We stood within three feet of each other, feeling the water, now and then one holding the other's hand, floating, our bodies prone, letting the heat ripple over our skin, and soon I felt the new person she'd promised move beneath my skin and take over my being. The heat and the pressure of the water totally relaxed me, sent tingles through my muscles, and worked wonders with my brain, cleansing it.

She asked me about myself and I told her. She asked about Papa and I told her he was a hard-working man who praised the Lord on Sunday and tried to live by His word during the rest of the week. She listened and nodded. "I do know that he's a very serious person," she said. I said that indeed he was; he read the Bible nightly.

I asked how she had known him. She said that it had been a long time ago, when he'd come to Decatur to sell meal his father had ground from corn at the mill on the mountain in the middle of The Forest, south of Town Creek near the community of Wren. "He was on a mission from his father, sent to town for a specific reason which he was bound and determined to complete. I found him a very attractive but totally serious young man," Prudence said. "Very much the way I find you."

"Oh?" I said. I'd never once thought that I was anything like Papa. I was his opposite. He was serious, I jovial. He was determined, I trifling.

"Look at your face," she said playfully. "Look at those sad eyes. They're the eyes of a boy who takes himself very seriously. You're the mirror image of John Reed. Don't you—take yourself seriously? Do you think that perhaps—because you strayed—you have sinned recently?"

"No," I answered too quickly.

192

Her smile did not vanish. "You look like a boy who needs a priest and a confessional booth. Something to wash away the evil and cleanse your soul."

"We're Presbyterian," I said.

"Even Presbyterians need forgiveness, now and then."

"You're teasing," I said.

"Yes, but only partly," she said.

Her eyes twinkled with such a lightness, I wanted to reach out for her, the way I'd done last night with Lacy. Then, as quickly as I'd thought of her, I tried to chase Lacy from my thoughts. I could not possibly think about a whore while I was talking to this lady.

"Well?" she said.

"What?"

"You want to tell me about your sins? Perhaps—if you would tell me—I could help."

I looked down into the murky water and shook my head. *Why is she doing this to me?* I asked.

She put her hand up, gently touched my chin with the tips of her long fingers, and whispered, "I'm sorry."

I pulled away from her. Suddenly a hurtful fever wrapped itself around my middle, replacing the sickness with a sorrow, a wanting to be with Lacy rather than this older, more mature, decent woman. She was too good, too perfect, too knowing. I felt suddenly that I didn't belong here, that I needed to be else-where, somewhere less exuberant and more commonplace, where I would feel less a stranger. For some reason, I'd been a stranger everywhere I'd been since I left my home in Town Creek. I thought: *What am I doing here? I don't deserve this.* I moved away from her, letting my body float away.

"I'm sorry," she said louder.

Behind me, I heard her swimming toward me. She grabbed my arm and pulled me to her.

When I turned, tears were leaking from my eyes like pus from a boil. I could not stop them. They hurt. They stung. They burned my eyes. They washed down saltily into the corners of my mouth as I thought not only about Lacy but old Katanzakis and poor Powtawee. I cried inside. I hurt. *God . . .*

"Really," she said softly. "Let me hold you." She pulled me toward her, but I broke away, jerking myself into deeper water. She held to my arm, applying pressure.

I looked around through the fog of my tears. Other people were holding each other, swimming as couples, standing and touching, none of them aware of the drama in this corner of the pool.

"I want to go up," I said, pulling away from her hold. "I feel too . . . too heavy. I feel like I can't move. It must be the medicinal qualities of the water. All of a sudden, I feel very sleepy. It's like . . ." I could not tell her what I was feeling. Too many feelings overcame me too quickly, all of them squeezing me, all at once. I wanted to escape. I wanted to be alone. I wanted to cry hard and feel every tear seep from my body. If I didn't go now, I was afraid what I might do next.

"You go ahead," she said. "I'll stay behind. I haven't had enough yet."

I took my towel and wiped it across my body. I glanced back toward her, standing in the water at a distance, looking away from me, gazing into the dark recesses of the cave. Perhaps she was thinking about the Indian princess. Perhaps she was listening for the echoes of the Indian princess's distant cries. I wanted to go to her and tell her everything was okay, that she'd done nothing to make me sad, that it was my own mind, my own memory, my own sorrowful, sinful ways that were making me feel this way. Instead, I walked away, climbed the long stairs to the suite, where I drank a pint of the smelly mineral water, got into my bed, and drifted into a deep sleep.

I was dreaming about flying through the sky in a beautiful multicolored balloon, floating high above the earth, wind blowing against my face as I marveled at the patterns below, feeling weightless, invigorated, free.

When my eyes opened her silhouette stood between my bed and the shade-drawn window where the late afternoon sun shone in a rosy striped haze. She moved toward me silently, drifting, like she was walking on a cloud. Her arms lifted. A thin filmlike gown draped from her shoulders. She shifted effortlessly, and the gown fell to the floor without a sound.

Wordless, she lifted the covers and slid between the sheets, her body turning onto mine, her breasts unleashed and pushing against my chest, her arms circling my body that heaved as I breathed deeply the suddenly scented air tingling with a fragrance of jasmine. Before I could speak her mouth covered mine and her tongue licked across my teeth. She tasted salty, and I reached around her and rubbed my palms against her back, holding her tightly, hoping that I was not dreaming, holding her like she was a buoy that would keep me afloat.

Hair smelling richly of lilac curtained my face into darkness while her lips eagerly devoured my mouth, my chin, my neck, and down.

I wiggled with the aching, gnawing pain of ecstasy, of wanting to satisfy the torturous longing that gripped me somewhere so deep I did not know its source, yet knowing I wanted it to continue, no matter what faced me on the other side, to grow, to enrapture my entire being with its mounting anguish, something that was so mysterious that I didn't understand it, yet I wanted to thrust myself totally into the darkness of her. The desire forced my body upward as my buttocks hoisted from the soft bed to meet her lips, soft as rose petals, engulfing me. It was a total thirst, unlike the time I had had with Lacy, unlike any time had ever been for me; it was not open and light but hidden in the black of night, surprising me with each new movement, each new hunger.

I tried to hold back, but like last night with Lacy, I spent quickly, squeezing my buttocks as tight as possible.

She slid away. I knew she was gone for good. I gasped for breath, knowing that I would be alone again, that she hated me for what I'd just done, that she would never want to see me again. I wanted to cry out for her to return, but I remained still and silent.

But she was back in a moment. Like Lacy, she had a hot wet rag that she applied to my body between my legs. Silently she worked, pushing me back and dropping the rag and kissing me again.

"Ohhh," I moaned as I hardened again.

I began twisting, but she held my shoulders and threw her leg over my middle and mounted me, lowering onto me, not like Lacy with a thrust but moving slowly, deliberately, easing me into her. Then she leaned down onto me, her breasts barely brushing my chest. I reached up and ran my fingers over them, feeling the nipples harden, feeling the smooth softness of the skin, then hugging her to me, kissing her, the sweetness of her now mixed with an animal-like musk. She breathed heavily against my cheek as I held her close.

As the room shaded into darker shadows, we made love a third time. We touched each other, urging each other, guiding, feeling, kissing, our bodies slick with sweat. After, she bathed me in the tub that sat high on legs, washing me with water that flowed from the mineral springs into the building. I did not feel the least bit self-conscious as she slid into the tub with me. I scrubbed her back and her breasts and her legs, making me want to do it again and again. She laughed and shook her head and said, "Wait. We have all night." Reluctantly, I acquiesced.

After I dressed in my room and she in hers, we met in the sitting room, where she held me and looked into my face and said, "I would never hurt you. Never. Not for anything in the world."

I did not know what to say. I gazed into her lovely face that glowed. She kissed my lips quickly. "I will never tease you again. Okay?"

I nodded.

"I did not mean to hurt you. What I said was . . ."

I put my forefinger to her lips. "Hush," I whispered.

She smiled and nodded. "Let's go eat," she said.

As I held the door open for her, I said, "And drink some French champagne with our Apalachicola oysters."

"You're learning fast," she said as she stepped out into the hallway, her bottom swishing from side to side with a new rhythm, a new light quickness in her step.

As we strolled across the lobby I noticed a wide man in a brocade vest and a perfectly tailored light gray suit standing next to a doorway leading into the dining room. He was checking a gold watch that hung from his broad body on a dangling fob.

Prudence slowed her step, turned her head slightly, and whispered, "That's Zachariah Ludlow, a banker from Hartselle. He's waiting for his wife, Agnes, who is the county's number one busybody, so we'll have to do a little creative thinking."

Her hand slipped onto my crooked arm as she said, "You lead the way, dear."

"Mr. Ludlow," she said as we neared the man, who pushed his watch back into its pocket. He looked up at me with an unsure frown.

"Zachariah, do you remember my nephew, Harold Reed?"

The man found a smile somewhere in his arsenal and shifted it onto the fat folds of his face. "Why, certainly," he said, extending his hand.

"How is Agnes?" Prudence asked.

Ludlow glanced into my face and, with an intimate wink, said, "We know how women are, don't we, Harold?"

I smiled and nodded.

"I swear I believe Agnes will be late for her own funeral," he said, pulling his pocket watch from his vest and examining the face again, then looking toward the stairway.

Inside the restaurant we were shown to our table on the far side of the room divided by pots filled with leafy plants, large square columns, and waist-high colorfully painted partitions.

As we passed several couples and a group of four, all of whom were craning their necks to check out our presence, Prudence stopped to introduce me.

Finally at the table, I held her chair, then settled myself and ordered the champagne. Hidden in a corner by a painted wall and a large plant, we relaxed as the waiter brought a silver bucket filled with ice and water into which he placed an already chilled bottle.

With our fluted glasses filled, the bubbles rising, Prudence raised her glass, touched mine, and said, "To a lovely week-end."

We drank together.

Prudence raised her glass and touched its rim to mine. "Here's to Mr. and Mrs. Ludlow and all the other busybodies in our county. I'm sure the gossips of Decatur are already filling the air with evil little words. Even if I did take us on a round-about circuitous route, they seem to have eyes everywhere."

I giggled, the bubbles tickling my throat and her words my mind.

"By this afternoon, after we were seen in the baths half-naked, Lord only knows what is being said."

We toasted ourselves again.

When the oysters were brought, laid out on a bed of ice, each in a pearl-colored half shell, I gazed at them with wonder.

"Watch me," she said. "Try to be as delicate as possible. But it is impossible to be entirely ladylike or gentlemanlike when eating oysters." She pushed a tiny fork into the body of one of the slimy little round gray organisms. Then she lifted the entire half shell to her mouth. She parted her lips and let the oyster slide into her mouth. She closed her lips, sucking the fork clean, and then she smacked her lips noisily.

I glanced around to see if anyone was watching.

She laughed lightly and shrugged her shoulders. "Like other exercises in the course of life, you have to make a noise—or the taste and appreciation are simply not enjoyed to the fullest."

I attempted to follow her instructions. However, when I tried to fork the oyster, it slid away. I reached out quickly and grabbed it with the tips of my fingers, gliding it back onto the shell.

She giggled.

I looked up into her face and knew she was not laughing at me. It was different from this afternoon in the hot baths. Now it was as though I were a part of her, and whatever she said or did was a part of me.

I picked up the oyster shell and put it to my lips. I saw then that I needed to break the oyster loose from the shell before slurping it up. I put it down, forked it, broke it loose, then brought it up again.

The oyster slid down my lower lip. Halfway down my chin, I grabbed it and pushed it up between my lips.

Inside my mouth, I thought at first of the slimy substance. Then I tasted the salty freshness, smelling it the way I had smelled her only minutes ago, the same kind of gamy sweetness. I bit down and felt the flavor explode within my mouth, filling it with a taste that I imagined was the flavor of the sea, where it had spent its entire life until now.

I swallowed the champagne behind the oyster, tasting the bubbles mix with the juice.

"It's good," I said.

She chuckled.

"It really is," I said with even more enthusiasm.

She smiled warmly, agreeing, then we began to eat in earnest, enjoying each flavor as one overflowed into the next.

I let her order for both of us. We had a small fresh salad of greens and tomato dressed with a touch of oil and vinegar, then our plates were filled with shrimp sautéed in garlic, butter, and lemon juice. Like the oysters, I had never before tasted shrimp. I had heard about them, but nobody in my family knew anything about seafood. And Mama had never ever cooked with garlic or lemon juice. She cooked with fatback or lard. This was an entirely new and delectable eating experience. After the last bite, we sopped the last speck of sauce from our plates with fresh bread baked in the hotel's kitchen.

During dinner, Prudence said, "Master Harold, you are enjoying the closest thing to sophistication that Alabama has to offer. The Grand Hotel on the eastern shore of Mobile Bay comes close. Once, years ago, the hotel at Fruithurst had a very good dining room with its own wine from vineyards on the hillsides along the Georgia border. A train carried tourists back and forth from Atlanta to Fruithurst. But there is nothing today like the Greerson, and I doubt if it will continue for many more years." Her final words sounded sad, an epitaph to grandeur.

With her words, I slowed my consumption, enjoying each taste.

"In the mid-nineteenth century, there were many large resorts and mineral baths around Alabama. There was one down at

Empire between here and Birmingham and another—Bailey Springs—north of Florence."

"I didn't know that," I said. "I've never heard of Bailey Springs."

"It was a thriving property. People from the East as far as Virginia, and from St. Louis and Memphis, Nashville and Louisville, came down to bathe in the restorative waters. They consulted physicians there, became healthy for at least a short while, then returned to their businesses and their homes, their churches and their garden clubs, whatever."

I smiled. I listened, taking in every word, thinking this was the way table conversation was meant to be: light and informative and entertaining. At home, whatever words passed across the table were hurried explanations of farming, commerce, troubles within our close-knit neighborhood, whoever was sick with what ailment, and whose son or daughter had gotten into trouble recently.

Gazing at her face in the muted light of the overhead lamp, my mind asked if it were really true that I had been with this woman an hour ago in the privacy of the hotel room on a bed, doing what we had done. It did not seem real. But here I was, fulfilling my voracious appetite for food and frivolous notions about the world. *How can life change so quickly? So thoroughly? So quickly?* My mind was abuzz with the thoughts of how life had suddenly been magnified for me. I had had no idea that I had been starving up to this point. Now I dwelled in a garden of delights, fruits growing bountifully, where all I had to do was reach out and pluck and partake.

"Would you like to retire to the men's library? To have a brandy and a smoke with Mr. Zachariah Ludlow?" Her voice danced with lightness.

I grinned from ear to ear.

"Or, would you . . ."

"The latter," I said.

Her rosy lips parted to show her sparkling teeth. Her eyes glistened.

I reached into the breast pocket of my coat where she had stored a number of bills. I took them out and extracted a twenty. Glancing into her face, I said, "I'll leave a generous tip."

Fifteen

After we returned to the suite, she invited me into her bed. Nearby was a bottle of dry white wine being chilled in a silver bucket filled with ice. Between lavender-scented sheets, I undressed her and kissed her the same way she had kissed me. We drank the wine and talked, my brain floating in a cloud of sensual flavors as I learned more in those heated minutes than I had in eleven years of school or sixteen years of life.

After I returned to my bed, I slept hard and didn't awaken until late the next morning.

As we rode back to Decatur the heavens clouded, thunder rumbled, and rain beat down onto the canvas roof of the buggy. As we crossed the marshy flatlands the geese did not make an appearance.

Before we arrived at the outskirts of the town, Prudence said, "I had a wonderful time, Harold. But that was there, and now we are here. Our lives must not become tangled in a dream. Not yours nor mine. I made a calculated assumption that you are mature enough to handle this. If anyone asks, you and I are cousins, but you regard me as an aunt. In *my* repertoire, you are my nephew who is visiting from a western province. If they ask, tell them your mother and I are first cousins once removed. That is, our grandmothers were sisters."

Her words resounded in my mind, especially the part about "our lives must not become entangled in a dream." I thought about her words throughout the lazy day as the rain peppered on the roof of the boardinghouse and when it continued into the night. I thought it was a sign when she moved the drummer out of my room, giving me privacy which I took as a promise of things to come. I dozed off and on through the afternoon. After having supper alone, when she dropped by my table to inquire about my health, I returned to my room, thinking she would come to me at any moment and drop the cool pretense. I tossed and tumbled. I awakened a dozen times, thinking of her, smelling her, feeling her touch, dreaming awful yet wonderful dreams.

Each time I awakened I thought she was with me. I opened my eyes and reached out. I grasped for her on the pillow. I searched the darkness but saw no one. I closed my eyes and felt the shame of my falsely aroused predicament.

When at last it was morning, I went down for breakfast, hoping I would see her and she would give me a sign of future promises. Surely her feelings did not remain at the Greerson Hotel and the Cave of the Wind. Surely she too thought about me as I was thinking about her. My brain did somersaults, thinking and planning how I could entice her to come to me or send for me.

I was sitting at the corner table in the dining room of the boardinghouse when a man with a small head and tiny doll-like hands entered, surveyed the room with a quick scan, regarded me, then moved toward a table in the opposite corner. I watched him step with the precision and lightness of a dancer on the balls of his feet. He was built like a child, but he had an old man's face: a high sloping brow covered with wrinkles, brown from an unforgiving sun, eyes sunk back into dark sockets, shaded by heavy black brows. His hair was thick and curly, black and professionally clipped above miniature ears.

Throughout breakfast I found him regarding me from time to time, taking notice of my features with the same scrutiny with which I had been studying him.

After we finished eating and I had fetched my shoeshine box, the little man met me in the front hallway. He stuck out his hand. "I'm Brother Preston Applewhite," he said. "I'm preaching an evangelistic message in my tent on the eastern side of town. I'd appreciate it if you and Mrs. Prudence would join me tonight at seven." I looked around. Prudence had been absent and was still nowhere to be seen. "I'm not sure about her, but I will try to attend," I said. After the last few days, I knew it would not hurt to have some spiritual guidance from whoever spoke The Word.

"You could start the day by giving me a first-class shine," he said.

Following him onto the porch, I dropped to my knees and began cleaning his black shoe that was caked with last night's mud. As I applied a thick coating of polish, he talked. "I've been talking with many of the good sisters of Decatur over the weekend, and I think it'd be a good thing if you and Mrs. Prudence attend my services. I will be preaching on the problem of the sinner in modern-day life. It seems that old-fashioned family values have been going astray in this community. It will be a good, hard sermon, aimed at an audience of sinners. I hope that it will have a cleansing effect on their souls."

When I glanced up into his miniature face, spitting on his leather and popping my rag, his little dark sunken eyes, framed in the thick brows, shone like coals on fire. His small mouth smiled wickedly, as only a preacher's can smile.

I rushed down to the depot to find customers crowding the waiting room. The word of my work had spread. A half-dozen men from various stations of commerce along Market Street were there specifically to have their shoes shined. "Will you consider staying in Decatur?" asked a lawyer named Odell Doss, who was said to be the best orator before a jury in Morgan County. I told him and others, including a man named

Seth Bell, who operated an investment property firm, that I had a particular mission to accomplish, and I meant to fulfill my promise to my father. "We know about your brother coming in Thursday," Mr. Doss said. Like Town Creek, nothing was a secret in Decatur.

Mr. Bell added, "We'd give you incentive to come back to Decatur, if you'd consider it. I'm told you are a barber as well as a bootblack." I told them I would certainly consider the offer: Norman Rocquemore, who owned several businesses in town, said he'd fix up a barber shop, outfit it with a pump-up chair and indoor plumbing, and let me have it with the first month's rent free of charge. I told him such a proposition sounded like a hard offer to refuse. Then the editor of the newspaper, *The Decatur Daily*, said he'd be at my stand three days a week: Monday, Wednesday, and Friday, if I'd remain at the depot. He was a well-dressed dude with a neatly trimmed mustache. Tipping me a half-dollar, he said, "If you have any trouble with anything, you call Editor Lee Sentell at the *Daily*. That clear?" I nodded and thanked him.

As I had previously, I watched the people getting off the southbound train. Knowing Papa had said Bosworth would not be here until Thursday, I still wanted to see for myself. Sure enough, Bosworth was not among the passengers. But two soldiers hobbled off the train. One walked with a crutch. His left leg had been amputated just below the knee. Watching him, I winced, wondering exactly what kind of injury Bosworth had sustained. I prayed that he would arrive in one piece. The other soldier walked okay, but there was an absent look in his eyes, and when his family came to greet him, he reached out with his hands to feel their faces with his fingers. Once again a swift sickness drifted through my stomach, realizing he was blind.

When I finished at the depot I walked a half-dozen blocks to The Tavern. By midmorning I had men lined up nearly a half-block, waiting to receive their shine. By noon my pockets were heavy with coins, and I had changed several dollar bills that I kept hidden in my inside pocket.

In the early afternoon, after the crowds thinned and business relaxed, I got to thinking about Powtawee and her situation. I stored my shoeshine box and set out walking. I found LaFayette Street and the cemetery, made my way through the hundreds of graves from 1888, and spotted the fresh blood-red gash of Katanzakis's grave near the big oak. I knelt next to the muddy soil beneath which he was buried. I placed my hand on the still-wet dirt. For an instant I thought I could feel his heart beating six feet below. I shut my eyes and prayed, asking God to help him fly through the sky higher than he'd ever flown, way up above the clouds. When I stood and turned and walked away, I felt as though he were looking down from somewhere far above me. I felt sure that he was up there, flying higher, waving his white cowboy hat, feeling the wind beat against his face.

Less than an hour later I sat next to Powtawee's bed. I described my dream of Katanzakis's heaven. She looked into my face with a blank stare. She said nothing. She lay in the crib in the rear room of the colored clinic and gazed upward. I tried to express my wish to help her with as much enthusiasm as I could muster, but my words did nothing to move her to joy.

I asked a barrage of questions, but if she had any idea what I was saying, she did not show it. As far as I could tell, I could have been speaking in a foreign tongue. No expression crossed her face. Her eyes seemed to gaze through me.

Dr. Albritton told me that Powtawee had stopped eating. If necessary, he said, they would force food into her system.

I shook my head, thinking that that was a horror which I had never thought possible.

"We never do it, except in rare and extreme cases, when we think the patient will die of starvation if we don't take such action," the young doctor said.

I told Powtawee that it would be best if she would eat of her own free will, but she continued to stare open-eyed into space. Her vision never focused on my face.

I reached out to touch her, but she rolled away.

I stood next to the bed for a long while, saying nothing, looking down at her, hoping she would say something to indicate that she felt my presence. But she still said nothing.

When I left, I felt empty and sad. I was not sure what I had wanted from her. Whatever it was, I had not received it. For my own good, I wanted to do something to help her, but it seemed that my presence was never even felt by her.

I passed the room where the white woman had fought with the men trying to hold her down. I peeped inside. She lay sleeping peacefully, her bruised and battered head bandaged. Beneath the covers her body rose and fell between heavy, labored breaths.

As I walked away from the clinic, my mind began to picture Lacy Beauchamp and Moccasin Alley, thinking about the time I'd had with Prudence Longshore, and thinking about the void she'd left when she failed to show in the middle of the night. In my sadness, I was a boy with a new itch, and I didn't know what to do now but hightail it straight to the Alley and the Starlight Club.

A crowd of four men were gathered on the street outside Powers Hardware Store. A heavyset man with thick gray muttonchop sideburns, Octavious Hicks, whom I had met at The Tavern with Prudence, and a slope-shouldered younger man with a long bent nose, Goodloe Littlejohn, whom Prudence had pointed out as "a pillar of the community," were laughing loud and hard. In the middle of the quartet of well-dressed gentlemen stood Pete Powers looking wide-eyed and frightened, like a wild animal being corralled. Pete's long arms were extended from each side of his round body with his large hands flapping against the sides of his baggy overalls. The other two men, watching and laughing, looked vaguely familiar, but I did not know their names.

As I neared, Pete's feet kicked at the mud where a snake snarled near his toes.

"Dance, dummy!" one of the men said, reaching down, grabbing the snake by the tail and shaking it toward Pete's feet.

Pete's face filled with fright, his limp hands shook, and his heavy-broganed feet rose and fell, picking up mud and splattering it. As he stumbled and fell back onto the dirt street, Goodloe Littlejohn bent down, picked up the snake and threw it toward Pete's legs. As the boy kicked wildly, the men laughed louder.

As mortified as I was of snakes, I rushed toward the group and reached down and grabbed the snake behind its head and jerked it away from Pete's legs. "Damn!" I declared, quickly throwing the snake across the road.

All four of the men nearly bent double with laughter.

Red-faced and short of breath, I stared angrily into their delighted faces. I couldn't believe their enjoyment. "What are you . . ." I began.

Octavious Hicks shook his heavy head. "It's only a play snake," he said. "It wouldn't hurt anybody."

"Just make-believe," put in Goodloe Littlejohn.

As Joseph Powers stomped out of his store, the four men stepped down the street, their laughter still creasing the early afternoon air. "What are you doing now?" Powers asked me, kneeling next to his still-frightened son, who sat in the mud in the middle of the street. The man glared up into my startled face. "What?!"

"Those men," I said. "They were making fun of Pete."

"You were all making fun of him!" Mr. Powers spat. "I don't know why you poke fun at the poor boy. I wouldn't do anything to harm you, and he surely wouldn't." He put his hands on Pete's shoulders and helped him up.

I tried to explain, but the man shook his head, dismissing me. He took the fat boy's trembling hands into his own and led him into the quiet darkness of the store, patting him on the back and shoulder, talking easily to him, telling him that everything was all right, okay, he would be safe inside, away from all the brutes on the street.

After I watched them disappear, feeling the heaviness overwhelming me even more than the moments after I left Powtawee, I walked down the narrow road that had been washed out with the Sunday rain. Gulleys slick with mud cut into the clay like wounds. I stayed on the far side, away from the entrance to McRae's Beer Hall and the teetering black cross that still dripped with rain water and swayed in the breeze from the river. Several Negro maids leaned over the railings of the rear stoops where they did laundry, regarding me with interested looks.

Inside the Starlight, Billy welcomed me. "A beer?" he asked.

"Please," I said.

After a sip or two, I looked around through the empty semi-darkness that smelled rank with last night's cigar and cigarette smoke, spilled beer, old perfume, and the blood of a man who'd caught a stool up-side his head, cutting a gash above his ear and bleeding onto the floor before the constable came and carried him and two others off to jail. Billy told me about the altercation while he mopped the floor.

"Is Sean O'Donohue still around?" I asked.

"Him and that little Scotsman, McCluskey, they're playing nightly for me until they get itchy feet and head for richer territory. They're a sight, those two foreigners. Folks come in just to hear them play and watch 'em dance a jig."

I smiled and sipped. I had to think about it more than a minute before I ventured, "Is Lacy around?"

"She's around somewhere," he said. "May be awake by now. She'll be over directly, I suppose. Or you could go over to Mimi's and have 'em wake her."

"No," I said. "I'll just wait."

He mumbled something and kept moving back and forth behind the bar, doing his work without words, washing glasses, toweling off the bar.

I was halfway through my second beer when Bubba and the crew from the railroad yard came in with the same rumbling noise they had displayed last Friday. While the others were pulling out chairs, sitting, and hollering orders to Billy, Bubba came over and slapped me across the back. "Hey, boy, how was that young pussy the other day?" He howled with laughter while I looked without expression into his round face. Thinking I'd be friendly, I nodded and said, "Just fine." He slapped me again and said, "I bet it was. I been eying that little ol' thing, only I ain't sure she could handle a big boy like me."

I said, "She probably does better with a little fellow like me."

Behind me, a feminine sound not much louder than the soft song of a quail in the bush said, "I'm a whole lot better with him, Bubba-boy," with a sarcastic twist.

Bubba looked through the darkness at the near-shapeless figure of Lacy Beauchamp standing next to the bar in the same ill-fitting fake-velvet blue dress she was wearing the other day. He howled with laughter so loud I thought he was going to burst his lungs. He bent forward, coughed, then said, "I might just give it a try before the night's over."

"You better save your money, Bubba," Lacy said, sliding onto a stool next to me.

Still laughing, he went to the table and sat with his gang. After a moment the entire group was laughing with him.

Lacy turned to me with a sullen face. "You didn't come back when you said you would," she said.

"I'm here," I said.

"You went off with that white-haired lady from the boarding-house."

I stared incredulously into her face, saying nothing.

"Sissy Little was downtown, buying supplies for Mimi. She said she saw you leave town Saturday morning in a high-fashion buggy with that tall woman with the silver hair."

I nodded. "That's Mrs. Prudence Longshore. She's my landlady." Then I remembered. "She's just like my aunt. Actually, she's my mama's first-cousin once removed."

Lacy Beauchamp screwed her face into a frown of disbelief. "That sounds like . . ."

I put up my hands. "Don't say it," I said.

"*Bullshit* is what I was going to say."

I smiled. "Have you ever seen her?"

"Sure, I've seen her," Lacy said. She turned away and gazed into the darkness where Bubba and the railroad workers sat. The same two women who'd joined them last Friday came in today and pulled chairs to their table.

"She's beautiful," Lacy said softly. "She's got the prettiest hair. In the sunlight, it shines just like polished silver."

I nodded. "She is pretty," I said.

"I saw her once driving her buggy to church on Sunday morning. She was sitting high and handsome, wearing a woolen suit the same color as her eyes. I'd never seen a woman wearing something so pretty. It fit perfect. And to think that she was once a Moccasin Alley girl . . ."

"What?!"

"I've heard talk."

"What kind of talk?"

"That she worked down here—years ago."

"That's insane."

"It's just talk."

"It's not true talk."

"How do you know that?" she asked.

"I can tell you it's not true. She's kin to me," I insisted. "Mama's first-cousin once removed."

Lacy laughed lightly, then she made a face. "What's wrong, farm boy? Your kin too good to work on Moccasin Alley?"

"It's not that."

"Y'all some kind of high-falutin' fancy folk?"

"I wouldn't say we're fancy. Not a-tall."

"What is it, then?"

"She's just so . . ." My voice trailed with my thoughts.

"She's too fine? Too perfect? Compared to me?" Lacy turned away and faced the door.

I reached out and touched her shoulder. "I didn't mean anything," I said.

She pivoted to face me. A quick sadness filled her eyes, her face. "You think a whore don't have feelings? You think you can talk about me just about any way you want, it don't affect me."

"I didn't say that," I said. I thought about how I had been hurt by the words Prudence had uttered in the water of the springs. "I'm sorry," I whispered.

I thought: *She looks so young.* The dress hung on her slender body. Her skin was smooth and olive, her hair black as coal, her eyes dark.

"I'm sorry," I repeated.

"I got feelings," she said.

"I know. I'm sorry. I didn't mean to say something cruel."

She blinked her eyes, reached over and took hold of my glass and lifted it to her lips. After a sip, she put it back. She looked into my face and said, "Where'd y'all go?"

"Down to the Cave of the Wind," I said.

"I've heard about that place."

"Hot springs, makes your skin tingle, and cures a person of all illnesses."

"I'd like to go there and wash myself."

"You're clean," I said.

"You don't know."

I looked at her from top to bottom, showing a new appreciation. I said nothing, but in my mind I was comparing her with Prudence, inch by inch, body for body.

"Like what you see?" she asked.

I nodded.

"You bring a five?"

I nodded.

"Want to start early?"

I nodded again.

"Buy me a sugar-beer?"

"What's that?"

"Just a beer. I'll fix the sugar."

I ordered and Billy brought it. She took a sugar pot and dipped out a spoonful and stirred it into her beer. Then she sipped. Smiling, she said, "It takes away the sour taste."

"I like the sour taste," I said.

"Most men do," she said.

IN HER LITTLE room in the rear of the house over the river swollen by the water from the weekend rain, we lay together with our sides touching. Feeling the slight liquid movement beneath us, I put my fingers on her thin arm and wrapped my fingers around it.

"I think you learned something from your first-cousin once removed," she said.

"My mama's first cousin . . ."

"Whatever."

Staring up into the rain-stained splotches on the gray ceiling, I said, "I don't know exactly what you mean."

"I feel something in you that wasn't there three days ago."

"Really?"

"The way you move. A strength. A confidence. You're more sure of yourself."

A growl of an engine roared outside. Water sloshed against pilings under Mimi's unpainted house. I held tighter to Lacy's arm as the room swayed. I knew my confidence and my surety would falter if the underpilings crumbled and we dropped into the water.

I turned my head to look questioningly into her face.

"It's a riverboat from Memphis," she said. "Steamboats come down the river after a big rain. The water comes up and they make it through the locks at Timberville and over the shoals. They'll come all the way down here. There'll be big times and big money on Moccasin Alley tonight. The men'll come in with their pockets jingling. You won't be able to stay all night."

"I paid my five dollars."

"And we started early."

"Oh," I said.

"I can't let you stay much later, when there's opportunity for some big money. Mimi wouldn't stand for it."

I didn't argue, but I held on to her arm. If the floor dropped much lower, I'd want to be gone.

"Lacy'll make her some big money tonight. Maybe even some traveling money."

"What do you mean, 'traveling money'?" I asked.

"Enough to hightail it out of here."

Waves lapped against the floor. The whole building rocked back and forth, like a swing, and I started to climb out of the bed.

She grabbed a-hold on my arms and pulled me down. "I like it like this," she said. She rose up onto her knees, turning toward me, bucking her bare bottom up and down.

"Hey," I said. "Don't do that." I slid my hands around her bottom and held to her, pulling her back onto the mattress.

"When the water's right up under my bed, that's when it's best," she said.

I swung over on top of her, ready.

She laughed lightly, not much louder than the waves. "You're something else, Harold Reed."

After, she rose on her elbow and looked down into my face. "What'd that aunt of yours do to you?"

"She's not my . . ."

She put the tip of her forefinger to my lips. "What'd she do?" she asked.

"Nothing," I said, remembering.

"That's the kind of nothing every young man needs," she said, smiling. "What'd you say y'all's kinship was?"

"She's my mother's first-cousin once removed."

"Oh," she said.

"Their grandmothers were first cousins," I said.

"I never knew anything about any of my relatives," she said. "I don't remember too much about my daddy, really and truly."

Later, in the dark, she asked about where I was from and how I got here and when my brother would come down from the North on the train. I talked, telling her.

Then she said, "I'm a mulatto. Some folks—like ol' Bubba over at the Starlight—call me a yeller-skin nigger. But I ain't. I'm a Mo-Wa."

"What's a Mo-Wa?" I asked.

"Indian. My mama was a little ol' brown-skin Indian down in a place called Buck's Bend on the Tombigbee River in south Alabama. My daddy—well, my daddy was a man."

I laughed.

"It ain't funny," she said.

Silently, I saddened.

"My ol' daddy beat my mama to a pulp in the days before I was born. Just for doing what she done: washing his clothes, keeping his house—whatever kind of house it was, made out of scrap-shit she found out in the mill yard in Saraland, doing for him, and letting him do her. Then he'd drink hogwash liquor and get the 'means' and come in like a hurricane, whupping everything he could get his hands on. She told me about it, later.

"She was a little mite of a woman and he was a big mean sonofabitch. He'd whup her, then he'd climb on her and do what he wanted with her."

Looking at her, I saw the hate working in her eyes. Her lips drew tight, showed a colorless line of nervous rancor seeping through her features, coursing through her veins and her memory. "I wasn't but a little girl playing with my rag doll when he'd stumble in smelling like rotgut, get a beady look in his eyes, fall onto his knees, jerk off my little britches, and start fingering me."

I reached out and lightly touched the smooth skin of her arm, trying to be of some comfort.

She pulled back, like my finger was a torch. She glared red-eyed into my face, blinking back tears. "When she came in, she tried to pull him off me. He just wheeled around and waylaid her with his fist, knocking her all the way across the room. Then he grabbed a-hold of my neck and pulled my face down onto him and said, 'Kiss it!' then, 'Lick it!' And all Mama did—or could do—was lay there bleeding, watching.

"He did that four or five times, then one afternoon, reeking of mash-liquor they made at the stills down in the swamps, he came in and jerked me around, pulled my legs apart, and raped me, tearing me up inside, jerking and carrying on like a crazy man about to burn up with a fire flaming way down inside him. I just laid there under him not moving, and I cried and cried. I clamped my eyes shut real tight, and I held on to my rag doll in my fists. All the while, he worked at putting that fire out, hurting me more and more with every jab.

"That night, me and Mama took off. We caught a ride down the river on a flatboat, stayed in Mobile until Mama found a man who promised to make life good for us in New Orleans. What Mama did was go to work in a whorehouse at the far end of Bourbon Street near Esplanade. I washed for her until the men started looking slant-eyed at me, making remarks about wanting me for their own.

"By that time, when I was twelve, I lit out up the Mississippi River with my own fancy man—a gambler from Natchez. Only he wasn't a very good gambler. He lost me in a game of seven-stud in Baton Rouge." She laughed a laugh that matched the rhythm of the lapping waves. "I was told that my body and soul were owned lock, stock, and barrel by a blues-singing nigger from Memphis, a man who had himself been beaten to a pulp many-a time. All across his back, he had scars on top of scars. A white man had beaten him when he was little and living on a plantation down in the Delta, expected to do the work of a full-growed man."

She put her head on my shoulder, nuzzled her face into my neck, and kissed me with tear-dampened lips. She grabbed a-hold on my arm and squeezed it while she cried.

I shuddered and ran my palm down her side, feeling her ribs and her slow, rhythmic breathing.

"He wasn't a bad man, but I hated being somebody's proper-ty, so I caught a ride on Beale Street, got on a boat down the Tennessee River, and ended up on Moccasin Alley. One day, I guess, when I get me a sack full of travelin' money, I'll catch me a ride out of here."

"Why don't you just leave?" I asked. "Walk out of here with me."

"With you?" She laughed like a tickled baby.

"You could go back to Town Creek with me and Bosworth," I said.

"Now, wouldn't I be something? Living in a fine little ol' Protestant town like Town Creek." She laughed again. "I bet yo' mama'd take me in and wash me up and take care of me. Her child's play-toy."

"No, no, no," I said. I rubbed her again and again. "It would-n't be like that. It'd never be like that."

"I ain't ever met a clean-cut white boy who didn't want to give me a bath," she said. "I saw it in your eyes when I came sashaying over to you when you were all cocked up there against the bar at the Starlight with a beer in your hand."

"Well, I . . ."

"Don't deny it, Harold Reed. You ain't a liar, are you?"

"No, I'm not."

"See, I can always tell."

"But if you came with me, Mama'd . . ."

She looked at me, her eyes questioning my sanity. "Yo' mama'd shit, is what yo' mama would do."

"Lacy . . ."

"Anyway, honey, I can't just walk down Moccasin Alley and out into the world," she said.

"Why can't you?"

"Did you see that cross down yonder next to McRae's Beer Hall?"

"The burned-black cross? I told you I did."

She nodded. "The hooded riders of the Ku Klux Klan burned that cross. They pulled a woman out of the beer hall and whipped her until she couldn't stand up. She was crying and moaning right out there on Moccasin Alley. She was beaten bloody and senseless."

"I heard she was a married woman," I said.

"She was a whore, just like me," Lacy Beauchamp said. "She got uppity and left Moccasin Alley, found her a millworker, married him, then came back down here to do a little business, make a little money, because her old man had lost his job and couldn't find another. The Ku Klux Klan found out about her, came down here, burned that cross, and whipped that woman so bad she ended up in a hospital for colored folks. The white doctors wouldn't touch her."

I cringed, thinking about Powtawee lying in the bed in the colored clinic, hurting and afraid. And then I thought about the white woman in the other room. Suddenly, in memory, I pictured the agony written across her twisted battered swollen face as she screamed and fought against the men trying to hold her down. "I think I saw her today," I said.

"You did?" she asked.

I told her about Powtawee and about the white woman in the room down the hall.

"Oh, Lord, Harold, that'd be me, if . . ."

I tried to pull her closer and hold her in my arms. "No," I said. "I wouldn't ever let that happen to you."

"This Indian girl, Powtawee, did you and her . . ."

I smiled and shook my head. "Oh, no, I just met her on the road. She came up out of nowhere, wanted to ride with us."

"We don't let Indians come down on Moccasin Alley," she said.

"You don't?"

"No."

"Why?"

"I don't know. It's a rule."

"Made by who?"

"How do I know? Not by me. It's a rule. Just like Negro men don't come down here screwing around."

"But you're . . ."

"They don't know I'm a Mo-Wa. They think I'm high-yeller. White men like a little color in their milk, if you know what I mean. But they don't want us messing around with no Negro men. They won't stand for it."

"With all your fire, it looks like you'd want to go out into the world and make something of yourself," I said with pious pride.

"A girl can't just walk out of Moccasin Alley," she said again. "Unless she's got plenty of money or a husband, like your . . . What'd you call her?"

I glared into her eyes. I knew what she was saying about Prudence couldn't be true. It was just some whore gossip, talked in the backrooms of places like Mimi's, or drunk-talk at the Starlight. It couldn't be true. Mrs. Prudence Longshore was a fine, upstanding person, a friend of Papa's.

"I heard it took her a long time to make it, but I'd say she's got her past way behind her now," Lacy said.

I didn't try to refute her words. I lay still.

But after her story I didn't feel like staying here in this place with her. My body ached, but not with the want of sex.

Suddenly I smelled the stench of lye soap boiling in a pot somewhere nearby.

I rolled out of bed and pulled on my underwear.

"You don't want to do it again?" she asked.

I looked over her skinny body, the brown nipples swollen above the slight mounds of her breasts, her ribs expanding beneath the almost translucent olive-tan skin. I reached over and touched her cheek and said, "I'd like to, but I'm suppose to go to church."

She started to laugh, but she rubbed her upper teeth against her lip. "Church?" she asked.

"To a revival meeting in a tent."

She looked at me like she didn't believe my words.

I shrugged. "That's where I'm going."

She smiled and shook her head slowly, looking into my face. "You're a strange boy, Harold Reed," she said.

Sixteen

On the front porch of the boardinghouse two drummers sat in rocking chairs, deep in a conversation about whether women should have the right to vote.

As I climbed the steps, I slowed my pace.

"Old stone-face Woodrow Wilson ought to keep his nose out-a our business," declared J. R. Ratliff of Selma, who had been selling wholesale hardware supplies to Mr. Powers at his store.

"And that wild and crazy bitch Julia Tutwiler should keep her mouth shut, if you ask me," said Rudolph Bolden of Montgomery, who had been peddling kitchen utensils to the same vendor.

"You know, we're staying at the establishment of the most radical suffragist in the Tennessee River valley, maybe even all of Alabama, with the exception of Miss Tutwiler," Ratliff said.

"Mrs. Prudence don't mean any harm," Bolden said.

"Just like Julia Tutwiler, she ought to keep her mouth shut, if you ask me," Ratliff said. "Women ought to keep quiet on political issues."

"Still, she runs the best boardinghouse in this part of the country."

If anybody knew boardinghouses, traveling salesmen surely did. They were experts. And since I'd been traveling, I figured that most of them also knew a little bit about a lot of things, or thought they did.

I walked past them, then stopped at the front door and turned. I started to say something when J. R. Ratliff looked over at me between puffs on his cigar. "You gonna go carousing again this evening?"

I immediately wondered why he was making it his business. Whatever I might decide to do with my night was my own business, not his. But I held my words inside and just stared through the cloud of smoke at his rugged face with its thick mustache and dark bespectacled eyes.

"I thought I'd see if Mrs. Prudence would like to go to the tent-preaching," I said.

"She and the preacher's already gone," said Bolden, who was lighting a roll-your-own cigarette that he'd licked properly before sticking the squeezed end between his lips.

"Brother Applewhite?" I asked.

"No, her regular preacher down at the Methodist church," Ratliff said.

"Dr. Alfred Summerall," I said.

"Yeah," Bolden said. "He picked her up in his buggy a few minutes ago."

"I guess the Methodists think they need a little more hellfire-and-damnation than they get on Sunday morning," Ratliff put in with a chuckle. "It'll probably do 'em a lot of good. You'd probably learn a lesson or two yourself, Mr. Reed, if you went to hear this little-bitty bantam rooster's preaching. They tell me he's pure full of it."

Without further comment, I moved aside to allow the implement salesman from Memphis entrance onto the porch. He was still wiping his mouth from a greasy supper. As he passed me, excusing himself, he belched loudly.

I grimaced, thinking he'd be a fine addition to the otherwise stimulating conversation that I had overheard. A fart or two from him would be a needed chorus to fill the gaps between their opinionated words.

"You think Mrs. Prudence is a radical suffragist?" I asked them, thinking I'd leave them with food for thought.

Ratliff nodded. "I know so," he said.

"She don't make no bones about it," said Bolden.

The implement salesman belched again as he sat in the third rocker.

"She's been writing letters to *The Decatur Daily* for more than a year, making her position clear as ice water," said Ratliff. "And that damn crazy editor prints 'em."

"And I've read her editorials in *The Montgomery Advertiser*. She and Mrs. Marie Bankhead Owen have been arguing the point in the press for a long while," Bolden added. "You know who Mrs. Owen is?"

I shook my head.

"She's the daughter of U.S. Senator John H. Bankhead of Jasper," Bolden informed me. "He's one of the most powerful politicians in our nation. Mrs. Owens is right bright, for a woman. She knows her place."

They might have been older and wiser than I, but I judged them both as know-it-alls whose thick skulls were set on hard beliefs that could never be penetrated by volumes of knowledge or an opposing point of view. Still, I figured I'd stir them up a bit with my own idea.

"You think this Mrs. Owen is correct in her stance against allowing women to vote?" I asked.

"She's a fine woman," Bolden said.

"So's Mrs. Prudence," I said.

"Mrs. Prudence is a fine business woman," Ratliff said pointedly. "And that unto itself is a rare item."

I smiled as I gazed into their faces.

"Maybe she thinks she's just as smart as some of the traveling men who stay at her establishment," I said.

Before either could reply, I added, "Maybe she thinks she could make just as good a choice politically as they do."

"Humph!" the man from Memphis grunted.

I pushed open the door and stepped inside before the others could take exception to my comment.

I draped my hat on an empty spot on the high hatrack and stepped through the semidarkness of the central hallway toward the stairs. "Mr. Reed?" a voice asked.

The wide-shouldered tall Negro woman, C. Q., stood in the doorway to the dining room.

"Yes, ma'am," I said.

"Mrs. Prudence asked me to put back some supper for you. Would you like to take it now, or . . ."

"Could I just have a biscuit to nibble on?" I asked.

"What about a pork chop in that biscuit?" C. Q. asked.

"Sounds good," I said. "I'll be down directly to get it. I'll eat it on my way to the tent revival."

"I'll have it ready for you," she said as I turned and continued my way up the stairs.

On the second floor I stopped before proceeding into alien territory. I listened closely and intently, thinking about what I was about to do. I'd never been one to sneak around and spy on people. I'd always thought that a person's privacy was his or her own affair. When you grow up in a large family there are very few secrets. What I planned now happened so fast in my mind that I didn't give it a second thought. If I'd thought on it, perhaps I would never have taken that first step into the darkness of her inner sanctum. But once I'd taken it, I couldn't turn back.

I listened for movements within the large high-ceilinged house where the rooms were twice as high and three times larger than the rooms in the small house where I grew up. Ours was an uneven piece of construction, beginning with the four main rooms Papa and his neighbors built, after he moved his young family from the foot of Reed Hill on the northernmost wilderness of The Forest to the flatland farm bordering Mr. Melvin Saunders's cottonfields. When a new child came into the world, Papa added a new room to the old building. In that manner, one room after another was stacked to the original house. When a traveler passed on the road he did not give the dwelling a second thought. With the porch running along the front and the rooms added along the back side, it just appeared to be your regular clapboard farmhouse, nothing more, nothing less.

But this place where I was now staying was a grand example of Victorian architecture, all of it planned from foundation to the high slanted roof, the rounded turret in the northwest corner that extended all the way up to the fourth floor, the gigantic eighteen rooms laid out in order that each could be entered from the central hallway near the stairs or from the rear hall that extended east and west on the southern side of the first three floors. Beneath was a cellar where canned goods could be kept cool even in the summer. At the very top of the turret was a sitting room reached only from Prudence's quarters. The house had been contracted by a wealthy plantation owner whose third wife, a woman nearly thirty years his junior, had insisted that part of her wedding gift be a home large enough to house them and the husband's nine children from his first two wives, who'd died in a farmhouse not unlike the one Papa had built.

The plantation owner, Oscar LaFayette, had been notorious as a selfish miser who would not even buy his children shoes to wear to church on Sundays. Then he fell in love with Margaret Beale, beautiful and barely sixteen, famous throughout the valley as a flirtatious belle whose beaux came courting from as far west as Tupelo, Mississippi, and as far east as Huntsville. Miss

Beale, a winsome small-boned woman with curly golden locks that hung to her freckled shoulders, was well aware of her power as the object of Mr. LaFayette's affections. And it was through her coquettish flirtations that she extracted promise after promise from Mr. LaFayette, who was forced to deliver before she would walk down the aisle to take his hand in matrimony.

One of the promises, fulfilled in 1878, a month before their wedding, was the construction of this massive and magnificent town house. Ten years later, after the birth of the couple's third child, all twelve children and the still-beautiful Mrs. LaFayette died in the fever epidemic that swept through Decatur like the plague, leaving the husband and father miserably sad and alone. He went into seclusion in the fourth-floor sitting room, where he died of starvation and heartbreak shortly before the turn of the century.

Two years after LaFayette's death, Andrew Dawson Longshore bought the place that had sat empty, gossiped about as a ghost house where so many people had died, then painted it in fresh, vibrant colors and refurnished it with new and antique furniture he and his own youthful bride, Prudence, picked out and purchased on their honeymoon in New Orleans. A. D. brought Prudence back to this house, where they were happy for almost a year before he drowned in the waters of the Tennessee River. Many neighbors rumored that his untimely death occurred because the ghost of Mr. LaFayette had followed him and perpetrated the drowning.

As I pushed open the door leading into Prudence's private suite, a creepy chill skittered down my back and shivered through my arms. Staying quiet, not moving, I heard C. Q. and her helpers downstairs in the kitchen cleaning up after supper. I heard boarders moving about slowly in their rooms, washing and getting ready for bed. There was a rhythmical hum of talk from the parlor where several were lingering into the night.

I moved into her rooms, closing the door carefully behind me. I struck a match and lit a lamp sitting on a chest of drawers. Next to it was a small round faded photograph. I picked it up and held it to the light and studied the portrait of a handsome woman resembling Prudence. She had the same finely carved chin and cheekbones, the same prominent nose and large bright eyes. Her hair was darker and her lips not quite as full.

After I placed the oval frame back in its original place, I moved toward the bed, where I sat on the tufted flowered spread, running my palm over the area where she would sleep. Without thinking, I lowered my body across the spread and put my head on the silky pillow and smelled her fragrance.

Running my hand over the smooth cloth, I felt myself becoming aroused. I sat up and looked around, half expecting someone to be watching.

"Prudence," I whispered. Only a few days ago I had never heard that word pronounced as some stranger's name. Now I was consumed with the sound and the images it evoked in my imagination, transferring me instantly to a dark place called Cave of the Wind. I wanted more than anything to stay here, to be with her, to live within these walls and become a part of her life. *Is life worth living elsewhere? Without her?*

As far as I was concerned, she could lock me up in the room with the ghost of Oscar LaFayette, and I would remain her prisoner forever. No one but she and I would ever know.

She'd given me everything I had ever wanted in life. With her, I would never again go to Moccasin Alley. With her, I would never miss Mama or Papa, Sister or Lucy or Ida Mae or Martin. I would meet Bosworth at the train Thursday and take him home. Then I would return to Decatur and Prudence and this house, these rooms, and I would be happy the rest of my life, with her. It was something I'd never dreamed about because I didn't know it existed until a few days ago, and now I couldn't live without that absent dream.

But she had turned me away. As cold as ice water in November, she had said, "No more." I shuddered and pulled myself upright. I smoothed the covers of the bed and stood.

Standing, I meandered the darkly private, orderly sanctuary of her living space: perused the great ghostly chifforobes that stood against two walls, opened the elaborately designed doors with inlaid wooden diamonds and starbursts, and gazed into the recess at the crowded wardrobe. I carefully closed the doors and went to the next and opened it and found more coats, dresses, suits, and the bottom lined with shoes. I pushed my face toward the clothes, whiffing them for her smell, knowing her body had been covered by them. These objects knew her as intimately as I, and I regarded them with reverence.

I moved beyond a black silk Chinese screen with painted magnolias in full blossom. Against the round wall of the turret room was a desk-style dressing table with a three-panel mirror. The way it faced, toward the west, she got ample morning light through high windows facing east. Standing here, looking down at the table covered with jars and boxes filled with cosmetics, her faint lavender fragrance touched my nostrils just as the aroma of her body had enticed me on the bed.

I went back to the chest of drawers. I opened the top drawer and gazed into the orderly rows of jewelry: several beaded necklaces, a diamond half-moon-shaped tiara that I touched with the tips of my fingers and thought how it would look resting atop her silver-colored hair, three bracelets in a row, and two rings sitting side by side. At the far end of the drawer was a gold box decorated with a hand-painted scene of a lake and woods, like the lake at the Greerson Hotel. I ran my fingers over it, feeling the smooth touch of the enamel. I flicked the tiny latch and it opened.

From the box I lifted several items that appeared to be baby toys. In my palm rested a round mother-of-pearl circle less than two inches in diameter, a tiny golden ring that would not fit even on my little finger, and a miniature necklace made of colorful green and red and yellow semiprecious stones. All three items lay in my open hand with room to spare. They looked as though they had been made for a doll. I put them aside and lifted a sheath of papers from the box.

At that moment I heard a sound outside the door.

Shifting quickly, I almost dropped the papers.

I held my breath, staring toward the dark door.

Someone stopped on the opposite side.

I wondered if C. Q. or one of the other workers had forgotten something.

If Prudence was returning . . .

I held my breath.

My fingers flicked through the papers that dropped to the floor.

"Dammit!" I whispered.

I fell to my knees on the Persian rug next to the bed. Quickly and nervously I retrieved the papers.

I remained on my knees for a long moment, still, listening.

Whoever was in the hallway continued on their way. Then I heard two sets of footsteps climbing the stairs.

I picked up the papers. Two were photographs with ragged edges. I carried them across the room to the lantern, where I turned them to the light and explored the images. In each three young women sat on a sofa. They were dressed in white gowns, simple in style, skirts falling to their ankles, bodices cut low across the tops of their breasts. The clothing was not revealing. The girls looked as ordinary as any girls might. They were staring seriously into the camera's lens. They looked almost frightened. None were smiling.

In the light I studied their faces. All were young. Not one could have been more than twenty. Perhaps younger. The girl in the middle resembled a very young Prudence; she had light-colored hair, long and straight, falling below her shoulders, her eyes big and bright, her chin upright and defiant, her cheekbones nearly as strong as now. The other girls were no older than she, and she looked like a baby with creamy soft skin and long slender arms.

As I surveyed the background, I wondered: the walls were papered in a pale pattern of curlicues, with a large rain-stained splotch forming circles within circles near the ceiling. I turned the photo, trying to view it better. Then I looked at the next one that must have been made in a sequence. The girls were pictured in a slightly different pose. Other than their bodies moving an inch or so and their expressions more moody, it appeared the same as the first. Again, I studied the background to see if it matched anything I had seen recently. As far as I could tell, the photos could have been made anywhere.

Looking from face to face, I saw no particular resemblance. They did not look like sisters. The other girls had darker hair. Their bodies were more full, not as tall and lithesome as hers.

In the last of the three photographs the girls had forced slight smiles onto their faces. Oddly, they did not appear happy at all. In fact, they looked like sad young women.

I tried to judge their ages but found myself wondering: *who? where? when?* and all the other unanswered questions.

Once again I heard sounds from the hallway. This time two of the house helpers were talking excitedly, doubtless chattering idle gossip as they climbed the stairs toward Prudence's rooms.

I hurriedly returned the photos to the box and the box to the drawer. With both hands steadying it, I squeezed the drawer shut.

I stood frozen, hearing them fumbling outside the door with whatever they were carrying. I knew that I had to douse the light and hide behind something.

My eyes searched through the room.

Outside the door one of the women laughed loudly as a hamper fell from her hands and dropped with a bang to the floor.

"Dammit!" one said.

The other laughed again.

"I'm glad Miss Prudence has gone to that preaching," one said. "We're nearly an hour late with the ironing."

"She'll get religion and won't mind our tardiness."

I stepped with a broad, silent stride across the room. I lifted the glass chimney from the lamp and blew.

The flame bounced.

For a moment, the flame swept down onto the round, delicately stitched doily.

I reached around the lamp and pushed my hand against the flame, killing it instantly.

Breathing deep, I ducked down behind the high chest just as the door opened and the young women stepped into the bedroom.

Lucky for me, they left the door open in order to see by the dim light of the hallway. They carried a large basket-style hamper across the room to the bed.

As they moved past me, I stepped behind them and sped out the door and down the stairs.

"Who's that?" one of the maids called from the top.

But I did not stop or turn or say a word.

On a table inside the dining room I found the porkchop and biscuit C. Q. had left for me. Then I picked my hat from the rack in the downstairs hallway, opened the front door, and nodded politely to the remaining two smokers who were talking on the porch.

Seventeen

When I parted the flaps of Brother Preston Applewhite's tent, a woman in a long robe stood behind the podium on the pulpit. The small preacher, dressed in a three-piece white suit, wearing white shoes and socks, and a three-inch-wide floppy white bowtie, was perched atop a three-foot-high stool behind the woman with her arms spread wide, her white robe hanging on each side, like an angel's wings. Her head bowed, she said loudly and distinctly, "Dear Lord, bless these sinners with Thy presence, let Your water wash through their hearts and make them generous."

Her final words, spoken before she pronounced, "Amen," was a signal for the volunteer ushers to begin passing their bowls.

In the fourth row among the crowd I recognized Mrs. Prudence's profile. Next to her sat the Methodist minister, Dr. Alfred Summerall, whose face was as solemn as it had been when he was funeralizing old Katanzakis. I wondered immediately if Dr. Summerall and the Methodists were part of Applewhite's tent show, what with the diminutive preacher staying at Mrs. Prudence's boardinghouse and having a great deal more knowledge about me and my circumstances than I wished for him to have.

To be on the safe side, I dropped a quarter into the collection plate, then waited for the money to be taken forward and for the little man with the old face to step onto a foot-high portable stand, lean into the podium, and say in his squeaky voice, "The Lord loves a sinner." Like the woman before him, he stretched his arms outward. His were shorter, more compact angel's wings. He looked out over his congregation. "You are all sinners," he accused.

He let his sentences hang in the air and stand alone for a moment before beginning the next. Practiced in his performance, after each small declaration he looked out over our heads. Now and then, after profound words spoken through his perfectly painted lips, he lowered his eyes to the lowly faces of those who sat and gazed up at him.

As he pronounced his words clearly, "I sayeth unto you," I looked around the crowd for other familiar faces. I saw two older women, Thelma Gooch and Audrey Crow, both of whom had been pointed out to me by Mrs. Prudence as good upstanding Christian citizens, although both tended to gossip whenever they had a chance, which was often. In a town the size of Decatur, a body gets to know a lot of people in a short time. Neither of these women, it seemed, had any regard for the truth. They trafficked in third-hand innuendo and accusation, not caring particularly who it might damage.

"I speak on sin," Applewhite said. He lowered his eyes to the big book open on the stand which he gripped with tiny, tension-taut fists.

Both Thelma Gooch and Audrey Crow dropped their turkey-necked chins. I noticed that they grasped hands that hung between them below chair-bottom level: Mrs. Gooch's left, Mrs. Crow's right.

"Yea, I sayeth unto you, just as the Lord sayeth in Proverbs," the preacher repeated the words of the Old Testament.

"Amen!" hummed the heavy man named Octavious Hicks, whom I still held in distrust after his display of rank humor, making fun of poor Pete Powers. Next to him was his friend, Goodloe Littlejohn, who in my estimation was no longer "a pillar of the community," as Mrs. Prudence had called him early in our acquaintance. Sitting three rows behind them was Jedediah Stokely, the hefty-shouldered blacksmith who'd looked over Jed's hooves and declared him in perfect shape for the trip back to Town Creek. At least he had not tried to hoodwink me with some mysterious ailment, the way Papa had warned me that some smitties might do to an innocent boy in a strange town.

It seemed that half of all the people I knew in Decatur were sitting under the tent, listening like good Christians to Brother Preston Applewhite's solemn words. Two rows in front of me was the newspaper editor, Lee Sentell, who nodded his head full of well-groomed dark brown hair in agreement with Applewhite's words.

"'A wise son heareth his father's instruction,'" Applewhite quoted, then looked out and stared directly into my eyes.

I thought instantly of Papa's warnings. His words came back to me as though I were sitting on the front porch, listening to his talk beneath the cloud of pipe smoke. I shivered slightly as I wondered.

"'. . . but a scorner heareth not rebuke,'" the preacher continued.

I wondered if he knew how exactly right-on-the-money he was. Perhaps he had pitched his tent in Town Creek last week. Perhaps he had spoken to Papa and Mama. Perhaps they had told him about me staying with Mrs. Prudence at her boardinghouse. Perhaps they let him know that I was a sin-filled young man away from home for the first time, out in the world, run amuck with new ideas of sin and sinning, up to my ears in sexual filth, ruining whatever reputation I once enjoyed, about to drown in the muck of my own making. Trying to be as discreet as possible, I lowered my face to my right shoulder and sniffed, wondering if I smelled of my particular sin.

The man next to me, a stranger, glared at me and frowned.

237

I was sure I still reeked of Lacy Beauchamp, her strong perfume and the raw animal flavor of her body, her wetness, her hair, and even her lipstick. I would never be able to cover it, not even with a gallon of bay rum and a jug of Mr. Guyton's favorite hair tonic. Nothing would ever hide what had been rubbing all over me.

"'He that keepeth his mouth keepeth his life,'" Applewhite read. Then he gazed out again. His eyes burned into my head with accusations.

I squirmed on the wooden bench, praying for an escape but seeing no path onto which I could make my retreat from the tent. He had me here, locked into a crowd beneath the warm canvas.

My eyes surveying the crowd, I noticed three separate large lanterns, big devices he must have found in some large city. I had never seen any lanterns quite so big. And I smelled the slight hint of oil that was being burned within their tubes.

"'. . . but he that openeth wide his lips shall have destruction,'" Applewhite told me, and I knew he had picked out this particular chapter and verse in order to send a shock through my sinful system. He knew, as any good preacher would know, that to communicate with my tainted soul he would have to wring it of all the sin it had soaked up in the last few days—which was considerable. I told myself that he could see through me like an Indian fisherman staring into the clear water of a mountain stream.

"'The soul of the sluggard desireth.'" Again, he separated his short sentences with brief but heavy pauses. Each was like a dagger thrust straight into my sorry soul.

"'. . . and hath nothing.'" He bit into each word. He allowed the final word to fall, like a dropped rock.

"'. . . but the soul of the diligent shall be made fat.'"

Once again, Octavious Hicks sang out, "Amen!" followed by Goodloe Littlejohn seconding the chorus with his own refrain.

"'Good understanding giveth favor,'" stated the preacher.

Thelma Gooch and Audrey Crow, still holding hands, nodded emphatically.

"'. . . but the way of transgressors is hard,'" the preacher said.

"Amen!"

"'Every prudent man dealeth with knowledge,'" he stated.

"Amen!"

"'. . . but a fool layeth open his folly.'"

"Amen!"

"'A wicked messenger falleth into mischief,'" he read.

I knew he had talked with Papa, Mrs. Prudence, and Lord only knew who else. Preston Applewhite was looking straight into my soul and was seeing mirrored there all of my personal mischief from Town Creek to Moccasin Alley: a long line of sinful encounters.

My mind raced through all of the pictures of sin that had happened to me during all of the days of my life. It was filled with one scene after another, all amounting to a mountain of sin under which I was buried, feeling it heavy against my chest. It was a wonder I would ever be able to find my way out from under such a huge heap of sorrow.

"'Evil pursueth sinners!'"

At that moment, while my brain was becoming cluttered with self-loathing, Mrs. Prudence shifted in her seat, turned her head, looked into my eyes, and smiled very softly.

With the thought that popped into my brain, I knew instantly that I would never find the road to righteousness. While the preacher stated, "'The highway of the upright is to depart from evil,'" my mind was traveling on a road leading straight to hell. There was no way on God's good earth that I would be able to clear away the clouds of evil and make room for a clean, good-living soul.

After the little man's final prayer, I walked away from the tent meeting silent and alone with the knowledge that I was surely lost and I would never find my way. He left me no out; I was damned to perdition. Each step of my lonely way was heavy. My feet operated while my mind was weighted down with the drudgery of sin.

One buggy and rider after another passed me as I walked away alone from the tent. With each step I felt the weight becoming heavier and heavier.

Less than a half-mile into town, Dr. Summerall's buggy halted at my side. With Mrs. Prudence sitting next to him, the Methodist minister offered a ride. "Sit on the back," he said, and I pulled myself up. I wondered if they too recognized me for what I truly was: a sinner drenched in damnation. If they did, they said nothing about it. In fact, neither said a word on the way. I figured they were thinking about the preacher's singling me out in the crowd and pointing his finger into my soul.

In front of the boardinghouse I slid off, then offered Mrs. Prudence a hand.

"Right fiery sermon tonight," Summerall said.

"Yes, sir, it was," I agreed.

Mrs. Prudence held her smile as she stepped down into my grip.

As I eased her onto the ground, horses stomped all around us like sudden claps of thunder. I turned and stared into the darkness at three hooded riders who surrounded us in an instant.

"What in the . . ." Summerall began.

"Ride on, preacher!" a big man on a wide horse ordered. From his saddle he unsnapped a whip and cracked it over the back of Dr. Summerall's horse, who danced against the road and trotted away, the preacher trying to gain control of the reins.

"Dr. Summerall!" Mrs. Prudence cried out.

Three more horsemen joined the intruders. All wore white hoods over their heads and white gowns hanging over their saddles. The horses pranced around us like we were a May pole.

"Sinful bitch!" the big man with the whip called out, his words snapping with the same quick sound as his whip.

One of the late arrivals, smaller than the others, sitting bunched on his horse's back with his gown covering his entire body, including his feet, said, "The Lord sayeth: 'He that spareth his rod hateth his son.'" There wasn't much doubt who he was. The sound of his voice and the choice of his biblical verse pointed directly at Applewhite.

As the words were spoken, the big man swung his whip through the air and down onto my right shoulder. I heard and saw it coming but could not move until it hit, dropping me to my knees with its quick power. As it hit, Prudence cried out and turned toward me.

"Sinful bastard!" the big man said.

He swung the whip again. This time it popped down across Prudence's back, knocking her off balance.

"You bastard!" I cursed and started to crawl toward him.

Another of the men kneed his horse, reining it into a circle, pushing it toward us, cutting us off from escape to the house. As he came close, he reached down and raked his hand across the back of Prudence's dress, grabbing it and ripping it.

The man's horse pushed against Prudence, who stumbled toward the picket fence that bordered her yard from the street.

I reached for the man, grabbed at his leg, but my hands slid down. I gathered the hem of his garment and jerked.

"Hey!" the man screamed as I kept pulling the gown, trying to snatch it from his body.

The whip hit Prudence again, turning her in a circle.

She screamed loudly as she fell to her knees, her hands trying to hold her dress up.

"What do you think . . ." I shouted. Before my words were finished, the whip whacked me again, this time across the face and neck, cutting and yanking me back away from the man whose hood was now only half-covering his upper body.

"You are sinners!" said the small man. His voice sounded exactly like the little preacher's words. I would know them anywhere.

"Applewhite, you're the sinner," I said.

"Sinner!" the big man swore again. He cocked his wrist.

The whip sang through the air, whistling its hateful sound, and landed again on Prudence, who was quivering with fright, trapped against the fence, her back against the rails like some torturing device. In her fright she was mumbling words I couldn't understand.

"Come on," I said, snatching her arm and pulling her toward the gate.

Two of the men jumped from their horses and blocked us before we ran two steps. They threw me against the fence. They tore again at Prudence's dress, pulling it down her back. They grabbed at her undergarments and tore them away, unclothing her above the waist.

"Sinner!" the big man said again.

"Jezebel!" another called.

"You filthy bastards!" I screamed, lowering my head and swinging my fists toward the two on the ground. I felt my knuckles slam against jaw and heard the man cry out.

Without looking up, I hit again and again, until the man stumbled and fell backward and I jumped on top of him and began slamming my fists into his face.

Prudence, weeping, tried to cover herself with her hands and arms, but the bullwhip landed, cutting a streak across her back, and she jerked and cried out.

"You belong where you started," the large man spat.

"You have no idea!" Prudence said.

"I know!" the man said.

The whip hissed and slapped down across her back, bending her double.

"Whore, bitch!" the man cursed and hit her again.

She dropped to her knees again.

The man I had pinned to the ground screamed for the others to hit me. As he did, I felt the whip cut across my shoulder again. I pushed up from Goodloe Littlejohn, whom I kicked in the side before he could roll away.

I lurched toward Prudence. I pulled off my jacket and handed it to her, trying to cover her. Then the whip came down on me, biting into my shoulder again.

I wheeled around and grabbed the whip. Holding it in my fist, I yanked.

The big man jolted forward in the saddle. He cursed under his breath as he attempted to pull the leather from my grip.

I didn't let go. I moved toward him, wrapping the leather around my hand as I stepped. Then I jerked again, trying to pull him from the horse.

This time I felt him give.

His weight leaned forward. If he had not let go, he would have fallen over the saddle horn.

I caught the handle, swung it over my head, and slapped it with all my strength. The whip snapped against the little man's gown, slapping against his leg before he could guide his horse away from me.

I swung again, this time hitting the big man, who pulled the reins so hard his horse's hooves beat against the roadbed as he backed away.

As I cracked the whip against the little man again, the one who had pulled Prudence's dress down came up behind me. He pinned my arms while Littlejohn pried the whip from my hands. After he threw the whip, handle-first, to the big rider, the two wrestled me to the ground and began kicking me in the ribs.

Prudence, trying to pull them from me, slipped and fell.

A man with a lantern stepped onto the porch of the boarding-house. He called out, "What's going on there?"

The whip hit Prudence again across the shoulders, tearing at her flesh, before she scampered away, through the gate, and toward the house, where another lantern was lighted and some-one came forward to help her up the front steps.

I was left alone, unable to escape, struggling on the ground, where I writhed as the whip came down repeatedly onto my back and shoulders.

Moments later, with a new blouse covering her body, Prudence stepped onto her front porch between two men with lanterns in their hands. She had a long-barrel gun pointed toward the road. "Which one wants to die?" she asked as she stepped down from the porch and moved toward them. "I may not be a good shot, but I can hit one of you."

By the time she was halfway across the yard, the men had mounted. All six turned westward and rode away in a fury.

Prudence dropped the gun and rushed to me. "Harold," she said, crying as she knelt next to me. When she touched my arm, I winced and jerked away.

"It hurts," I managed.

A half-dozen boarders were standing on the porch in their night clothes.

"Mrs. Prudence, are you all right?"

The men lifted me and carried me into the house, where she and a pharmaceutical salesman from Mobile tore away the rest of my shirt and swabbed my wounds gently with medicine. Then he ministered to her back and shoulders. Before the man helped me up the stairs to my room, Prudence picked thick green leaves from a plant growing in a pot in her kitchen window. She squeezed the juice from the leaves onto the lesions along my shoulders, back, and neck, then applied the liquid to her own wounds.

I slept restlessly, tossing and tumbling. Each time I rolled onto my side I awakened with pain jolting through my ribcage. Each time I awakened I listened intently for sounds from outside. Once I thought I heard the sounds of horses on the road, but when I listened with more intensity I realized it was only my imagination.

Eighteen

I awakened early, hurting. I washed my wounds in the cool water in the pitcher in my room. Then I lay back down and tried to rest, but my body ached and my mind would not relax. Angry and anxious, I wanted to seek relief in revenge. I lay in bed hurting, thinking about striking back at last night's attackers. I knew two of them, perhaps three. Still, I contained myself, waiting until the other boarders had finished eating before I came down to the dining room.

I was sitting at a table next to the bank of windows looking out over the sunny spring flower garden, thinking about ways we could hit back at Brother Applewhite and the others.

Prudence swept through the wide doorway and strode directly to my table. As she moved toward me, a near-silent shiver of petticoats sounded beneath her long skirt, a quickening, nervous sound that irritated my ears. She pulled a chair out and sat, her face without expression aimed at me like her eyes were staring down the sight of a gun.

I gazed into her face, seeing more than a woman who had been hurt by a Klansman's whip. Her eyes were afire with anger. Her lips were pulled tight against her teeth. A quiver jerked with a tic at the top of her jaw, as if in pain.

"Harold!" she said, a cold biting two-syllable sound.

I did not dare say a word. I could almost hear the wheels of her mind turning as she determined exactly what to say next. I knew she wasn't thinking about my hurt or her own hurt from the whip.

"I am very disappointed," she said distinctly. Her words cut through me to the quick, jarring my insides.

I felt a shudder of cold reality ripple through my insides. I had almost forgotten about my adventure into her suite. I clutched my lips together tightly, trying to think what I could say, what excuse I could make.

"Why?" she asked, her voice squeezing painfully from deep within her throat. Her Adam's apple quivered, like her jaw.

I held my spoon awkwardly in my fingers. Then I passed it from one hand to the other, almost dropping it.

"Why'd you go into my private quarters? Why'd you ramble through my things?" The sound of pain flavored every word.

My vision shifted. I stared down at the spoon that sparkled in the morning light. My throat tightened.

I wanted to deny her accusation. I wanted to spit out a lie and make it all right. I wanted to cover for my foolishness.

"Harold?" I'd never heard my name pronounced in that intensely personal way, questioning, accusing, pointing.

Then I gazed up into her tortured face with a fake innocence, as though I had no idea what she was talking about.

"You could have stepped up to me and slapped me in the face, if you wanted to hurt me."

"I didn't," I said. My mind scrambled words. There was no explanation.

Her eyes watered as she leaned toward me across the breakfast table. She stretched her long-fingered hands over the table top, palms down. "Harold, I never lock the door to my rooms. I trust people. I especially trust you. I never once thought you'd . . ." Her voice broke in the middle of the last sentence.

I felt something inside my chest crash as I opened my mouth and started to explain. But the words wouldn't come. I felt suddenly more naked than I'd been in the bedroom at the Greerson Hotel. I felt as though all of my secrets, all of my doubts, all of my inner thoughts had spilled out on the table. My own eyes watered. My throat was constricted. I reached out with both hands and took hold of the glass of water and brought it to my lips. I gulped.

When I put the glass down, I said, "I'm sorry." The words lay in the narrow space between us.

Tears ran down the valleys between her eyes and nose. She blinked. She brought a cloth napkin to her face.

I handed her my clean handkerchief.

Then I used my own napkin to wipe my face.

"Why?" she asked again.

"I don't know," I uttered.

"What were you looking for?" she asked.

"Something," I said.

"What?"

"A girl down on Moccasin Alley. She said . . ."

Prudence turned in her chair. She looked away toward a commotion in the hallway.

C. Q. came into the dining room and stopped when she saw us.

"C. Q., see what's the matter out there," Prudence said.

"Yes, ma'am," the big woman said and stepped toward the hall.

The sun shone through the bank of windows onto Prudence's silver hair that sparkled like the spoon in my hand.

She lowered her head until she stared at the oak floor. "What girl? What about Moccasin Alley?"

"Just a girl down there. She said she'd heard gossip. She said you'd once lived down there. I thought maybe . . ."

Prudence swiveled in the chair to stare straight into my face. Her face was now clean of tears. It had a newly scrubbed look. Her eyes were as bright as the first time I'd looked into them. "Do you want me to tell you about a time long ago? A time before I was married? And a time after I was married and when I became a widow?" she asked directly. "Do you want to know *every*thing about me?"

The spoon dropped. It hit the table and lay there. I swallowed hard and did not answer her question.

"What do you think you know? You and your damned little whore?"

"I . . . I don't know."

"No, you don't!" she said sharply. "You don't know anything. Absolutely nothing!"

"I saw the pictures of you and the others."

"Girls? You think it shows me as a young whore? Is that what you think, Harold Reed? After we've been together, like a man and a woman. After I let down all of my guards. After I gave you . . ." She hesitated, her wide eyes gazing into my eyes. "Everything," she whispered. Her eyes glistened. "Your deceit, your dirty, awful thoughts. Do you know that *you* hurt me worse than a Ku Klux Klan whip? Worse than they could ever hurt me."

I felt suddenly dirty, and guilty. I'd been where I should not have been. I'd sneaked into her room and uncovered something she wished to keep hidden. I had invaded her private world. I was a thief, a burglar, a criminal who had stolen something dear and precious from her. Now I didn't want to know. I wanted to turn away from her. I wanted to walk out into the garden and keep on going. I wanted to go home and stay and never leave. I wanted to be safe. If only Bosworth would come.

I swallowed hard.

She slid her chair away from the table. She leaned toward me and reached out to me and took my hand in hers. "Come," she said.

Although I wanted to stay put, although I wanted to break and run, I had no choice but to go with her. She led me, not relinquishing my hand from her grip, out of the dining room, up the stairs, and to the closed door of her suite. She turned the knob with her left hand while holding mine in her right. Then she pulled me into the darkness, then letting go to light a lamp, then swishing across the room to her bedside table to light another.

She turned slowly, deliberately, and looked at me and said, "Sit," and I did.

I felt worse than a naughty schoolboy being scolded. I sat with my knees together and my hands on my knees.

She went to the chest of drawers that I had opened last night. She reached into the top drawer and lifted out the gold box into which I had plundered. She gently raised the lid, reached inside, and extracted the tiny necklace and the pearl playthings.

She held them in her palm extended toward me. "These were the last items A. D. bought for me. They were for our baby."

I gazed down at the miniature jewelry and the teething ring.

"When A. D. died, I was pregnant," she said. "After his death, I . . . I had a miscarriage and lost the little boy."

I felt a knot swell in my chest. I wanted to cry but couldn't.

I watched silently as she put the baby things aside and reached back into the box and withdrew the photographs.

She brought them to me and thrust them toward me. "Look," she said, her word soft as silk and sharp as a penknife.

I took them from her, holding them with the tips of shaky fingers.

"Does that look like Moccasin Alley?" she asked.

I shrugged, staring into the faded sepia images of the three young women posed on the sofa in front of the bare rain-stained wall.

"If it looks like Moccasin Alley to you, Harold, you've got a perverted, warped imagination."

I looked from the photo to her face that was still drawn tight, twitching and uncompromising, her eyes glazed with anger.

She snapped her pointed forefinger at the edge of the photographs fanned at the ends of my fingers. "That's a poor, pitiful place, and those were my friends," she managed, her voice breaking again.

"I . . ." I started, but I didn't know what to say.

"That's a poor, pitiful place where I lived as a girl, where I grew up." She covered her face with my handkerchief. She did not turn away. When she took her hands down, she blinked and said, "My parents were killed when I was a little girl. The only thing I have left of them is that picture of my mother." She gestured toward the oval photograph in the gold frame on the table next to my chair.

"The State of Tennessee put me in this orphanage in Nashville. That's where I grew up, with my friends, until I came down here and met Andrew Dawson Longshore, the most decent, sweetest, kindest man." She laughed through her tears. "I didn't even have a name. They called me Prudence. Plain and simple Prudence." She snatched the pictures from my hand and waved them in the air. "That's all! Just Prudence. The others? They were Purity and Honour. Prudence, Purity, and Honour. Whores?" She laughed again. "We were the furthest thing from whoredom you could find. And I tell you one thing, I'm no stranger to the righteous indignation of a sorry man's snapping whip. We had religion beat into our poor pitiful bodies every day of our lives." Her shoulders shaking, she turned away and faced the far wall, blew her nose, and shook her head.

When she turned to face me again, her face was once again flushed and full with a scrubbed glow. "Why, Harold? Because I rebuffed you? Or because I gave myself to you? I trusted you completely. I gave you everything I had. Then I told you we had to go back to the lives we'd always known? Wasn't it enough? Couldn't you live with what you'd been given? Couldn't you be satisfied?"

I shook my head. I didn't know how to answer. I didn't know what to say. I felt so foreign to myself, my brain so cluttered, my motives so impure. I had no answers.

"No, of course not," she whispered.

Once again, she shook the photographs. "These are my memories. They're terrible memories. Nightmares. That's why I keep them tucked away at the bottom of this box. I can't look at them without shuddering. That time of adolescence should have been precious to all of us. It should have been a sweet time. But it wasn't. It was horrible. In the name of Christianity, the master beat us to make us pray. And he beat us while we prayed. He said that our pain would make us believe stronger and that we would know that God is almighty."

She thrust them toward me again.

I did not reach out for them.

"Take them," she insisted.

I took them.

"Look at the faces, Harold."

I looked. Once again, I saw the slight change from photo to photo, the faces and the poses.

"We were told: 'Don't look so sad! Smile! Look happy!' But we weren't happy. We were sad. Our bellies were growling. Our insides were about to erupt. We were poor children—fourteen years old—about to be turned loose into a world that you have no idea even exists. While we were there at the house, at night we would cling to each other in the bed where we all slept together. We could hold each other in our misery. But the same day this picture was made we were made to walk away with two dollars in each of our pockets. You have never had to face anything like that. Oh, you think you're alone on the road, traveling from Town Creek to Decatur. But you will go home. You will have your brothers and your sisters, your Mama and Papa. We had no one, no place, no nothing, except ourselves. And we knew that soon we'd go our separate ways. Then we wouldn't even have each other. Each would have to face her own solitude, her own fate, separate and apart from the others. It'd be up to each one of us to make our way.

"Those other girls—Purity, she joined the Catholic church and became a nun over in Memphis, and Honour, she married a man from Louisville. That's all I know. I wish I had a long story about each one. But we went our separate ways. Word drifted back now and then from some drummer who didn't know he was telling me something about my own history, or from another traveler from the north or the west. It's funny what a small world it is, listening to people who've been places and heard people talking, telling their stories of life in another place. They don't have the slightest idea they are touching you, giving you something of yourself that was taken away a long time ago."

I sat without moving, staring into the old pictures of the scrub-faced young women. Staring into Prudence's face, I realized it was a mask. I put what she'd told me with the vision of youth that she portrayed for the camera, and it all became more and more blurred with the layer upon layer of realization. Still, it made me wonder, but I did not ask the questions.

After a few moments or an hour, she rose and went back to the chest of drawers. She reached into the dark chasm, fixed her hands on another object and brought it out into the light that now poured through the high windows of the round turret-room.

My eyes riveted on a box that was smaller than the first, thinner and more fragile. It was covered by a thin coat of mother-of-pearl that looked almost real in the bright light.

When she handed it to me I held it in extended fingers that vibrated with nervousness.

"Open it," she said.

My fingers shook as I fumbled with the tiny latch.

"Here," she said, and she took it and opened it. She reached inside and tenderly extracted a sheath of three-by-five frayed-edge papers and again pushed them toward me, saying, "You didn't find these. I suppose the girls scared you before you got to them."

With my hands still shaking, I could barely focus on the slight images on the photos that were even more faded than the first ones. At least a dozen photographs showed a girl or girls in loose-fitting dresses or skimpy revealing underwear, each trying to be sexually alluring but failing in the attempt, each wearing a smile that was even more false than the expressions of the girls at the orphanage. Then there was a picture of a dozen girls lined up like a school class with a tall, elegant-looking woman in the center. Behind them was a wooden building I recognized as Mimi's on the bank of the river. The girls stood on the dirt road of Moccasin Alley, in front of the door leading to the place of constant twilight. When I turned the rectangular paper at an angle, catching a stream of light from the windows, I saw that the tall woman was a younger version of Prudence. As I gazed into the image, I frowned.

She sat, sinking onto the bed. She sighed audibly.

I looked from the photo to her shadowed face.

She stared directly into my eyes. "So, now you see my terrible past. After A. D. died, he left me this house." She chuckled a sarcastic half-laugh. "It's a great house, but it takes a lot of money for its upkeep. It was money I didn't have. Oh, he left me a little, but it was gone soon after the funeral. There I was: a poor grieving girl who'd barely had time to fall in love before my wonderful husband died because of some silly male-bragging challenge. Before I knew it, I was devastated with debts. An overzealous banker approved a loan, then he expected to make nightly calls on me in my boudoir. That would be my payment for his generosity." She arched her brows and slapped her hands down on the mattress. "When I said, 'No,' he started foreclosure proceedings. I had stupidly put this house up as collateral against the loan.

"That's when I met my legislator friend . . ."

"Mr. John D. Lawrence." I knew there had been something very familiar about their attitude toward each other that day after Katanzakis's funeral when he came to our table at The Tavern.

She nodded. "Ol' John D. was infatuated or in love or whatever you might call it with a pretty little girl who worked in a place down on Moccasin Alley. He was a highly respected planter, businessman, and politician. He couldn't afford to be aboveboard in his dealings with this bordello on the water, owned by a tyrant who enjoyed not only taking out sexual favors from the girls, but holding them in bondage, beating them, and making them do whatever risqué and disgusting acts he desired. The object of John D.'s affections had complained to her lover, who made demands on the proprietor, who indicated without compromise that if John D. didn't mind his manners and keep his mouth shut, he would find himself exposed to the county's gentry."

I listened, looking into the woman whom I had loved and whom I had hurt. I started toward her, but she put up her hands, shaking her head. "Listen," she said.

"But . . ." I took her hands in mine.

She shook her head again and withdrew her hands. She took a deep breath. "My banker friend could not keep his own mouth shut about our situation. At some men's thing—on a hunt or at a horse race north of the river, or somewhere—he drunkenly told the story about how he had me in a fix and how he was going to own my fine downtown Victorian home very soon, unless I began submitting to his demands. A few days later, John D. came to see me. He became my financial adviser, so to speak. In exchange for my cooperation in a business deal, he gave me cash to pay off my loan at the bank."

"Your cooperation?"

"I became his business partner. He furnished the money and became the silent partner when I bought the place on Moccasin Alley, and dismissed the whoremaster and began running the establishment without outside assistance. John D. could visit any time he wished in the dark of night or in the light of morning. His little lover was treated like a princess, as were all of the girls who worked for me. In time, John D. found other romantic interests, the girl took off for greener pastures in the North somewhere. We made a pile of money. With a handshake, we sold Mimi the real estate and dissolved our business partnership."

Again, after a few moments or an hour, she said, "Now, you can go. You've heard all my stories. You've done your damage."

"But . . ."

"You'll be gone day after tomorrow," she said. "You'll have another story to add to your collection about what happened on your trip to the faraway town of Decatur. You can brag to all your friends that you've had a real woman who once owned a whorehouse. You'll all laugh and have a lot of fun, talking about me and whoever else you've met on your journey."

Her words rang in my ears, stinging, I said, "I've got to get Bosworth Thursday morning. I'll take him back to Mama and Papa at Town Creek. Then I'll come back here to be with you. I promise I'll never say a word about Moccasin Alley or what you've been through."

She shook her head, smiling lightly. "Go to your room, Harold. Wash your face."

"I'll come back," I said again. "I promise."

Nineteen

Although my body still ached from the whipping and kicking, and my brain still rang numb from her words, I gathered my shoeshine material and hiked to the depot, where I met the Tuesday morning travelers. I shined shoes for an hour before moving to The Tavern, where I continued my work until after lunch.

From a woman who could barely speak English I bought a bouquet of yellow flowers. I carried them to the colored clinic, where the nurse told me she had persuaded Powtawee to drink a glass of juice and eat a half-bowl of oatmeal for breakfast. I gave her the flowers for Powtawee. She smiled and said that was nice. Then I followed her through the rear hallway.

At the door to the room where the battered woman had lain, I stopped and peered inside. Seeing only an empty bed, I turned questioningly to the nurse, who shrugged and said, "She left last night with a stranger."

"That's all?" I asked. "You just let her go?"

"We couldn't keep her here against her will. The man came, they talked, and they left together."

"You didn't know who he was?"

She shook her head.

"He could have been anybody," I said hopelessly.

The woman shrugged.

I followed her to the place where Powtawee lay behind the bars of the crib. I went directly to her and held the flowers in front of her face.

I waved the flowers from side to side, saying, "These are for you, Powtawee," but she showed no sign of recognition, staring straight ahead. "I want you to feel better," I said.

The nurse took the flowers and put them into a plain glass vase and placed the vase in a nearby window. They were the only thing of any color within the drab walls.

I sat for another hour, looking at the girl who was now breathing without the raspy sound.

Later I gave the nurse three dollars and told her to buy something special for Powtawee to eat, something sweet. She smiled and nodded and said she would.

LATE TUESDAY afternoon I walked back to Moccasin Alley. I told myself I was not going to visit with Lacy Beauchamp, but I reckon I was lying. I went straight to Mimi's and pulled a dollar from my pocket.

Mimi looked at the greenback, then up into my face. "Who do you want?" she asked.

"Lacy," I said.

"Lacy's not here," she said.

"She over at the Starlight?" I turned.

"No," she said.

I turned back to her. "Where?"

"She's gone."

"Just like that?" I asked. It seemed to me that people were moving out of Decatur in droves. First, the battered woman at the colored clinic. Now, Lacy.

"We don't keep the girls locked up. If they don't owe me money, they're free to go."

"But she said she couldn't go just anywhere. She said girls from Moccasin Alley couldn't go downtown or . . ."

"She made some money the other night, paid me what she owed me. After that, she was free to leave, anytime she wanted. She hightailed it yesterday with an old boy from Chattanooga. I guess she took a liking to him." She shrugged. "When the girls get itchy, nobody can stop 'em from moving on."

I stood there dumbfounded, looking into the woman's face, thinking about what Lacy had told me.

"Sugar, don't feel hurt," Mimi said. "Whores lie sometimes, just like everybody else."

Still hurting and feeling low, I took my dollar back, walked across the Alley to the Starlight Club and paid for a beer. After a while, Bubba and the boys from the L&N shop came in as randy and boisterous as ever. I nodded and said, "Howdy," and Bubba came over.

"You still fucking around with that little ol' skinny girl?" he asked.

I let his words skip past me without comment.

He was full of himself, but I was sure he didn't mean any real harm. "I'd like to buy you and your friends a drink," I said.

"What you want?" he asked suspiciously.

"I just want to be friendly."

He shrugged and eyed me with a sly look.

Then he shrugged. "We all drink beer."

Bubba was a section foreman with the Louisville & Nashville Railroad. Two of his friends were shop men and one was an engineer. They all introduced themselves and said they lived over in Railroad Town, where they worked. I told them this was next to my last night in Decatur and I'd like to do a little something for them, since they had all been my drinking companions, so to speak.

We all shook hands and they asked me to join their table.

261

When the women came in—Sue Ann and Louise—I bought their drinks too. We had several rounds before I told them about my Monday night experience.

After I ended with a description of Mrs. Prudence holding her gun on the hooded riders, Bubba said, "Well, I'm a sonofabitch. They sound like a bunch of sorry bastards."

"And you say one of 'em was that preacher with the tent revival out on the road to Priceville?" asked Leon, a shop worker.

"Yep," I said. "He was short, like a midget, and had a squeaky voice, was quoting the same words from the Old Testament he'd been talking in the tent, and he never showed up again at the boardinghouse."

Bubba nodded. "Just like a damn no-account jackleg preacher to throw in with the Ku Klux."

"Reckon he might be the Mystic Klud?" asked Leon.

"The what?" Bubba said.

"The Mystic Klud. That's what they call the KKK preacher or chaplain."

"How the hell you know that?"

"I rode with 'em once, up in Pulaski, Tennessee," Leon said. "They told me they were the ghosts of the Confederacy, but they weren't nothing but a bunch of chickenshit rednecks, if you ask me. You could-a bought the whole lot of 'em for a little more'n a dime."

"I hate those sonsofbitches," said Matthew, the engineer. "Any bastard that'll hide behind a mask to do his dirty work is a sorry asshole. Not worth being called a man."

"I was hoping maybe y'all'd feel this way," I said. "I've been wondering if y'all might help me with a little mischief tomorrow night. I was thinking we'd give the revival another visit and show 'em a thing or two."

"Why don't we go tonight?" Bubba asked. "You already got us all riled up over this thing."

"I've thought about it. If we let 'em go ahead and have their meeting tonight, they'll think they've scared us half to death. If nothing happens tonight, they won't expect nothing tomorrow. It'll come as a big surprise."

"We'll catch 'em with their pants down," Matthew said.

Bubba and the boys said they'd like nothing better than to scare the wits out of a bunch of Ku Klux Klan and some holier-than-thou townspeople to boot. "Everybody up yonder in town looks down on folks from Railroad Town or Moccasin Alley," Bubba said. Sue Ann and Louise said they'd like to join in the fun, but they had some hard work in front of them tonight and tomorrow on account of the bunch of stevedores who were in town to unload and reload the steamboats that had made it through the shoals. I told them we understood their situation. I figured they probably had to do double-time now that Lacy had walked away from the job.

About that time, O'Donohue and McCluskey showed up, played a ditty that Bubba and Sue Ann did a little pigeonwing buck dance to, then Leon and Louise took the floor and bounced their heels with what they called a double-shuffle. Bubba told the musicians about the predicament, and O'Donohue said he'd throw in with us as long as he could count on being back before eleven on Wednesday. He said that was when the real dancers showed up at the Starlight and appreciated some rhythm. He'd like to get all the donations that some new blood from the riverboats would be bringing with them. McCluskey said he'd have to bow out of the ruckus on account of his bad heart and blood pressure problems. A week or so ago, a barber over in Mooresville had bled him pale, weakening him thoroughly, and he still looked ravaged from that experience.

Before I left, I promised to meet them at the Starlight before nightfall on Wednesday.

I HAD SUPPER alone at the boardinghouse. C. Q. told me Prudence was taking her meal by herself in her private quarters. "She doesn't want to be disturbed," she added.

I picked at my meal, stared out the windows at the darkening flower garden and the outbuildings beyond. Tomorrow would be a long day of waiting. I already felt ill at ease, my patience wearing thin, my body still aching. I imagined that Prudence had been bathing her wounds in the juice of the aloe plant. When I thought about it, a picture of her body, full and voluptuous, formed in my brain and teased me with its amazing memory.

In the hallway outside the dining room I hesitated. I listened to the men outside, talking and smoking. They were arguing about the necessity of children working in the coal mines of north-central Alabama. I moved toward the stairs and started climbing.

I put my ear to the door of her rooms. Hearing nothing, I knocked. Then I waited. Then I knocked again.

Prudence cracked the door an inch and gazed through the opening. "Go away," she said.

"Please let me talk with you," I begged.

"Go away. Go to sleep. Don't come back." She shut the door.

"Please," I said, talking into the door.

"I mean it, Harold. Go away," she said again.

I went to my room and lay on the bed. I stared up into the shadowy ceiling and thought about her. I wanted her so badly I could feel her and smell her. When I closed my eyes, my lips and tongue could taste her. She was here with me, her body touching mine from the ends of my toes to the slope of my forehead. I could feel the pressure of her hands against my back, the warmth of her thighs squeezing, the tickle of her hair falling over my face.

My awakening dreams of her almost drove me back to her closed door. I wondered if I might go insane, thinking about her.

I shook my head and buried my face in the pillow, believing that I could smell her fragrance just as I had smelled it last night on the bed in her room. I breathed deep and imagined her nearness.

After a long while of thinking about her, I chased her from my brain. In a swirl of agony, I thought about Lacy and wondered where she was at this very moment. And I thought about Powtawee and even prayed for her to find a path back to life. It wouldn't be easy. Nothing is.

I balled my fists out of pure frustration and slammed them into a pillow. Then I rolled over and closed my eyes. But I couldn't sleep.

I continued to think, until my brain went numb.

AT BREAKFAST on Wednesday morning I was hoping Prudence would enter the dining room and sit next to me, but she never showed. I stuck my head in the kitchen, but she was not there. In the barn beyond the flower garden I found Roscoe greasing the axles on the old buggy I would use tomorrow to transport Bosworth home to Town Creek. It was ample-sized and had a wide thick-cushioned leather seat. "It ought to be a fairly comfortable ride," Roscoe said, and I agreed. Before I left, I rubbed Jed's nose and patted Jenny on the flank. "We'll be going home tomorrow," I told them, but they were anxious to get out of the stall and into the paddock where thick clover awaited their hunger. I asked Roscoe if he had three or four large knives I could borrow for a project I had in mind for tonight. He frowned, thinking. "I've got a machete I use to trim back the hedges," he said. "It's right sharp. And I'll ask C. Q. about some knives." I nodded and told him I'd appreciate his help.

I went to the depot. I was determined to pass the day as always, working and meeting people.

Today, fewer people exited the train. Nobody seemed to need or want a shoeshine. I had time on my hands. I walked down the street and lingered across the way from the hardware store and hoped that the deaf-and-dumb boy would come out. If he did, I would give him a piece of hard candy I had purchased from the vendor at the depot. But he didn't come out. I ate the candy and wandered away toward The Tavern.

Once again, the crowds that had gathered here yesterday seemed to have dispersed. I wondered about Wednesday. *What's so different about today?* It was only a day. Nothing more, nothing less. A beautiful sunshine-drenched day in April. Springtime. People should be milling about downtown. It was no president's birthday. No one was celebrating the founding of a nation or the remembrance of a historical occasion. Yet very few people were on the street.

A woman in a flowered dress carrying a matching parasol and wearing a wide-brimmed bonnet sashayed through the portico and entered The Tavern behind a man in a three-piece white linen suit. They looked like an Easter parade on New York's Fifth Avenue, something I'd seen featured on the pages of *The Saturday Evening Post* last summer. Remembering the food that had arrived on fashionable platters when I'd eaten noon dinner with Prudence and O'Donohue, I figured that surely Decatur had arrived as a society contender along with Memphis, Louisville, and Charleston, which were often written about as the top places to visit in the South, where people of wealth and position enjoyed tourist activities.

Finding only one customer to have his black shoes shined before entering the hotel-restaurant, I stepped on down the street in search of a way to spend my day.

Three boys no older than I were standing in an alley, pitching pennies into the wedge of the side of a brick building. The one whose penny stopped closest to the building won all three of the tossed coins.

I watched from a distance, shoving my hands deep into the pockets of my overalls, feeling the weight of my coins and the bulge of my paper money. I squeezed my fingers around my fortune, considerably more than I had when I first arrived in this town in a fury, trying to save poor Powtawee's life. I sure as heck wasn't about to lose my hard-earned money in a game of chance with some fast-talking city boys.

As I thought about my Indian friend, I picked up the speed of my step. I walked down the elevated wooden sidewalk, careful not to step on the creases between the wide boards. When I got to the end of the raised walk, I stepped off and looked back where I had walked, in the shade beneath the overhanging cover. I smiled, thinking that I had accomplished the simple feat, not allowing my brogans to touch the spaces between the boards.

For the first time this morning, I smiled, thinking I had been foolish but feeling the necessity to be foolish. I laughed aloud at myself, then looked around to check and see if anyone was watching. I was glad to see that no one was paying the first bit of attention to me.

At the colored clinic I made my way to Powtawee's room without escort. The flowers still sat on the window sill. I drew a chair close to her bed and leaned toward her, gripping the bars of her crib with my hands. She lay unmoving, staring open-eyed at the ceiling. "Powtawee," I whispered. She didn't move. "This is my last visit," I said. "In the morning I'll be meeting my brother, Bosworth, who's coming in on the train. I'll be taking him home to Mama and Papa in Town Creek."

I hesitated, looking around.

"If you want to go with us, tell me," I said.

I waited.

Still, she did not move.

"If you want, I'll take you. There'll be room on the buggy Mrs. Prudence has fixed for us. There's a place behind the seat where you would fit. It might not be the most comfortable ride in the world, but it'll transport you without too many problems. Once there, Mama'll take care of you. She's good at nursing."

Again, I waited for her to respond.

She didn't.

I breathed deep and let the air out through my nose. I held to the bars and stared into her darkly splotched face. I knew that in the last few days she had endured more pain and suffering than most people had to take in an entire lifetime. I had no idea how old she was, but she could not have been too many years older than I. No matter, she was still a girl.

I wanted to take her and hold her and rock her in my arms and tell her truthfully that there would be no more pain, but I knew that would be a lie. And she would know it too. I guess that was the biggest problem with being here and offering her what I hoped would be the promise of a paradise: both of us knew it was a lie. Yet I had to say it. I had to try.

I said it again, but she did not show compliance or understanding. She remained mute and untouchable.

I reached through the bars and touched her bare arm.

She did not jerk away.

I rubbed my fingers along her forearm, stroking gently. Moments later I lowered my hand to her palm and surrounded her fingers with my own. "I do care, Powtawee," I said.

I closed my eyes, hoping I would not cry.

At that instant, when I wasn't watching, her hand closed on mine. She squeezed my fingers.

When I opened my eyes, I saw a tear drop from the corner of her eye and roll down the valley of her nose to the corner of her mouth. I squeezed my grip on her hand, returning her meager caress.

I stayed like that for a long time: my hand resting in her hand. She did not squeeze again. No more tears were shed.

Finally, I stood. I leaned over the top of the railing on the side of her bed. I looked down into her dark eyes. "I'll come back," I lied. As an afterthought, perhaps trying to soothe my own conscience, I took a sheath of dollars from my pocket and slid it into her palm. "This will help, if you need anything," I said. Then I turned and walked out without looking back.

I DID NOT stop until I arrived at the Starlight Club. I bought Bubba and his friends beer. We were toasting the downfall of hypocrisy and the Ku Klux Klan when O'Donohue arrived.

"I've got to back out of the fun," the Irishman said. "McCluskey's got us an early gig aboard a party boat that pulled in this morning after an all-night sail from somewhere up North."

"They're going about things backwards, aren't they?" Bubba asked.

"A bunch of gamblers and whores from east Tennessee," O'Donohue said. "They've been sleeping all day. They'll party all night. Came rolling in at mid-morning. Loaded with mountain moonshine."

"The *Rebel Belle*?"

"That's it," O'Donohue said. "There'll be some high times on that boat by nightfall."

"Y'all'll be back here by eleven?" Billy the bartender asked. He knew his crowd and didn't want them to miss the music. By eleven, he knew, O'Donohue and McCluskey would be warmed up enough to make the drinkers lively.

"Let's go wreck us a revival meeting," Bubba shouted.

I grinned. Bubba and his boys were ready. Together, we marched out of the Starlight, up Moccasin Alley to Main Street, and into the residential area to Prudence's boardinghouse. We rounded the picket fence, went through the gate to the barn, and found it gray with the long shadows of twilight.

"Roscoe?" I called.

There was no reply.

I called again.

"Roscoe, you got the machetes ready?" I asked into the darkness.

"Y'all wait here," I told Bubba. I went into the barn and found the buggy waiting. Behind it was the fancy surrey. Somewhere deep in the barn I heard Prudence's big mare Judy stomp against the floor of her stall and blow a night snort from her haughty nose. "Roscoe?" I called again.

I listened.

From outside, Bubba called, "Harold, somebody out here wants you."

I returned to the waiting men.

At the back door of the boardinghouse, C. Q. stood with a lantern. "Mr. Harold?" she said.

"What is it, C. Q.?"

"Miss Prudence wants you inside."

"But she told me . . ."

"She says she wants to see you now."

I glanced toward Bubba, who shrugged.

"I'll see you in a minute, boys," I said, and went into the house.

In the kitchen, C. Q. stood next to the table where she had neatly folded a stack of white cloth hoods and gowns the laundry woman had fashioned from old sheets and pillowcases. I picked one up and let it fall from my fingers. Examining it, I nodded my approval. Then C. Q. said, "Miss Prudence said for you to go straight up to her room."

"What's she want?" I asked.

C. Q. shrugged and pointed me toward the wide hallway. I dropped the hood onto the stack and walked through the house to the stairs.

At the closed door to Prudence's room, I knocked and waited, trying to imagine what she wanted with me.

After a moment, the door opened. She stood inside the room wearing a long dressing gown pulled tight around her neck and draping to her ankles. "Come in, Harold," she said softly.

She glided across the floor and sat in her chair and gestured for me to sit opposite her.

I sat and waited, glancing around the shadowed room in the light of the lamps. It had become eerily familiar to me by now. The moments of my being here alone, a burglar stealing memories, drifted through my mind without ease.

"Roscoe and C. Q. both told me you planned to do something tonight," she said in a whispery voice.

I hung my head and wondered how I would tell her what I had planned. It suddenly seemed as ill-advised as my trip into these quarters night before last.

"Roscoe said you wanted knives and machetes," she said evenly.

I swallowed hard, still not knowing exactly what to say about my planned journey into revenge.

"Were you going to attack the Reverend and his flock? Planning to do it like the Ku Klux Klan? Wearing hoods and robes?" she asked. The words sounded almost comical, coming from her.

I cleared my throat. "We're going to scare them," I said.

"With knives and machetes?"

"Me and some boys from down on Moccasin Alley, we're gonna cut the tent down around them, let it fall on 'em, put 'em in the dark, and whip them."

"Whip them?" She pronounced the words so distinctly, they stung. "Like they whipped us? With the same kind of vengeance? Hiding behind a disguise?"

"I want to strike back," I said. Now my voice had dropped to a whisper. "I thought you'd appreciate our taking revenge on the people who attacked us. I want to treat them the way they treated us. I even thought you might go with us—if I could talk to you more, let you know what we're planning to do."

"Why would I do that?" she asked.

"They said terrible things. They beat you. They were the ones hiding with hoods over their heads," I said.

"Harold, did you tell these men from Moccasin Alley about me?"

"No," I said. I almost said, "ma'am," but I didn't.

"You didn't tell them that I was once a madam down there?"

"No, I didn't. I'll never tell anyone. But I did tell them about the Reverend and about the Ku Kluxers."

"Those are evil people, Harold." She sat back, staring at me across the abyss of only a few feet, her voice now like a magnified, booming shout penetrating my ears. Her words echoed inside me as she repeated them: "They are evil. If you do the same things they do, you will be evil. You will be just as bad as they are. Does that make what you do right?"

She hushed. Her eyes bore into me from across that short expanse of space between us.

I squirmed in the chair, trying to think of some explanation, some excuse for my plans, something to pull me up and make me righteous. "Don't you believe in revenge?"

"Smartly aimed, revenge might sometimes be justified. But I don't think your plan is very smart."

Her words hit me like a fist. I felt the power of them.

"You think I'm being dumb?" I asked.

"I think you're rushing into something that you haven't thoroughly thought about."

"I thought about it all day yesterday and all day today."

"Time is not always an adequate measure of thought."

"Every time my shoulder hurt, I thought about what I could do to them."

"What if you hurt someone?" she asked.

"We don't plan to . . ."

"What if the tent caught fire? What if people are burned? Killed?"

"But that's not . . ."

"What if you kill someone?"

"I'd never kill anyone."

"What if the tent fell onto one of those lanterns and it caught fire? What if people got caught under the tent and couldn't get out—with smoke and flames everywhere?"

Suddenly I was reduced to a boy. I felt myself shirking back into the disguise of youth, a mask I had worn until recently, a masquerade that I had been comfortable wearing as an extra-layered garment. Until this moment I thought I had discarded it for the more vulnerable nakedness of adulthood. But now I felt myself saying, "No, ma'am," in a timid, child-like voice.

"What would happen if you killed someone?"

Her words pierced my brain, opening it like a jagged wound. I didn't answer.

"What would you say to the families of your victims? What would you say to their wives? Their children?"

My fingers, laying in my lap, became entangled.

"Even Ku Klux Klansmen have families. Even those hypocrites who preach one set of rules and live by another have someone who cares for them—someone who is innocent of their corruption."

I swallowed hard.

"Do you have answers made up for them? Can you explain your way out of such a heavy, horrible guilt that such violence would bring, Harold?"

I looked away from her. I stared down into my lap at my knotted hands. I could not speak. I had no answers.

"Have you thought that, because of your actions on one night of your young life, you would suffer horrible guilt every night for the rest of your life? Would you be able to sleep after doing something so dreadful?"

I remained mute. The words sank into my being and lay there.

"Are you prepared to face the consequences of your actions?" she asked.

I felt so foolish, I wanted to run from her. It was worse than last night. It hurt with a deeper pain. My insides wanted to erupt as they had after seeing the limp dead body of poor Katanzakis hanging in the tree. Only now it was my own plan, my own immature thoughts, that made me sick.

After a few moments that seemed to extend into eternity, Prudence rose and stepped toward me, her footsteps as light as air. She reached out and put a hand on my shoulder, barely touching, the weight heavy. "Go back to Moccasin Alley with your friends, Harold. Have yourself some fun on your last night in Decatur. Enjoy yourself, but not at someone else's expense."

I wanted to say, "Yes, ma'am," obediently. I raised my face to look at her. I opened my mouth. But I said nothing.

I wanted to grab her and hold her. I wanted her to hold me. If I lurched for her, would she hold me?

For a moment I thought I was going to cry. I prayed I wouldn't. My throat was tight and dry. My head was filled with thoughts. I remained silent.

She moved slowly away from me, turning toward the round turret and the windows that showed the light of the moon.

I stood and walked silently to the door, where I stopped and turned. Looking at her silhouette, I tried desperately to compose a series of words that would mean everything to her and to me and to us. But words failed me. I swallowed again, opened the door, and stepped out into the hallway.

When I told the men we had to return to Moccasin Alley, Bubba questioned me. The others asked *Why?* and I told them that the Reverend Mr. Applewhite had moved his tent revival on to Mooresville. I said we should have gone and done our deed last night. They shrugged and shook their heads and said they wished we had done it then. I told them not to worry, I would pay for all the beer tonight.

After I had cooled their emotions—and had felt a cooling down within myself—and after we started our trek back toward Moccasin Alley, a strange feeling swept through my body. Suddenly my bones and blood seemed cleaner, clearer, lighter somehow. It was almost like the way Pawpa explained the sensations that came over him when he had been baptized by Preacher Sims in Reed Creek on the mountain in The Forest. I was a different person than I had been an hour earlier. I moved with a new freedom that manifested itself in the spring of my step and the joy of my voice.

At the Starlight we drank and caroused. I sat in the broad lap of a big woman from Mimi's but didn't go across the road with her. Maggie, a whore from a place called Miss Irene's, showed me a step, and I danced with her and discovered that I could move without terrible awkwardness while I held her heavy shoulders and felt her palms pressing against my back.

I was enjoying the revelry. O'Donohue and McCluskey brought their party to the Starlight, adding to the merriment. Toes were tapping as the couples bucked their heels against the naked floor. I knew that I was not drunk, although the scene was intoxicating with the rhythmical sounds and the thick smells of strong perfume mixed with the tart fragrance of corn whiskey and the freedom of movement.

Suddenly the picture of Brother Applewhite and his congregation came into my mind like the black-and-white screen of a moving picture show. The look on his pious face when he spread his white-clad arms burned into my brain. I seethed as I listened to the gay music but heard the echoes of the preacher's sad, soiled, hypocritical words.

I could not stand it another moment. Although Prudence's words had calmed me previously, now I felt the anger of the Klan's nighttime visit burning down deep inside. I stood and looked around as though I had wandered into a strange place and had no idea where I was—lost in the familiarity of this dungeon.

Bubba, who'd been fraternizing with one of Mimi's new girls who'd arrived this morning from Birmingham, stepped toward me and scrunched his face. "What's wrong, Harold?"

"I'm going to the revival," I said.

"But you said . . ."

"I lied, Bubba."

"But you told us . . ."

"I know what-all I said, Bubba."

"You're going anyway?"

"I'm going. I'm not asking y'all to go. This is my concern. I'm not going to hurt anyone. I'm not going to raise a fist. But I am going to have my say. I've got to do that."

"Those people might hurt you," Bubba said.

"I doubt it," I said. My view of the night became bright as mid-day. I was without doubt for the first time in my young life.

Bubba shook his head. "Didn't they whip you?"

"While they were hiding behind masks," I said. "They're a bunch of low-life cowards. That's what they are."

"Still . . ."

"I'm going to confront them," I said. I started toward the door.

Billy the bartender said, "Hey, Harold. Take it easy. See you around?"

I smiled. They all knew me on Moccasin Alley. I'd been here less than a week, but it was like I'd been raised among these unpainted uneven buildings along the waterfront. Like me, they slanted sideways without appropriate design or planned architecture. I was a fixture here, like the green-shaded lamps and the boys from Railroad Town and the salesmen who detoured from Main Street looking for a good time.

"I'll see you around," I answered, as though I meant it.

I strode purposefully, taking long fast strides up and out of Moccasin Alley. With each step, keeping time with the quick beat of O'Donohue's fiddle that faded behind me, my brain raced with the plans of what I would do when I entered Applewhite's tent.

As I passed Powell's Hardware, heading eastward, I heard the sounds of movement behind me.

I did not turn to see who was following.

I picked up my pace.

Thoughts of robed Klansmen swooping down on me in the darkness rushed through my brain. I could see them, like the other night, lashing out with their whips, the leather tongues wrapping around my ankles, jerking, flinging me off balance, then others holding me down, clamping my shoulders to the ground while others in hoods unclothed me and kicked me, toes beating against me while I writhed and rolled on my hips, unable to escape.

As I thought about my Klan enemies, I moved up into the residential area, the footfalls growing heavier behind me. I circled behind Mrs. Prudence's house to the dark rear doorway. Stopping, I reached for the knob.

I stood still, breathing heavy in the damp humid darkness.

I gasped and held my breath, waiting and wondering, hesitating before I turned it.

"Harold," a voice said behind me.

I let go of the knob, turned, and gazed through the darkness. Shadowy figures gathered in the yard.

"Harold!" the voice said again.

"Bubba," I said. "Is that you?"

"Me and the boys. We'll do whatever you tell us."

"But we'd like to beat the shit outa those Ku Kluxers," Raymond said.

I smiled. "Y'all stay where you are. I've got to fetch something. I'll be right out." I turned the knob that clicked open. I stepped inside. In the darkness of the kitchen I saw the stack of white sheets and pillowcases still sitting where C. Q. had placed them earlier. I gathered them into my hands, stepped back outside, and handed them out to Bubba and his crew.

I ran to the barn where I found among Roscoe's tack a long leather whip, a buggy whip, and a pair of freshly soaped leather straps. I brought them back and handed them out to

Bubba, Leon, and Raymond, keeping the long whip for myself, wrapping it in a circle and letting it hang from my left hand.

As we walked down the road toward the field where Applewhite's tent glowed in the night we slipped into our covering. As we moved across the field, I took a deep breath. The night air expanded my lungs with a refreshing coolness, giving me new life, not unlike the smelly warm water of the Cave of the Wind.

I said a few words to them, then I turned, stiff and straight, like a soldier, and marched toward my destination, hoping with each step that I could find the courage to face those who had hidden behind masks when they attacked me and Prudence.

Twenty

When I pulled back the flap and entered the revival meeting, Brother Preston Applewhite was standing on the wooden box that held him up above the podium where he could look down on his congregation. His arms were outstretched, his eyes squeezed shut, and he was praying in a loud, commanding voice. He was clad in the same three-piece white suit he was wearing Monday night.

As I marched down the center aisle, mumbles and sighs rippled through the audience. I took wide strides, just as I had when I was walking through the town, determined. I stepped onto the stage with heavy feet.

"Praise be to God almighty!" Applewhite shouted when he opened his eyes and found me standing with feet spread beneath the sheet that was as white as his three-piece suit. His eyes widened when he recognized the whip extended from my raised fist.

"Glory!" he said loudly.

Some of the audience smiled, thinking we were part of the performance, but among those who knew something was terribly wrong were Octavious Hicks, whose girth and height matched those of the large rider from Monday night, and Goodloe Littlejohn, who also shifted nervously on his bench and reached inside his coat.

As he reached, I motioned toward Littlejohn. Bubba, covered by the sheet and pillowcase, stepped to Littlejohn's side and followed his hand that disappeared beneath his waistcoat. An instant later, Bubba extracted a five-inch-long Derringer that could have done some damage if it were aimed into someone's face from a distance of no more than five feet. Otherwise, it was more a toy than a weapon. When Bubba tossed it into a dark corner of the tent, Littlejohn eked an angry sound from his throat and started to rise, but Bubba pushed him roughly back onto the bench. Littlejohn's eyes blazing, he looked around toward Leon, who was standing no more than ten feet away with the leather reins cocked and ready to swing. Hidden behind his hood, Leon looked even more menacing than he was in overalls.

When Brother Preston Applewhite objected to my sudden appearance, I stepped onto the podium, reached out, took his wide lapels in my fists, and lifted him onto his tiptoes. His eyes widened, like they were about to pop from his skull.

"Put me down! Put me down!" Applewhite screamed.

I shifted my hold. I slid my hands under his armpits and lifted again. He was as easy to lift as a hundred-pound sack of potatoes and not as difficult as a freshly stuffed and wired bale of cotton. I picked him up from the wooden box, his feet kicking like a wind-up toy. I almost laughed.

Several members of the congregation chuckled.

Leon laughed loudly, as did Bubba.

When I put Applewhite down, he stumbled backward, toppling from the stage onto the ground. He scrambled in the dirt until he steadied himself on his knees. Balanced on hands and knees, he looked up at me like a scared rabbit, not sure whether to scamper away or attack.

I pointed toward Applewhite. "This man is a liar!" I swore. "He has a knowledge of the Bible, but he does not tell it truthfully. He is a hypocrite. He is a Ku Klux Klansman who hides behind a hood and gown. He is a stinking coward to boot."

"What do you think you are?" shouted Octavious Hicks.

Bubba stepped toward Hicks, swishing the buggy whip through the air. It hissed before it fell onto Hicks's shoulder.

"Oh! Dammit, man!" Hicks grabbed for the whip, but Bubba jerked it back too fast for his hands. Hicks grasped his own shoulder and held onto it and moaned. Anger boiled through his gnarled teeth.

"On Monday night the Reverend Preston Applewhite preached Proverbs from the Old Testament. He read all the hell-fire and damnation words and phrases. But he left out the most important words of all," I said. I reached deep inside myself to find the words, the thoughts, the images. I always knew the words were within me. I could always speak them to a horse or into the wind. I could talk up a blue streak when I had a shoeshine rag in my hands or hand-operated clippers between the fingers of my right hand. But I had never been one to make speeches to the public. In a classroom, I found it difficult to stand before my peers and speak my mind. When I spoke, my words stammered. My voice shook with the same vibration that flickered in my fingers and hands.

Once, in the third grade, when we were ordered to memorize Edgar Allen Poe's "The Raven," I refused to stand before the class and say the words. It was not because I couldn't; it was because I was afraid to stand in front of everyone and repeat the words; I knew that I would fail miserably. Rather than attempt and fail, I accepted the F Mrs. Leland wrote on my report card and the spanking Papa gave me for not doing what I had been told to do.

But now, hiding behind the sheet with the holes cut for my eyes and for my mouth, I spoke with power and conviction and insistence.

"On Monday night, Reverend Applewhite damned the world for being 'slothful' and 'ignorant' and 'sluggard' and 'evil,' to name only a few of the sins that so easily and eagerly fell from his lips. He enjoys damning others. He loves to point his finger and assign blame elsewhere."

I looked toward the men who had accompanied me. They were standing in a semicircle from the left side, across the back of the tent, to the right side where Bubba's presence anchored them. They all nodded with approval as I spoke.

Then I turned my attention back to the congregation and to Applewhite. "After preaching his sermon of wrath and perdition, setting a fire of hatred and cruelty in the souls of evil-hearted men, he turned these men loose to ride the night on their horses under the cowardly cloaks of anonymity with which I now address you."

There was another nervous shifting as I stared directly into the faces of Hicks and Littlejohn.

I raised my whip high in the air, swished it in their direction, flicking my wrist just before the tip end of the whip reached them, popping it in the thick humid air that smelled of coal oil from the lanterns and the harsh odor of the canvas tent.

As the two men wiggled in their seats, I raised my voice until it boomed out over them all. "I tell you: there is the punishment of hellfire and damnation—especially to those who do not realize the importance of redemption. 'Yea tho' I speaketh unto you, the truth of poverty and shame and hypocrisy runs through mankind like a fever.'"

I slowed my speech, having no idea what I was quoting but thinking that it sounded good and correct, strong and true, tough and hard.

As I slowed, Thelma Gooch and Audrey Crow rose together from their seats and said, "This is enough!" in unison.

I nodded toward Leon, who stepped to the end of their bench and threw his entire arm over his shoulder, bringing with it the twin inch-wide strips of leather, which popped loudly against the women's backsides.

"Oh!" screamed Thelma Gooch.

"That hurts!" shouted Audrey Crow.

"Sit down!" I ordered.

Leon swung his leather reins again, this time catching both women across the shoulders.

I knew it did not hurt them. I could barely hear the slaps of the leather against the material of their dresses. Perhaps it stung slightly. Leon did not swing *that* hard. But they looked as scared as I had been on Monday night.

They sat, shivering and grumbling.

"Hypocrisy and deliberate falsehoods are the worst crimes against humanity!" I shouted.

I repeated my words, wanting them to sink in with repetition.

Bubba and his men nodded with my words.

"It is worse than the dreaded *vomita negra*—the black vomit!" I said.

"Ehhh!" Thelma Gooch groaned.

"Let you without sin cast the first stone!" I screamed, then turned and shut off the lantern sitting on the front left corner of the stage, casting that part of the tent into quick shadows.

At the moment the darkness fell on them, the newspaper editor, Lee Sentell, said, "The man speaks the truth."

"Like hell!" Octavious Hicks pronounced.

"Put out the other lamps," said Bubba, who doused the lantern near his side.

Leon went to the lantern in the rear and was trying to put it out when I moved through the front of the tent, struggled to reach under my sheet and take my knife from the bib of my overalls.

Bubba and Raymond were heaving against the center pole, pushing it away from the crowd. When it began to drop, they hustled toward the rear opening.

As I cut the taut rope that ran from the tent to a stake in the hard ground, I saw Leon through the opening. He knelt to turn the lever and kill the flame of his lantern, but it did not go out immediately. As he struggled, Octavious Hicks stepped onto the bench, wheeled around, and pushed past several startled couples sitting on the next row. Moving swiftly for a man his size, he hooked the loose ends of Leon's reins and jerked them.

Taken aback, Leon pulled with the force of his shoulders and arms that had thickened through the years of working in the railroad shop. His strength yanked Hicks off his feet and pulled the big man into the dirt.

Then Leon turned again to the flame, but the crowd had begun moving among themselves like panic-stricken sheep. They pushed against Leon and the lantern tumbled. Fire spilled onto trampled grass. Leon began stomping, hollering for help.

Goodloe Littlejohn rushed toward his friend, Octavious Hicks. I moved toward them, thinking I'd give them each one last kick in the rear on behalf of Pete Powers.

Thelma Gooch and Audrey Crow held to each other, crying out for the Lord to help them.

The woman in white ran to Brother Preston Applewhite, enveloping him in her arms, as the tent fell over them.

At that moment, Bubba and I stepped onto the tumbling sides of the tent and began whipping at the lumps that rose and fell beneath the canvas.

"Oh, please, let us out!" screamed Thelma Gooch.

"Please!" shouted Audrey Crow.

After another long moment, I grabbed the women by their arms and pulled them from the black darkness under the fallen tent. When they were free of the tent, they ran past me and climbed onto their buggy, where their horse was nervously stomping against the ground. They disappeared into the night,

Thelma Gooch popping the reins of her harness against the horse's backside.

On the far side of the tent, Leon shouted for help.

"The fire!" Bubba said. He rushed toward the flames that licked into the night.

Leon stomped the blaze, holding it back.

Bubba pulled the sheet from his head and wadded it into a big ball, which he slammed against the flames. I did likewise, forgetting my disguise, using it to smother the fire.

As the flame died, Leon swung his reins onto the canvas.

Another person screamed.

Applewhite and his assistant were crawling toward the rear of the tent. I ran toward them, popping my whip onto the canvas near their heads. He screamed. His voice squeaked like a rusty axle. I hit again. This time he cried out a profanity. I slapped the whip onto the swollen hill of canvas. Although I didn't hit him directly, the sound of his cry shrieked, echoing agony.

Moments later, Bubba, the railroad crew, and I marched across the field, hearing behind us the wails and cries of the people still struggling to find their way out from the darkness.

We shook hands and slapped each other's shoulders, saying our goodbyes in the wide boulevard in front of the depot. I thanked them for their help, but they all said they'd had the time of their life and appreciated my including them. "And one thing's for sure," Bubba said.

"What's that?"

"If you ever quit barbering, you'd make one helluva preacher."

Leon agreed. "Man, you string words together like a sure-enough hard-shell minister. You sure you ain't got the calling?"

I chuckled and thanked them again and moved along toward the boarding house. Bubba and his boys headed back to Moccasin Alley to have another drink and toast their good time.

ALTHOUGH I WAS weary, I lay awake for a long while. I stared up into the shadows cast upon the ceiling of the room by the reflection of the moon.

An hour or so later I heard the sounds of men on the street below. The men were talking, but I could not make out their words. Horses' hooves beat on the hard dirt street. I wondered what I'd do if they came inside. I wondered what Prudence would do.

Moments later my doubts disappeared as the sounds faded into the night.

Before tonight I had never hidden my face behind a mask. Not seriously. Only when I was a little boy playing with my friends, Raiford Bradford and Peter Morgan. I had never known how much bravery and stupidity such anonymity gave a person. Hidden, you can do anything. Behind a mask, you can speak out as you have never spoken before. No wonder men can hate so freely, commit acts of violence, burn their neighbor's house, whip a woman, and spew hateful messages into the air. Hidden, man can free the devil that sleeps dormant in the brightness of daylight. In the dark, it is easy to release the savage monster that lies in repose within us all.

I had spoken out to those frightened people. They probably didn't remember one word I said. But that was not the point, was it? I knew all too well that they would remember the night. Editor Sentell would write about it in his newspaper. It would soon become part of the lore of this country.

I slept, knowing that tomorrow I had a journey to finish. I couldn't wait to see Bosworth and listen to him tell his story about what happened in the war. I hoped with all my heart that he would tell me about being a hero. He could make all my stories true, which would give me the satisfaction of being a truthful person, like Bosworth and like Papa.

BOOK THREE
The Road Home

Twenty-One

I near-about didn't recognize him. His head, sitting atop a thin little neck that poked up from a bony frame, looked as though it had shrunk since the last time I had seen him. His eyes, hidden deep in dark sockets, looked like the eyes of a frightened sparrow hiding in the shadows of a thick bush. His sallow skin lay like smooth-cured bleached cowhide against high cheekbones and a narrow, pointed chin. His mouth seemed too perfect for a man's face with its delicate curves, its heart-shaped pout. His neck extended up from the loose collar of the faded brown tunic that hung over the frail and stiff body, down to the leggings wrapped tightly around his ankles and calves.

My eyes quickly scanned him, from shoes scuffed but polished bright brown down to the thin soles, all the way up to the square set of his doughboy's campaign hat pulled snug to the tops of his ears. His complexion was so pale it seemed translucent. A network of veins, tiny pink and blue ribbons, mapped beneath the surface of his face.

When he raised his right hand to wave, it was bandaged. The tape disappeared up his sleeve. Long, slender, almost feminine fingers stuck from the splotched gauze covering his wrist and palm. As his hand reached shoulder-high I saw the shadow of pain cross his face.

He spoke my name and I went to him. He stepped down from the opening between two passenger cars. I met him as he opened his arms and pulled me to his skinny body, enveloping me. "My, how you've grown, Harold," he said, his voice a light whisper, like a cool morning breeze, barely audible.

"I guess I have," I said, feeling his arms holding me, his hands on my back.

His freshly shaven face, smooth as Lacy's breast, brushed against my neck, leaving a hint of bay rum.

Pushing me back to arm's length, he said, "You've filled out."

His eyes looked me over, then suddenly saddened.

He glanced around, through the vanishing crowd in the angular shadows beneath the large train shed. "I half-expected Mama and Papa," he said in a voice so forlorn it made me quiver.

I pulled from his grip and stared into his disappointed face. "You know how it is, with planting, the crops, everything on the place an emergency this time of the year, everything having to be done at the last minute, like there won't ever be a tomorrow," I said, trying to think of a long list of reasons. There was no way I could have foreseen his displeasure with my lone appearance. "We had a hard rain Sunday, and it kept up pretty steady all night," I added. "Crops'll be popping up before you know it."

"Well, yes, I suppose," he said, seeming to understand, to remember. He turned and collected a large piece of luggage from a uniformed red-cap porter.

Bosworth slid a coin into the man's hand. I nodded, thinking he too had changed in the past two years.

He moved with a brittle step, his knees stiff, but he would not allow me to take the bag from his left hand.

When I glanced down at his right, he held up the bandaged fist. "My *home-free* wound," he said, his face creasing into a smile. "That's what the boys in the hospital call their injuries. Home-free wounds," he repeated.

"Oh," I said, and moved aside two boxes in the back of the buggy, where I'd loaded my belongings.

He reached up with his left hand, took hold of the seat, and lifted his left leg, poised to pull himself up. I saw him wince. "Can I help?" I asked, but he pulled away when I tried to lend a hand. I drew back.

I retreated to the rear of the buggy, where I busied myself putting his bag among the things I'd accumulated during my short stay in Decatur. I watched, through the webbing I had fixed to protect our baggage, as he struggled to climb aboard. Then I went to the opposite side and climbed up, settling myself next to him.

"That's Jed and Jenny," Bosworth said.

"Yes," I said. "I rode Jed and led Jenny along behind. I thought it'd be easier on both of us, if they pulled us along on the buggy, rather than having to ride 'em back." Having witnessed his awkward movements, I was glad that Prudence had provided the buggy for our use. Papa had been smart to include it in his telegram.

Bosworth nodded.

As I snapped the reins lightly over the animals' backs, Bosworth's nerves jumped. He grabbed the bottom of the spring-held seat. "Okay?" I asked. He nodded but did not release his grip.

As I drove west on Market Street, I asked, "Is there anything you need in town, before we head toward home?"

"No," he said.

In front of the hardware store Pete Powers stood with the broom in his hands. His eyes followed as we rode by. I smiled and raised my hand. For an instant, I thought a smile moved onto his face, then his father appeared and glared toward me as he took Pete by the shoulder and led him into the safety of the store.

As we rolled past the mouth of Moccasin Alley my thoughts raced through numerous pictures frozen into my memory. I knew they would never go away. I held them there, captured forever.

Bosworth said nothing else for a long time. We put the town behind us in silence. I kept thinking he'd ask about Mama and Papa, about Sister and Lucy, Ida Mae and the rest. I thought he might ask about the home place, Town Creek, how we'd done on the baseball diamond last summer, but he didn't. He sat straight, his back like an unyielding rod, leaning when the buggy leaned, his eyes fixed on the horizon over the tips of the animals' ears.

Finally I couldn't stand it any longer. I was about to burst with thought. I couldn't help it. I wanted to know where he'd been, what he'd done, all the sights he'd seen, Europe, France, Paris, New Jersey, Maryland, the train ride south, all of it.

I asked my questions, then allowed periods of silence to fall around us, filled only by the squeaking of the wheels and groaning of the axles, the twitters of birds in the distance, and an occasional yawn or fart from Jed or Jenny. Bosworth said nothing. He sat straight on the seat, his back stiff, his head bobbing as we shuffled over a bridge or hit some holes in the road. Once, nearly two hours into our journey home, he announced that he needed to pee. I reined in, let the animals graze, and joined Bosworth in relieving ourselves next to a tree.

I asked if he was hungry for a sandwich or biscuit with some jam that C. Q. had packed, but he shook his head.

In a short time we were on the road again.

To fill the silence, I decided to tell him about my trip, beginning with Mama and Papa saying goodbye in the dark outside of our house in Town Creek. I expanded the descriptions, editing to make them as sharp and visual as possible, making the words full and fanciful, entertaining, giving them an airish

296

quality, like Katanzakis's colorful high-flying balloon, so that Bosworth could see and hear and feel everything that had happened. I was telling about the balloon being picked up by the strong winds out of the northwest, sailing through the black air with thunder and lightning crashing all around. I told about seeing something fall from the balloon, then seeing the balloon itself disappear into the trees. "Everything happened so fast it made my head swim," I commented. After having said the words, I felt him shivering on the seat only inches from me. When I looked, his entire body was shaking. His lips were trembling. Tears were flooding his eyes, washing down the flat planes of his cheeks.

I pulled to a stop, then turned to him, opening my arms and shifting on the seat to pull him to me, preparing to cradle him like Mama used to comfort me on stormy nights or after nightmares. I thought that perhaps I had been too successful in my telling about the tragic happening. I thought that he was crying for Anthony Katanzakis and the Indian girl Powtawee.

When I held him, his body vibrated to an almost lifeless respite, until his head lay against my shoulder, girl-like. I heard him say something but did not understand the words. I pulled away and he raised his head. He stared into my face with red-rimmed, hurting eyes. His lips moved. I watched them carefully to determine his message.

When he repeated his words, I heard him say, "They called me Boz." He nodded, as though to reassure himself. "They did. They called me Boz."

I smiled gently. "That's good, Bosworth. They had a nickname for you. You want me to call you Boz?"

He shook his head slowly, his eyes filling with tears again.

I reached behind our seat and dug a canteen from the provisions C. Q. had packed. I uncapped the metal container and handed it to him. He drank several swallows. Then he blinked and took another swallow and handed it back.

I had a swallow before clicking my tongue in my cheek and slapping the reins lightly across Jed and Jenny's backs.

We rolled over ridges between fields, through meadows alive with flocks of doves flying together like fast-moving clouds, individuals darting and diving out of the pack now and then, but mostly staying together as a whole, like the Canada geese Prudence and I had seen on our way to the Cave of the Wind. In the fields tiny plants formed long rows, barely peeping up from the blood-red soil that had been doused by Sunday's rain, now basking in the bright warm spring sunlight. New life was beginning to sprout across the valley.

As we rolled, Bosworth sucked air into his lungs and came to life. "My buddies called me Boz," he repeated. He waited, then he started talking again, low and easy, in a cadence, his voice keeping time with the jingle of the harness that shook as the animals stepped. "In boot camp at a place called Campbell, Kansas, we marched morning, noon, and night. It was worse than Papa shaking you out of bed at six in the morning. A bugle blasted at five. We jumped up, got dressed, double-timed to breakfast, where eggs and mushy oats and dry sausage was shoveled onto your tray. Sergeant Atwater marched between the tables while you ate. If you didn't eat fast enough, he hit his baton next to your tray, slamming it down hard and loud." Out of the corner of my eye I saw Bosworth flinch. I hugged my elbows close to my ribs, feeling the pang of his hurt. I didn't say a word, listening.

In excruciating detail, he told the story of long hot days, sweltering nights that turned suddenly chilly when a breeze would blow out of the north and sweep down on the camp across the flat Kansas countryside. He told about making friends with a slow-witted hillbilly boy from Arkansas and how that boy named Ralph Sims stirred the anger of the bull-headed Sergeant Atwater, who forced them to dig ditches half the night and fill the holes the next morning. Once again, Bosworth quivered like he was freezing. But it wasn't cold. If anything, it was hot. The sun was warm on our backs. I had shed my jacket hours ago. But he still sat straight on the seat with his loose-fitting woolen tunic fastened from his waist to the knot of his Adam's apple.

I kept us moving, but neither Jed nor Jenny put much effort into pulling us along. They moved in short, idle steps, like they too were listening to every detail of his story. I didn't hasten them.

Bosworth described the monotony of the long days under the Kansas summer sun. When he finally got his group of soldiers across the country to New Jersey and aboard a ship heading for Europe, I was mighty glad to have that tedious journey behind. It was like that first day of my own journey from Town Creek, until I finally met the pair of pilgrims heading for Pontotoc, Mississippi, with a loose wheel on their wagon.

Words flowed from Bosworth's mouth, but he never once turned his head to look in my direction. I glanced toward him now and then, but he looked straight ahead, the fingers of his left hand wrapped around his bandaged right hand. He did not speak with overflowing emotion. In fact, he seemed near emotionless, although his words bore sharply into me as they were spoken in a quiet tone. And now and then he trembled suddenly, quivering, then stopped, took a quick breath, then went on with his words.

I listened, feeling the depth and horror of the war as it had affected this boy whom I had known only as an older brother, who knew more than I and who had gone off to school when I was still a child. Then he came home for a short while, gathered a few things, and said goodbye before heading off to the army. I had known him only as someone who had comforted me when

I was little, when I hurt myself doing something stupid; I knew him as someone who'd been there, like a shadow, carrying his squirrel gun and bringing home his kill, sitting silently on the back porch next to the well box, skinning and cleaning the animals. I had never known him as a living, breathing, suffering, loving person, but now he was allowing me to enter his world, where he had undergone the worst kind of torture a man could possibly imagine.

Listening to him, I wondered about myself and asked myself if I could make such a strong decision as the one he made: to go off and fight for my country, and I remembered Papa's words, "He wasn't a slacker."

His outfit was one of the first to arrive in northern France. "They told us we were there to fight the enemy: Kaiser Wilhelm's army. It was a name without a face, something they told us to hate, something we were told existed to capture us and kill us. Hatred festered, like a boil on your backside, unseen but felt every second of every day. It rubbed and rubbed, and the hurt got worse and worse."

Bosworth drew a picture of hateful drudgery, quick and senseless violence, death in poppy fields and in a river valley, in hillside vineyards and in a picturesque tiny town laced with cobblestone streets and blooming flowers, and his friend, the boy from Harrison, Arkansas, Ralph Sims, killing soldier after German soldier, then being blown to smithereens while he himself stood within arm's distance of my brother. Telling it, Bosworth shivered again, and his voice quivered.

Then he told more, story after story of death and destruction, until I thought I could not stand to hear another word. I closed my eyes and tried to picture it. The verbal agony came in waves of words that poured steadily and quietly from his mouth and memory.

"Once, in a forest called Argonne that looked a lot like the woods where Pawpa and Mawma live, I ran up on a German soldier. He was no more than ten feet from me. We stared at each other. He was no older'n you, Harold: sixteen or seventeen at most. I looked straight into his eyes, like the startled eyes of a deer that walked up on me one time up near the river years ago. I never told y'all about that. I was out there looking for some squirrels with my single-shot four-ten. Me and the German soldier were the same way that me and the deer was: startled and scared of each other. Like with the deer, I just turned and walked away." He laughed an empty laugh that hung in the air and stayed with me. Again, I wondered if I would have had the courage to turn and walk away.

"I walked all over France. I went where they told me to go, where they guided me. I never told anybody about the German boy 'til I got back to the United States to the hospital in Maryland. There, they told me to talk. They said, 'The more you talk, the more you'll heal.'" Then he laughed again that same empty laugh that echoed through the stillness.

We passed the Walker plantation, Home Sweet Home, at the beginning of twilight, when the colors of the sunlight in the far distance started changing from a general brightness to a great round ball. I made the decision to keep on moving down the road. I judged that Bosworth didn't want to talk army experiences with the old general, and he probably wouldn't want to hear about all the glory of the Confederacy or a grand, noble war like the Spanish-American conflict. After the distant heavens played a symphony of colors for us, constantly changing from red to orange to blue to purple, we camped under a live oak. We ate cold fried chicken and potato salad. We washed it down with a jug of lukewarm tea.

Bosworth stretched out on one side of the fire. I lay opposite him. In the middle of the night I awakened and rolled over and gazed through the last smoke of the coals, under the star-filled sky, at the mound of man snoring beneath the cover of his blanket.

An hour later, when I heard a scream like the pained yawl of a wounded animal, I bolted upright. I jumped to my feet and rushed to him. Twisted into the fetal position, his body shook and shivered. I felt his forehead. It was burning with fever. I fed him the last of the tea. He choked as he swallowed. I took the canteen and dampened a rag and applied it to his face. He opened his eyes and looked up into my face. Eyes wild, unfocused, like the eyes of a trapped varmint, he sprang from me like a frightened cat.

He ran into the dark woods. Shocked, I called to him, but he did not stop. I ran after him through the woods dappled with moonlight. I slowed, listening. He had gained ground on me. I heard a thud. He hit a tree. I pushed ahead, running as fast as I could until my foot stepped into a hole and I tumbled forward. Briars scratched at my hands and arms and face. I pushed up and took off again, following behind his uneven footfalls.

Then I heard nothing. "Bosworth!" I called. "Listen to me, Bosworth. You have to come back. You have to go home. It's too late to turn around. If I don't bring you home, Papa'll shoot me, I swear he will." I hushed. I listened.

Again, I heard nothing.

I moved slowly ahead through the darkness.

I picked my bare foot up, stepped out, pressed it down against damp leaves, then stepped again.

I stopped. I listened.

Ahead, somewhere in the underbrush, I heard weeping, a deep-chested cry that tore at me worse than the briars.

"Boz," I said in almost a whisper as I moved toward the base of a great oak where he lay wrapped around a thick root that extruded from the cool ground. "Boz," I said again.

I crouched next to him. He lifted his head, tears streaming down his cheeks, his lips quivering. He pressed his cheek against my knees. I folded to the floor of the forest and took him in my arms as he said, "Afraid," in the high-pitched voice of a little boy. I held him as he shook and cried. Once again, he said, "Afraid," like a frightened four-year-old.

We stayed like that for the rest of the night, I holding him in my arms like a baby, he dozing, waking, crying, hugging, then dozing again.

At first light, I led him back to the campsite. I made coffee. Holding the cup with both hands, he sipped. He looked across the fire at me and nodded, pleased, smiling.

I helped him up into the buggy. Then we got underway, moving slowly toward home. He sat next to me and said nothing.

I talked. I told him all about Town Creek, my job at Mr. Guyton's barber shop. I told him about Decatur and Mrs. Prudence's boardinghouse. I told him about going to the train station every morning, shining men's shoes and waiting for him to return. But I didn't tell him about Moccasin Alley and Lacy Beauchamp. Nor did I tell him about the Greerson Hotel and the Cave of the Wind.

Twenty-Two

When we moved into sight of the house late that afternoon, Bosworth smiled. Soon we caught a whiff of pork smoldering on coals in the pit between the house and the barn. Papa had dug the pit and started the meat cooking early in the morning, preparing for a family celebration.

Mama was the first to sense our arrival. She came out onto the front porch and called a greeting, waving her arms in the air. Papa was next, followed by Sister and Lucy. Even Martin was there, with his wife Mabel and their baby, Little John. Old Louisa Dot stood next to the house in her long flour-sack dress and sunbonnet, grinning a near-toothless grin of pure happiness. They all hugged and kissed Bosworth, who kept smiling and thanking them, all the while looking around to make sure that I remained nearby. He said he wished Ida Mae had been there, but she had a month of school to go before she could come home for the summer.

We all ate too much, sitting around on the back porch and out in the yard between the house and the pit, in the shade of the chinaberry tree and the fig tree whose fruit was plentiful and would be ripe in a little more than a month. The meat was succulent and tangy with Papa's special brown sauce. Some of the folks who lived down Bynum Road near old Louisa stopped and clapped Bosworth on the back and told him how glad they were that he was back home for good. Mrs. Ella Louis, whose son Tommy had been killed by the Kaiser's army in a forest in Germany, heard the word and came up on her buggy. She stepped across the yard and hugged Bosworth. She shed a tear

305

or two as she hugged Mama and said how lucky she was to have her boy home.

That first night, Bosworth and I slept in the same bed in the back bedroom. I was tired to the bone and slept hard. I had the feeling that I had accomplished something major in life, and now it was over. I awakened early in the morning and didn't hear his sound. I started to rise, then saw the dark outline of his body at the window, peering out. I said nothing. I lay back and watched his unmoving body. He sat there a long time, still and silent, I watching. I imagined he was just glad to be home, wanting to see the sun come up across the fields outside. After a while, I dropped off again and dozed until daybreak. That extra little bit of time was the best sleep I'd ever had, up to then. It was a confident, reassuring sleep.

Bosworth stayed close to the house for a few days. He went with me to the barber shop on his third day home. He sat in a straight-back chair opposite Mr. Guyton and answered questions the men asked about France and Paris and the army, but I noticed he never filled in the details about his friend from Arkansas or about the misery and the horror, about the loss that I knew still gnawed at his insides.

ON THE EVENING after we returned, I told Mama and Papa about much of my trip. I told them about the tragic happenings with Anthony Katanzakis and Powtawee. I told them how nice Mrs. Prudence was to us, how she'd arranged for the Greek adventurer's funeral and had gone to see about Powtawee more than once. I didn't say a word about our trip to the Greerson Hotel and the Cave of the Wind. I left out the part about Moccasin Alley and the night the Ku Kluxers came after us and about my retaliation.

306

We'd been home a week when Papa followed me to the barn one morning and stood behind me, while I settled myself on the stool and put my hands to Bossy's teats and began squeezing streams of fresh warm milk that splashed with a brusque metallic sharpness into my galvanized pail. "Was Mrs. Prudence all right?" Papa asked.

"She was wonderful," I said, Bossy's teat slipping from my fingers, the stream of milk missing the edge of the bucket.

"Really?" Papa said. "Wonderful, eh?"

I nodded. I grabbed the slippery teat and jerked it downward, squeezing and hitting the target with the solid stream of milk as Bossy stomped her rear hooves against the hard ground and made a quick sound of displeasure in her throat. Behind me, Papa walked away. A few minutes later I heard him enter the outhouse, slamming the door behind him. When he finished his business he came back into the barn while I was finishing my chores. "Did she say anything in particular?" Papa asked. "Anything specific?" he added.

"She's a very nice lady," I said.

"Yes," he said, adding, "she is."

Then I said, "She's happy with her life. She has a very nice preacher." Then I added, "She took me to a place called Cave of the Wind."

He said, "Oh," and kind of held it inside, like he was remembering something. I said no more and he did not ask other questions. When I stood and started toward the house with the pail of fresh milk, he just stared into my eyes and nodded silently. I saw something in his face I'd never seen before, but I didn't ask him about it, and I allowed it to sit in memory.

IN THE AFTERNOONS Bosworth sat on the front porch of the house. He watched the wagons and buggies and cars pass.

When people waved, he waved back. A group of boys and girls came to play. They hid in the hedges around the porch and they called to him. When they gestured for him to come he answered their call. He ran into the yard and played hide-and-seek with the children.

Within a few weeks I noticed how he was beginning to move with more ease. He put away his uniform and wore overalls. Eating Mama's cooking, he began to fill out, and his complexion became more ruddy than pale. He took off the bandage and his wound healed slowly in the fresh air, leaving a long wide scar down his arm and across his hand.

One afternoon when I came home and sat on the porch with him I watched as he joined the children, running and laughing. Tall and lean, he looked like an athlete, but remained awkward, even gawky, like a big long-legged bird moving about the yard. I walked down from the porch and called. When I had them all gathered around me I asked if they would like to play baseball in the open field across the road from our house.

I found several old gloves stiff from lack of play, a scuffed ball, and a bat that hadn't been used in years.

"I've never been much of a baseball player," Bosworth said.

"You can pitch," I said. "With long arms like yours, you'll be a natural."

Bosworth smiled and said he'd give it a try.

I allocated positions to each of the children. Bosworth took his place on the mound we built up from loose red clay and packed down hard and solid by jumping up and down on it. We piled rocks for bases. I kicked down high grass for home plate, squared off with the bat raised off my right shoulder, and waited for his first pitch.

It came in slow and high. I let it pass.

As Bosworth went into his second windup, folding his elbows, fingering the ball, shrugging his shoulders, the catcher cheered him on.

This time he stretched a long skinny leg out, stepping toward me in a slow, exaggerated step, and then he unwound slowly, meticulously, and he whizzed the ball straight across the plate, just above my knees.

I swung too late, missing the ball altogether.

"Strike one!" the catcher called.

In the field the kids were slapping their fists into their gloves, like a staccato beat of a drum. They continued slapping knuckles against leather as they bent low, squatted, and prepared to catch whatever I hit.

"You got 'im, Bosworth," they called. "You got 'im!"

I waited for the next one.

It came fast, waist-high.

I swung and connected.

I dropped the bat and started running toward first base.

Bosworth leaned down, bending at the waist, his bare right hand grabbing for the bouncing ball. He snatched it in his fingers, snapped his wrist, and sent the ball directly into the glove of the first baseman.

I was out by a full stride.

When I stopped beyond the base, I bent forward, blowing wind. When I looked up and across the field, Bosworth was standing tall in all of his glory, glove cocked, face coated with sweat. He slapped his right fist into his glove and called, "All right, boys, come on, let's play ball."

THE NEXT AFTERNOON when I got home after school and work, Bosworth was waiting on the porch with his glove, the ball, and the bat. The younger boys were standing at their places in the field. The original group had been joined by a half-dozen more, all eager to play.

It was a beautiful spring afternoon in Town Creek, Alabama. The daffodils and dandelions were blooming bright yellow in the last of the day's brilliant sunlight. Great golden splotches glittered across the outfield as my brother lifted his leg, cocked his arm, and prepared to pitch to the next batter.

Mama and Papa stepped out onto the porch and watched across the hedges as Bosworth went into his windup and pitched like he had been built for the sport. Papa even came across the road and stood along the third-base line and watched with pride shining in his eyes while his oldest son struck out three batters in a row.

The kids who played with him loved Bosworth. They called him The Boz. As he developed he got better and better, faster with more control, until he was playing with the adult team that traveled to Bynum and Bear Creek and even as far away as Muscle Shoals for Saturday afternoon games. People from miles around traveled to wherever the team was playing just to watch Bosworth pitch. Word spread. He became popular among the fans across the Tennessee River valley of north Alabama.

Bosworth worked alongside Papa at the cotton gin for a while. Then, the next year, he returned to college for some refresher courses. While there, he was recruited to pitch for the school team. Later, in the spring, he went for tryouts with a farm club in northeast Georgia, and folks there started talking about the big leagues. But halfway through the summer the manager judged Bosworth was not good enough to make it with the big city teams and cut him loose. He settled in a small Georgia town, married a local woman who'd accompanied a girl friend to see him play ball, and they had two children. On weekends, Bosworth pitched with a team of young men who worked in a textile mill.

I visited a time or two. Once, late at night, after Bosworth and the kids had gone to bed, his wife Irene told me that now and then he had some bad nights. "I couldn't tell the others what I tell you, Harold," she said confidentially. "You're special to Bosworth. You know more about him than the others know." In the night, when thunder rumbled and lightning flashed, she said, Bosworth moaned like a frightened animal. He shook and shivered until Irene held him in her arms. She rocked him back and forth, like he was a little boy, until his eyes closed and his breathing became slow and steady. She stared into my face, like I knew, and said, "He never talks about it, but I know it's the war, returning."

I nodded.

"You gave him the one thing he can still hold on to, when the world turns sour on him," she said in a near whisper. "For a while, he had the dream of being a great pitcher of baseball. It swam around in his head and gave him a new life that nothing else provided. He loved it. Still does. When he gets out there in the bright sunlight, goes into his windup, and rolls his long arm through the air, I can see a dream-like trance in his eyes. Oh, he doesn't hold out any possibilities of anything impossible. But it's the sweetest memory he's got to cling to."

That night as I lay in the darkened room of that strange house, the picture of my oldest brother came to me as it always did now, when I thought about him: of a tall, skinny, limber-legged boy standing on the red clay pitcher's mound, a ball cocked in his long-fingered hand, the bright sun of early summer shining on his freckled face in the center of a wide green field dappled with splotches of bright yellow flowers. When he goes into his wind-up, I gasp at the sight, like watching a graceful dancer float through liquid motions, finally stepping up and out, his arm flinging forward, releasing the ball that I can barely see, like a thin streak, then hearing the staccato thud as it hits the catcher's mitt in a puff of dust.

AFTER A WHILE, I heard that Miss Annie Walker learned about the Indian girl Powtawee's predicament and drove her buggy into Decatur and visited her at the colored clinic. I was told that Miss Annie encouraged Powtawee to go to school to learn what she needed to know to return to her own people and teach them about the world.

Now and then I'd hear from a traveler who'd been to Decatur that Mrs. Prudence Longshore was doing fine. "She's a very handsome woman," a tall man from Atlanta commented from the barber's chair where I was cutting his hair. I told him that I certainly agreed with his assessment.

BEFORE THE spring of 1919 I was a boy satisfied to be living quietly on the edge of civilization. After my trip to Decatur I became eager to experience new adventures. I dreamed about distant places filled with strange and interesting people. I set my sights on a far horizon, a purple haze glowing with possibilities, a simple, almost silent, always sensuous, and mysterious sound, beckoning. When I traveled, I listened to the poetry of the road resonate in the atmosphere, and its echo kept me company, even when I was alone.

About the Author

WAYNE GREENHAW lived in Town Creek, Alabama, as a child and has returned there often during his life.

In his teens he studied writing at the Instituto Allende in San Miguel de Allende, Mexico. Later he studied writing under the legendary Hudson Strode at the University of Alabama.

As a columnist and reporter, he has published hundreds of articles in regional, national, and international publications, including *The New York Times*, *Atlantic Monthly*, *Reader's Digest*, and *The Writer* magazine. He contributed six chapters for a *Guide to Mexico*.

Greenhaw, who was a Nieman Fellow at Harvard, has published fifteen books of fiction and nonfiction. He has worked on prize-winning TV productions, and two plays he wrote have been produced. He has worked as an editor and has taught journalism and creative writing

Greenhaw lives in Montgomery with his wife, Sally.

Also by Wayne Greenhaw

NONFICTION

Alabama: A State of Mind, Community Communications and the
  Business Council of Alabama, 2000

Alabama on My Mind: A Collection, Sycamore Press, 1986*

Alabama: Portrait of a State, Black Belt Press, 1998*

Elephants in the Cottonfields: Ronald Reagan and the New Republican South,
  Macmillan, 1981

Flying High: Inside Big-Time Drug Smuggling, Dodd Mead, 1984

The Making of a Hero: Lt. William L. Calley and the My Lai Massacre,
  Touchstone, 1971

Montgomery: Center Stage in the South, Windsor Publications, 1990

Montgomery: The Biography of a City, The Advertiser Company, 1993

My Heart Is in the Earth: True Stories of Alabama and Mexico, River City
  Publishing, 2001*

Watch Out for George Wallace, Prentice-Hall, 1976

NOVELS

Beyond the Night, Black Belt Press, 1999*

The Golfer, J. B. Lippincott, 1968, also Sycamore Press, 1991*

Hard Travelin', Touchstone, 1971

King of Country, Black Belt Press, 1994*

DRAMA

Rose: A Southern Lady, a one-actress play

The Spirit Tree, a play in two acts

SHORT STORIES

Tombigbee and Other Stories, Sycamore Press, 1991*

Titles marked with an asterisk (*) are available from River City
Publishing. Phone toll-free 1 (877) 408-7078, or 265-6753 local, or order
via e-mail at sales@rivercitypublishing.com.